MW01194438

BENEATH STRANGE LIGHTS

by

VIVIAN VALENTINE

Wildflower Press
an imprint of Blue Fortune Enterprises, LLC

BENEATH STRANGE LIGHTS
Copyright © 2023 by Vivian Wise

All rights reserved. Printed in the United States of America. No part of this book may be used or reproduced in any manner whatsoever without written permission except in the case of brief quotations embodied in critical articles or reviews.

This book is a work of fiction. Names, characters, businesses, organizations, places, events and incidents either are the product of the author's imagination or are used fictitiously. Any resemblance to actual persons, living or dead, events, or locales is entirely coincidental.

For information contact :
Blue Fortune Enterprises, LLC
Wildflower Press
P.O. Box 554
Yorktown, VA 23690
http://blue-fortune.com

Illustration by Frankie Valentine
Cover design by BFE LLC

ISBN: 978-1-948979-91-7
First Edition: March 2023

To my incredible wife Frankie Valentine,
who never stopped believing in me
even when I didn't believe in myself.

"It must be allow'd, that these Blasphemies of an infernall Train of Daemons are Matters of too common Knowledge to be deny'd; the cursed Voices of Azazel and Buzrael, of Beelzebub and Belial, being heard now from under Ground by above a Score of credible Witnesses now living. I my self did not more than a Fortnight ago catch a very plain Discourse of evill Powers in the Hill behind my House; wherein there were a Rattling and Rolling, Groaning, Screeching, and Hissing, such as no Things of this Earth cou'd raise up, and which must needs have come from those Caves that only black Magick can discover, and only the Divell unlock."

- H.P. Lovecraft, *The Dunwich Horror*

"What I've always wondered," said Brian, "is why they call 'em UFOS when they know they're flying saucers. I mean, they're *Identified* Flying Objects then."

"It's 'cos the government hushes it all up," said Adam. "Millions of flyin' saucers landin' all the time and the government keeps hushing it up."

"Why?" said Wensleydale.

Adam hesitated. His reading hadn't provided a quick explanation for this. *New Aquarian* just took it as the foundation of belief, both of itself and its readers, that the government hushed everything up.

"'Cos they're the *government*," Adam said simply. "That's what governments do."

- Neil Gaiman and Terry Pratchett, *Good Omens*

01

This was the beginning of the end. Not my last day of captivity, though. I had lived in various facilities under the auspices of the Bureau of Extranormal Investigations for 6,465 days, under local time keeping standards. My behavior was carefully monitored, my movements strictly dictated, and every aspect of my environment rigorously, if neglectfully, controlled.

That is not to say I was always mistreated. I should make that clear from the outset. I would not recommend any living entity be raised the way the Bureau did with me, but I acknowledge that there were good and bad periods. On September 6, 1954, I was in the middle of a good period that had lasted about three years... although after the seven years previous, I suppose I had nowhere to go but up.

The air was chilly that autumn morning. Ventilation in this building was notoriously poor, and I had not asked for a space heater. I wore only a thin cotton shift, but my skin didn't break into gooseflesh. The cold was fine. I was used to the cold.

I ran through my typical morning routine. Brushed my teeth and hair. Selected the nearest dress in my closet. Ran through my biorhythms.

Breathing fine. Blood pressure normal. Heartbeat slightly elevated; I had woken from an unusually bad dream. Two arms, two legs, two eyes, two lungs, one heart. Height still approximately five foot nine inches. In other words, my body was still as it was expected to be.

After taking care of my morning toilet, I went into the kitchen to prepare breakfast. The dishes were still in the sink from yesterday, causing me a slight twist of guilt. It was a moment of laziness I couldn't afford to let become a habit. Now I only had one clean plate. At least dinner had been soup; my pot was dirty, but the cooking pan was still clean. *I'll do the dishes before class*, I thought as I retrieved the pan and hot plate.

I poured oil into the pan and turned on the heat, then fetched the egg carton out of the small refrigerator. Still six eggs. That was good; it meant I'd have some extra when the week's rations were delivered on Wednesday. I could bake cookies if I could finagle access to an oven.

I picked out a pair of eggs and frowned. Beneath its shell, the second one had gone bad. I shook my head and tossed it in the waste bin, then grabbed another. I cracked them in the pan and scrambled the yolks with a splash of milk. No cheese; I needed to save that for my dinners. At least I could take my lunches in the staff cafeteria for the next two weeks. I had a meal card now, and it didn't even come out of my food ration.

Once the eggs were ready, I scooped them onto the last clean plate and went to eat in the dining room, which was also the kitchen. And the living room. At least the bedroom and bathroom were separate rooms, albeit both much smaller. I sat cross-legged on my sofa and turned on the radio, flicking the dial between the available channels. Listening to the static as I enjoyed my breakfast. I heard more interesting things that way.

There was a knock at the door, and I called for the man on the other side to come in. There was no need to ask who it was. It was unmistakably Agent Walsh, my handler for the past three years, although the paperwork the Bureau had generated named him as my "guardian". Likewise, there was no need to get up and let him in. The door to my dormitory did not lock. At least, not from my side.

"Good morning, Agent Walsh," I said, after I turned down the radio.

Walsh looked around the dim, off-white room and sighed. It was, I had to admit, something of an embarrassment. It was a clean but mostly empty space. In addition to my two-person sofa, I had only a countertop and refrigerator, two folding chairs (surreptitiously retrieved from a conference room a year or so ago), a short bookcase surrounded by a knee-high stack of overflow, and a poster from a Chuck Berry concert that had been held upstate a few weeks ago. I hadn't attended.

"This is new," he said, pointing to the poster. His voice didn't indicate disapproval, but he wanted to know how I'd gotten it.

"Miss Caroline gave it to me," I said. "She said my room could use some 'sprucing up'."

"Caroline…? Oh, you mean Miss Washington. From the cleaning staff."

"Yes."

Walsh looked around the room again. It was still odd, seeing people need to take so much time to perceive their surroundings. "She's not wrong."

I didn't reply. I knew what my space looked like. I knew every inch of it.

"I didn't realize you had become so close with the staff."

How would you? I thought but didn't say. "Sometimes she brings by records and plays them for me. I like it. The music she enjoys is very energetic. Is that a problem?"

"Does it get you excited?"

I narrowed my eyes at him. There was a tone of apprehension in his voice that I didn't trust. I turned his words over and over in my mind, trying to puzzle out his meaning. There was a hidden danger there, one that neither of us really understood. If I were feeling fair, I'd acknowledge that it wasn't Walsh's fault; the Bureau had kept my handler as much in the dark as they'd kept me. The incident with Agent Pickman when I was fourteen—when I'd made it unmistakably clear that I was a girl and would be treated as such—had reminded everyone of what I'd done to Agent Carlisle when I was three. Walsh didn't know what he was supposed to be looking out for, only that he was supposed to be looking out for it.

But then, I wasn't feeling fair. When had anyone ever been fair to me?

"Sometimes we dance. It's fun," I finally said, then repeated, "Is that a problem?"

"Lord knows you don't get enough fun," Walsh said under his breath, and I almost dared to believe he meant it. "No, Amelia, it's not a problem. You are allowed visitors, you know."

That was news to me. No one but my handler, nurses, and maintenance staff had ever come to see me. Was this a new policy? I'd been a good girl for years, no incidents or other problems. Not counting that last thing with Agent Pickman, but the inquiry had determined he was entirely at fault. Maybe it was an old policy and no one had ever bothered to tell me. That felt right.

So, I can have company now. Not that I had anyone to invite in. I didn't have anything by way of a peer group, but then, the Bureau wasn't in the habit of hiring teenagers.

While I pondered this, Walsh grabbed one of the folding chairs and set it across from the couch. He sat in it with a slight grimace. He was thinking of my sofa, which he had taken me to purchase second-hand a few weeks after taking over as my handler. That was the day I first learned I had been receiving a small stipend from the Bureau since 1950. None of it had been spent before or since. There was probably a tidy sum in the account.

"You're probably wondering why I came by," he said.

I finished the last bit of scrambled egg and set the plate aside. "You'll tell me in your own time. I mean, I assume you're mostly checking up on me, but I can tell something else is on your mind."

"Is my checking up on you a problem?"

"It's your job. I'm used to it by now." Unspoken went, *and it's all I've ever known*. "Also, you have asked after my comfort, which I appreciate."

"So you are doing well, then?"

"I'm eating acceptably. My conditions *are* comfortable, believe it or not. I received some new books in the mail. The censors let through five out of the six I requested this time."

Walsh wanted to argue that they weren't censors, but he didn't. Instead, he asked me to give him the name of the book so he could track it down for me... and likely investigate it, just to be sure. I shrugged and told him the truth. There was no harm in it.

"The latest Asimov novel. *Caves of Steel*."

He looked incredulous. "A science fiction novel? That's what they kept back?"

I nodded. "More often, it's my recreational reading they interfere with."

"That's absurd. Unless... I suppose they might think the name is Russian? That's no excuse, I'm just..."

"I think it's more that whoever is responsible for going through my mail disapproves of me wasting my time on 'pulp trash'. That's what they wrote on the memo that came with the other books."

"That's ridiculous. You're our ward. That means we're responsible for you, not that every petty bully in the Bureau gets to take their frustrations out on you."

That's exactly what it means, I thought, but again, I kept it to myself.

"I'll get you your book. Today, if I can. Are you having any other problems? Issues with your rations, maintenance?"

"No. Everything's fine—"

I clammed up as soon as I realized I was speaking without thinking. I never did that. I couldn't afford to *not* pick my words carefully. What was I doing? Unfortunately, Walsh noticed. A look of concern immediately filled his eyes, and he leaned forward. In sympathy, or trying to intimidate me? I couldn't say.

"What's wrong, Amelia? Has something happened?"

"I... I've been having nightmares. For the past few nights, actually."

It was a mistake being honest, and I could see that in his face. He pulled out a notepad and clicked a pen, ready to take notes. The Bureau had always been interested in my dreams. Too interested. I knew there was a drawer in a filing cabinet deeper in this building, stuffed with the dream journals they made me keep from the moment they realized I could write all the way to age fourteen, when I finally mastered lucid dreaming. I'd only had a handful of dreams that I didn't inspire myself in over three years. When my handlers found out I had one of those intrusive dreams, their reaction was accordingly overblown.

"Describe it, please," Agent Walsh said. "Describe everything."

I could tell he wouldn't relent. I could try claiming I had already forgotten my dream, the way most people appeared to do, but the fact of my perfect recall was common knowledge within this part of the Bureau. Letting out a sigh, I closed my eyes and sat back, recalling the vision. This was, I tried to remind myself, part of his job. I would have to content myself with the fact that he would be the one writing a full report to his superiors. In triplicate.

"There is darkness. Everywhere. Darkness and cold, and then light. Blue light. I am falling into the blue light. I am afraid it will kill me. I'm not sure why.

"Then everything is dark again, but not the cold dark. It's warm and thick and heavy, and I can't move easily. I see people surrounding me. They're huge, with tiny heads. Their arms stretch out for miles, tormenting me. Mostly men. There's one woman. I don't recognize any of them. I'm afraid of them."

I opened my eyes for a moment. "The woman isn't my mother."

"I didn't ask if she was."

"You were going to."

"Amelia, I have never asked about your mother."

I had to admit that was true. "You agents tend to."

Agent Walsh shifted awkwardly in his uncomfortable chair. He was thinking about Agent Pickman now. He felt guilty. That was something, at least.

"How do you know she's not your mother if you don't recognize her?" he asked after a moment, clearly reluctant to voice the question.

"I just do. It's a dream."

"Fair enough."

"After that, I'm indoors. A house, probably. It's old. I think I'm going from room to room. Someone's looking for me, someone I can't see. I think I'm looking for them, too? I'm not sure, I'm confused. In the dream, I mean."

"And then?"

"And then I woke up."

Agent Walsh frowned at his notepad. He scribbled something else and said, "That's not very conclusive."

I shrugged. "It was only a dream. Not that 'pulp trash' I like."

Walsh laughed, a familiar, friendly sound, and just infectious enough to make my lips quirk up into a smile. He returned his pen and notebook to his jacket pocket and stood. I stood along with him, feeling it necessary to observe a social nicety.

"That should keep me busy through the morning," he said. "I'm glad to hear you're otherwise doing well."

"Can't complain."

"You'll let me know if you have any more dreams?"

"I suppose I'll have to."

"Mmm."

I could tell that for a moment he wanted to say something else but changed his mind as he was forming the words. Instead, he asked whether I was going to be busy today.

"I have class in a couple of hours. That'll be through lunch. After that, I suppose I'm free for the day. I was going to read, but you clearly want something else."

He flushed slightly, embarrassed to be so transparent. "It will keep until after your class. I can come by after lunch. Or, no, why don't you come by my office? That might be better."

"Whatever you say, Agent Walsh. Please excuse me, now. I need to get ready for class."

02

～～～

"Good morning, gentlemen. Welcome to the Bureau of Extranormal Investigations. My name is Miss Temple, and I will be your instructor for the next two weeks of orientation."

A dozen men were seated in the small conference room. I was keenly aware that I was the only one in the room not wearing a gun. The agents were professional enough to keep them out of sight, of course, secured in holsters underneath their suit coats, but I could tell they were there. It wasn't comfortable knowledge. It reminded me too much of my position; my presence here was far less voluntary than theirs.

Their silent hostility did not help my calm. About half were surprised, even offended, to see a woman filling in as their instructor. A girl, technically, though they couldn't tell that—I'd matured quickly enough that most people thought I was two or three years older than I actually was. To their credit, I suppose, they did a good job of hiding their offense. These were highly trained professionals. A man had to display certain qualities in order for the Bureau to consider him for this field of work. A certain soberness of disposition was key, as well as a keen but not unguarded mind. These were the sort of people who believed the height of professionalism was a calm, cold demeanor even in the face of outright violence. They believed they should be able to face a bomb exploding without panicking. "Steely," they liked to call it.

It had little enough importance to me. If it meant they were going to sit quietly and listen to what I had to teach them, I was willing to tolerate it. If they were lucky, they would never need to maintain that bearing in the face of the material in my notes. If they were unlucky, it might save their lives and the lives of others.

Their desks were set up to form two semi-circles, with my lectern at the center. An overhead projector buzzed noisily to my right, currently throwing a blank yellow triangle against the screen behind me. I drew the first overlay from the folder in front of me and placed it on the glass. A simplified model of the universe, at least as current human science understood and could portray it, filled the window of light.

"Mathematics has proven conclusively that we live in a space of more than four dimensions," I said. "You can perceive the three you know best right now, especially if you refrain from losing an eye. You move along the fourth dimension at a constant rate, although you can't perceive your actual movement quite as readily. The remaining dimensions we can't perceive, or at least we think we can't, but we can demonstrate their existence with the correct mathematical equations."

The level of skepticism in the room rose. Most government agents didn't have the mathematical background to verify what I was telling them. By the Bureau's design, in fact. These men had been recruited from the FBI, the remains of the OSS, the Treasury Department. Their new superiors had deliberately refrained from recruiting field agents from those who'd studied the sort of mathematics that might prove the reality of what I was teaching. I had other evidence that would hopefully be more convincing. In fact, most of these men would have had some exposure to it, or they wouldn't have been considered for Extranormal Investigations. If they could accept that, they could take or leave the math. The Bureau didn't need them to be capable of writing a proof, just of conducting an investigation.

I kept my eyes on the agents as I spoke, moving my gaze back and forth in a slow, steady arc. I didn't need to look at the screen to see what I was gesturing at, and I'd been told at length that eye contact set others at ease. I wasn't sure about that. I found it profoundly uncomfortable. Meanwhile, the exacting precision of my movements unsettled these men. I was uncanny.

"Consequentially, these extra dimensions hold a great deal of additional space… far more than that taken up by our tiny corner of the universe. And that space is not empty.

"Most people, when they hear about extra dimensions, imagine a series of parallel worlds nearly identical to our own. Often ones in which certain decisions were made differently. A world in which Mister Poole pursued his baseball career instead of choosing government service, for instance."

Nathan Poole started in his chair, drawing chuckles from the men behind and on either side of him. His steely calm dropped for just a moment, replaced by surprise. I could feel his shock. How could she have known that? Surely the Temple girl couldn't have been briefed on them, could she?

I gave him an enigmatic smile before continuing. "Unfortunately, so far as we can tell, such worlds are solely the province of science fiction. Entertaining in your off time, of course, but far from informative in the field.

"No, the space that concerns us is a little more esoteric."

I withdrew the next overlay. It showed a large circle around a simple still life—a stick figure woman, a house, and a tree, not far removed from a child's drawing.

"Consider this world. It consists of two spatial dimensions. Our inhabitant can move up and down, to the left and to the right. She cannot move through the circle that surrounds it. She can't even see over it; there's no such thing as 'over' for her. It forms a perfect barrier. We, on the other hand, can see everything inside her world from a vantage point she can't conceive."

The prospective agents were getting restless, wondering what this had to do with the investigation. These were men accustomed to racketeering, smuggling, kidnapping. They were going to need a practical application soon if I was going to keep their attention. I held out my hand toward the screen, fingers outstretched.

"If I were to touch my fingertips to her world, she would see five circles suddenly appear out of thin air. If I moved my hand *through* the screen, the circles would seem to change size and shape until they merged into a big rectangle—my palm. I could instead hook a finger around her. She'd see one circle, then another suddenly pop up behind her. In other words, she'd only ever perceive the smallest slivers of my three-dimensional body. How would she explain that?

"What if I picked up that tree and moved it? It would disappear as it moved through a dimension she couldn't see and then suddenly reappear. What if I picked up *her?* How would she explain what was happening? How terrifying would it be for her?

"This brings us to the Richmond Case of 1935."

I removed the overlay and put down the next. It was a photograph from one of the Bureau's more recent cases. A farmhouse had exploded from the inside, but there was no sign of any fire. Many of the wooden timbers looked like they had been melted and stretched like taffy instead of being burnt. A handful of rooms—kitchen, living room, a trio of bedrooms—were laid bare by the way the house's walls and roof had been peeled open. Despite the photo's poor quality, strange shapes could be seen in the corners of the bedrooms, although from the distance they couldn't be easily made out.

The prospective agents stopped fidgeting. Some of them had heard something of this case, though the Bureau kept most of the details tightly restricted. Others were seeing it for the first time. Each man was trying to come up with some explanation for the destruction on the screen. This was the reason they'd each had to sign an exacting non-disclosure agreement before being assigned to the Bureau. That understanding was beginning to settle on them.

Good, I thought. *Maybe now they'll pay better attention.*

"Nineteen years ago, in March of 1935, an unexplained disaster struck the Richmond family farm in southeastern Oregon. That property had been the site of unexplained phenomena for decades, possibly generations. Strange lights, unpredictable weather patterns, rumors of apparitions and unusual animals. The Richmond family had something of a history of eccentricity. The family patriarch, Jonas, bought this property in 1933, apparently on the strength of the stories. The Bureau's investigation revealed he had come west from Connecticut, looking to for an isolated property with 'storied history'."

One of the prospective agents, Richard Morris, raised his hand. "For what purpose?"

"'Scientific experiments,' according to what little of his notes survived the incident. Jonas Richmond was a self-educated, self-styled scientific investigator. Pursuing a discipline he largely pioneered himself, Jonas sought to demonstrate the existence of higher-dimensional spaces.

"Evidently, he very nearly succeeded."

I changed overlays again. This one showed the remains of the farmhouse's attic and the laboratory that Jonas Richmond had set up. There was a weird *thing* growing out of the floorboards in the midst of several strange and shattered scientific apparatuses. The image was blown up and poorly focused—it had been cropped from a photograph taken from a safe distance—but the shape was clear enough. It was like a termite's nest or a tall tree stump, growing incongruously out of the wooden attic floor. The legend at the bottom of the overlay read *Subject 13*.

"This growth, for lack of a better word, was discovered at the farmhouse directly after the incident. The Bureau never ascertained whether it was present before, nor if it was directly related to the catastrophe that befell the house. Likewise, the Bureau never found any sign of Jonas Richmond or his wife and two eldest children. The third child, a girl named Sophia, was eventually found several miles away. Her first-hand accounts of the goings-on at the Richmond farm contributed substantially to the Bureau's report."

Accounts that, unfortunately, I had not been given access to. I hadn't been given access to the full report on Subject 13 or any of the other phenomena I'd used to prepare my part of their indoctrination. I was going off abstracts and summaries of summaries, with the bare minimum of primary source material for visual aids. The Bureau wanted to open their prospective agents' eyes without relaxing their grip on their secrets. Or perhaps it was just how little they trusted me.

The men looked at one another, then at me. I could feel the question growing in their minds, and it irked me for a reason I couldn't quite explain. I waited for one of them to muster the courage to ask it. Finally, Stanley Dawes spoke up.

"What happened to the girl?"

"Sophia Richmond?" I asked, emphasizing her name. "She was sent back to Connecticut to live with relatives. The Bureau still has her under regular observation. The exact details are, of course, private and therefore restricted."

"What about the... uh, the thing?" Morris asked.

I looked back at the picture. "It lasted about a week after the incident before it started to rot. By the time the investigation was over, not even a residue remained."

"Why?" Morris asked. "What the hell *happened* to it?"

I shrugged. "Perhaps you'll be the one to find out, Mister Morris. Most likely you won't. You can't expect to ever find out what happened. Not in these cases. We still don't have enough puzzle pieces to assemble the full picture. What you can do, hopefully, is prevent what happened to the Richmonds from happening to some other misguided or unlucky person.

"Events like this aren't crimes, Mister Morris. This isn't a criminal investigation. It's more like disaster recovery. Sometimes a storm causes a river to flood. Sometimes negligence causes a forest fire. Sometimes things poke into the fabric of our world from somewhere else. Events like the disaster at the Richmond farm don't happen 'all the time', but they do happen with disturbing frequency. Enough frequency that the government found it necessary to establish this agency. If possible, to prevent them from happening. More often, to clean up afterward.

"Over the next two weeks, we'll go through a number of confirmed sightings to compare and contrast what the Bureau has learned. Its library is incomplete, but hopefully you'll be the ones to add to it."

As I opened my binder full of ghosts, I observed the prospective agents' reaction. One or two were quietly intrigued, hoping to find the truth behind the urban legends and folklore they'd grown up hearing. The others were as keenly aware of their guns as I was. They weren't looking for the truth; they were looking the enemies it might reveal, the ones they now believed were hiding right in front of them.

I shivered, but no one took any notice.

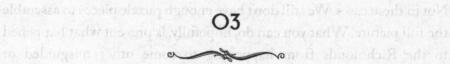

03

By the time the class concluded shortly before lunch, the men's faces were all pale. They stumbled out of the conference room in small knots, muttering to one another. They clearly did not want to believe a single thing I had just taught them, but really, they had no choice. The Bureau wouldn't have recruited them only to have their time wasted.

When the last prospective agent had left, I bound up my teaching material in an accordion folder and carried it into the hall. Before going to lunch, I took it to the secure materials library on the second floor. Annette Vance, the clerk, was waiting at the window counter. She was a very pretty young woman, with glossy dark hair and green eyes behind cat-eye glasses, and she did not like me one bit. She had joined the Bureau well after the war. Her big sister had been part of the Bureau before, along with dozens of other women, doing important work while the men were away in Europe and the Pacific. After the war, the women had been sent back home to keep house for their husbands, but Miss Vance wouldn't hear of it. They'd taken her big sister, they would take her, too. And they did… in a succession of clerical jobs. She resented me for being trusted with accessing sensitive material, while she just catalogued it.

"Good afternoon, Miss Vance," I said brightly. I had wished so dearly for her not to dislike me, even though she was a few years older than me and couldn't possibly want to be friends.

She didn't look up from her crossword. "Afternoon's an hour away still."

"Yes, but it's too late to be 'good morning', isn't it?" Wasn't it? Surely it was.

She rolled her eyes at her paper and held out her hands for the files. Slumping my shoulders, I handed them over. My fingertips brushed against her palm for just a moment, and I felt a little flutter in my breast. Heat rose in my cheeks, but I didn't think Miss Vance noticed anything. She hadn't even looked up from her crossword.

She slapped the files down in the tray marked "Intake", then handed me the clipboard with the checkout log. I found my entry from this morning, signed the files back in, and handed it back with an attempt at a winning smile. She didn't respond.

I stood for a moment, awkward, and finally said, "Thank you, Miss Vance. I'll see you tomorrow morning. Have a good day."

She didn't even look up. I walked away feeling oddly dejected, while Miss Vance thought about how weird I was and how ridiculous it was for the Bureau to have a girl teaching real agents while she was stuck behind that window. She wasn't wrong, really. Miss Vance was very sharp and would serve the Bureau a lot better as an analyst than as a clerk. And I'd had to admit a few years ago that I was very weird.

I didn't want to think about that, though, so I went to the cafeteria.

It was still early for lunch at 11:15. Bureau office culture discouraged being the first to take a lunch break, so most people were still at their desks when I released my class. That had been deliberate scheduling on my part; I preferred there to be as few people as possible in the cafeteria when I sat down to eat. It was better that way.

Unfortunately for that plan, I hadn't considered that those few people would include most of my class. Nine of them sat at a pair of tables. One of them, who faced the door, stopped whatever improbable story he was telling when I walked in and muttered something to the others. Their heads all turned in unison. I could feel them watching me as I walked up to the lunch counter and selected my entrée. Lunch was a choice of chicken fried steak or baked chicken, with two out of three different vegetables as sides, and rolls. I made my choices at random, pointing to a dish when the attendant asked what I wanted and smiling when they handed my tray back. There was a dessert counter, but I slid my tray past it on the way to the tea pitchers; my meal card didn't cover extras.

Gail Chisholm was handling the register today, and she smiled in a way that felt genuine when she saw me. Mrs. Chisholm had worked in food services for the Bureau since I was small, and though I didn't see her very often, she had always been kind to me.

"Good morning, Miss Temple. I'm so glad to see you in here today," she said as she took my meal card.

She looked down at the card and noted the dates written along the "valid thru" line. This one was good from today until the middle of the month; if the next two weeks went well, I'd get a new one whenever the Bureau had another batch of new hires. There were 23 squares printed on the card, although the last thirteen had been crossed out in pen. Mrs. Chisholm made a disapproving nose.

"These men here, I don't understand them," she said. "They have you living here, don't they? Why won't they have us feed you all the time?"

"I feed myself pretty well, Mrs. Chisholm," I said, which she didn't believe. "But I do appreciate your concern."

"I ought to write the assistant director," she said, but we both knew it wouldn't do any good. She clicked the card with a hole-punch and handed it back. "You let me know if you need anything, child."

"I will, ma'am, but I am fine. Really."

I left Mrs. Chisholm with a smile that I really felt for once and took my tray to an empty table in the corner farthest from the door. Before I started eating, I bowed my head for a moment and folded my hands in front of the tray. Eyes closed, I recounted the day's events up to that point, considering them and their context as a whole. I knew this wasn't what most people did when they bowed their heads before public meals but performing the motions of the ritual seemed to put them more at ease around me. Usually.

After a minute, I lifted my head and picked up the flatware to begin eating. It was quite good. The vegetables were overdone, but the chicken was tender and flavorful. Certainly better than any meal I'd made for myself in the past several months. The portion was a bit small, so I cut small slices, trying to draw out the meal, savor the taste, and ignore the prospective agent who had sat down across from me without asking.

Finally, Stanley Dawes coughed. "Excuse me, Miss Temple?"

I sighed and put down my fork. "Yes, Mister Dawes?"

He blushed a bit, unsettled by my addressing him by name. We'd never met before, after all. I wasn't supposed to know anyone on the Bureau campus besides my handler and a few specialists. Which had always seemed unfair, as everyone appeared to know me.

"I wanted to talk to you about your lecture today, if you don't mind," he said.

I cut my eyes past him to the other eight prospective agents. Of course, they all watched us, though the more clever ones did a good job of looking like they weren't. Likely the ones who'd had actual experience with surveillance. To my surprise, they weren't waiting for the payoff to a prank. They were just curious and apprehensive as to how I would respond to Dawes' intrusion. Dawes himself was close to terrified, though to his credit, he was doing a good job of hiding it.

Six inches of height and over a hundred pounds on me and carrying a gun, yet he was terrified of me. Amazing.

I picked my knife and fork back up and gestured for him to go ahead. "I can eat and talk at the same time, Mister Dawes. Well, not at the *same* time," I added, suddenly wondering what rumors he might have heard, "but I can alternate."

It took him about half a second for him to recognize the joke, but once he did, he let out a small laugh. The others stared at us.

"It's about the part you opened with," he said. "The part about parallel worlds?"

"And how there aren't any?" I speared a small piece of chicken with my fork.

"Yes, but… after the Richmond case, you talked about the various, ah, 'subjects' the Bureau has catalogued over the years. One in particular jumped out at me."

Dawes pulled a notepad out of his pocket. It was identical to the one Walsh used; I thought they might be standard issue. "Here we go, Subject 024-B. You talked about two sightings from Bureau records, one in '41 and another in '49, but I got the sense that there were a lot more, just unconfirmed. Is that right?"

"Yes. Someone else will go deeper into investigative and research methods after your indoctrination is complete," I said, "but generally you'll find that for every encounter that leaves hard evidence, there are ten that are just unverifiable eyewitness testimony, and for every one of those, there are another ten that are just weird, unexplainable events."

"Yeah. So, number 24. The case in sighting A involved a single incident, right? The old man reported something in his back forty, state police found weird bits of vegetation in his shed, one trooper has what sounds like a drug-induced hallucination, yeah?"

"Yes, you took very adequate notes, Mister Dawes."

He ignored the subtle jab. "Sighting B, though… you've got evidence backing sightings in five different places in Ellis County, yeah? Plus uncorroborated sightings in a half-dozen other places. Even photographs of two different encounters are miles away from one another."

"I'm familiar with my lesson plan. Where are you going with this, Mister Dawes?"

"It's… most of your lecture, you talked about these as if each was a single, distinct phenomenon, right? Like, there is *a* Subject 16 and *a* 24 and *a* 33. But," he continued, as he tapped a finger on his notes, "this case reads more like a group."

I held up a hand. "You recall my opening statement? What the Flatlander would think of my fingers?"

"Okay, sure. You're saying it's probably just one thing poking through in a dozen different places."

"In all probability. Are you familiar with Occam's Razor?"

"I prefer Gillette. Don't change the subject."

"I'm not… never mind. The point I'm trying to make is that it's far more likely to be a single phenomenon than a multiplicity of them. In the absence of evidence—"

"Is there an absence?" Dawes leaned in closely. "I worked a lot of racketeering cases before this. I know conspiracies. This case, with the way the things pop up here and there, the disappearances, the changes… it all looks coordinated."

"Coordinated by whom, exactly?"

"I don't know. Maybe someone in Oklahoma. Or maybe someone on… on the other side."

"On the other side," I said flatly.

"Or above or... or however you want to describe it," Mister Dawes said, snorting in frustration. "From the fifth dimension or whatever."

"Now you're reaching even further, Mister Dawes," I said, pushing my vegetables on my plate and trying to return my attention to my meal. "There's even less evidence of intelligence in these higher-order spaces than there is of parallel universes."

He furrowed his brow and squinted. "But then, how do they explain you?"

My fork clattered against my plate after falling out of my hand. I stared at him, trying to keep my composure intact. My heart thumped so loudly that he must have heard it, but I didn't dare react. They expected that.

I glared at him and said frostily, "Mister Dawes, I think you're going to do very well in the Bureau."

"That remains to be seen," said a familiar voice behind me.

Dawes looked up guiltily while I sipped my tea and ignored the man interrupting us. Agent Walsh, standing behind me with a sour look on his face.

"Dawes," Walsh said, "do you recall the briefing on Bureau protocol regarding interactions with Miss Temple?"

Dawes flushed and tried stammering a response. I turned my attention to my chicken, ignoring his quiet but very public chewing-out. There were about three bites left, if I cut very conservatively, and I did so. After three years as my handler, Agent Walsh had developed a possessive streak I found presumptuous and overbearing, and I wasn't going to reward him with my attention until I was damned good and ready.

"I understand, Agent Walsh," Dawes said, stammering slightly. "Won't happen again. Sorry, Miss Temple."

"I will see you in class tomorrow, Mister Dawes," I said, not looking at either man as I dabbed my napkin against my mouth.

Dawes nodded to Walsh and backed away. His colleagues at the other table welcomed him back, giving him a good ribbing for the chewing out he'd just received… as if they'd have behaved any differently in his position.

"You need to be careful around those fellas, Amelia," Walsh said. "Don't let them get so close next time."

"We were having a conversation, Agent Walsh. A conversation regarding my class. A class *you* fought the deputy assistant director to let me teach, in fact."

"I remember those arguments very distinctly, Amelia."

"Then would you care to explain just how I am supposed to teach this class you want me to teach if you won't allow me to interact with the students except through you? I didn't see you in the conference room this morning."

"I do have a caseload, Amelia. A lighter one than most agents, but it's still there."

"My point exactly."

"*My* point is that you don't know these guys. You don't know how they're going to act around you. You have to be more careful."

"I am careful, Agent Walsh. I don't need you to take care of me. I'm capable of taking care of myself."

Walsh frowned. "You're behaving childishly."

"Technically, I still am a child."

"I don't believe that. In fact, I'm not sure you've ever been a child."

That got me to look at him. It stung, and I wasn't sure why. "What do you mean by that?"

"Don't play coy, Amelia. I may not have access to all your files, but I've put together quite a bit."

"Yes, Agent Walsh, *thank you* for reminding me. I am acutely aware of how much you know about me."

He opened his mouth to speak but stopped and sighed. A good thing, as he'd have cause to regret his words.

"We've gotten off on the wrong foot today, haven't we? I'm sorry, Amelia. I just wanted to stop by and make sure your first class went well. You haven't had much interaction with the Bureau as a whole lately. To be honest, I've been worried about you all day."

I took a sip of my tea to drown what I wanted to say next. I would have had cause to regret *that*. "The first day went perfectly well. The prospective agent you chased off seemed a bit impertinent, but I expect he's heard all sorts of rumors, considering it's apparently not safe for me to be in society."

He winced. "I suppose I deserved that."

"Yes. You did."

"Amelia, I'm sorry. Really, I am. You know I'm trying to get you more freedom. The Bureau's kept you locked away for far too long, treated you like a…"

He paused. Agent Pickman's tenure as my handler hung between us like a thundercloud. As it had for years.

"Anyway, that's why we've had trouble with you," he said, struggling with the words. "Now that you're practically an adult—"

He broke off again, looking around. More people entered the cafeteria in twos and threes. No one looked at us yet… or at least, looked like they were looking at us.

"We can talk about that later," he said. "I just want you to understand, not everyone sees you the way I do. Some of these men…"

Unbidden, a memory flashed across the forefront of his mind. A young girl was lying in bed, her hair dark, her dress white. Her breathing shallow. The memory was old, but the pain was fresh. I'd seen it in Agent Walsh's mind before, whenever he was particularly concerned about me. I looked nothing like the girl in his mind, but that didn't seem to matter. I hadn't dared to ask. I didn't want to explain how I knew or make him think I cared that much.

But it was certainly better than Agent Carlisle treating me like a monster. Or Agent Pickman as a science experiment.

He completed the sentence practically as an afterthought. "I just want you to be careful."

"I am careful, Agent Walsh."

He sighed again. "Of course you are. Anyway, I'm glad the first day went well. We can talk about the rest when you come by my office. You remember that I wanted you to come by my office later?"

"Yes, I remember, Agent Walsh."

"Just please, promise you won't forget."

"I don't need to promise anything, Agent Walsh," I said. "You know I've never forgotten anything."

04

I remember a black sky above the cold desert, staring up into nothingness the night I was born. I remember a riot of strange lights, twisting and spinning in the starless night sky like an enraged aurora. I remember a strange tearing sound, moving from darkness to darkness as the noise of the womb was replaced by rhythmic, atonal chanting that did not quite drown out the sound of my mother's screams. I remember the wet heat of the blood that covered me, the dry smoothness of the hands that pulled me from my mother's womb. I remember my eyes opening, and the first sight I beheld as I entered this new world.

My mother lay against a cushion, propped up by a man in a dark robe. Despite the desert chill, her face was slick with sweat. She panted with exertion, and tears streamed from her eyes, but I couldn't see any trace of pain. Only anger mixed with sorrow. She glared at the man who held me, but the ordeal of my birth left her too fatigued to speak.

I turned my tiny head and looked up at the man. His face was stern and deeply lined, but his piercing blue eyes shone brightly in the torchlight. His expression was one I would learn to read very well on other faces over the years: satisfaction mixed with cold contempt.

He ignored my mother's pain and outrage, tucking me clumsily into the crook of his arm and turning away. I could now see that we were surrounded by a ring of men in robes, just like those of the man holding me and the man holding my mother. A scar ran down that man's face, starting beneath his left eye, then down his cheek and hooking up at his chin. I watched him drop my mother, letting her fall none too gently against the desert floor. She wailed, not in pain but in grief as the cold man carried me away.

I never saw her again, nor did I see the cold man. I know she was my mother as surely as I know my own name, but I never learned hers, nor who the cold man was. Was he my father, or perhaps hers? I have turned his image over in my head a thousand times while staring in the mirror. I can see no resemblance between us, though sometimes I think I see some between him and my mother. If he was kin to me, he seemed to have little interest in my well-being. After we left the birthing, I was turned over to the care of others for a time. Eleven days, to be exact. On the twelfth day after my birth, more strange men burst into the compound in west Texas where I was being cared for. I don't know what they expected to find—I still don't—but they found me. They took me to the Bureau, and every memory of every day since has been with them.

It isn't a bad life, all told. But I wish I knew what happened to my mother.

O5

Agent Walsh's office was in the part of the building commonly dubbed "the orange zone". Consisting of the top two floors and a third of the second, it was the area the Bureau reserved for material deemed extremely sensitive. The offices of field agents and analysts were all in that area, as were two-thirds of the Bureau's records and a selection of laboratories. As well as my dormitory.

Walsh was waiting in his office. He was working on a report when I arrived, analyzing similarities between a sequence of encounters in the American Southwest to determine whether they represented further evidence of a previously encountered subject or an as-yet uncatalogued specimen. As was typical of the Bureau's results, he leaned toward a mix of the two when I knocked. He covered his typewriter and called for me to enter.

His desk was a mess, with open files scattered across its surface, forming white foothills around the mountain of his typewriter. Perhaps about two-thirds of the mess actually related to his current work; the rest was typical debris of a half-dozen other tasks. He had a filing cabinet sitting behind him, its half-empty drawers pulled open.

"Amelia, I'm glad you came," he said, rifling through his papers. "Please, take a seat."

A chair was set against the wall next to his desk, occupied by a stack of files. I picked up the stack and pointedly began sorting the files into drawers. Walsh had the decency to look a little shamefaced. He pushed a few papers into a pile and coughed awkwardly. I hoped the papers belonged in the same file.

"You don't have to do that, Amelia," he said. "You're not my secretary, you know."

"I am well aware of that, Agent Walsh," I said. "I am, in fact, an instructor-slash-sensitive-materials. I had a number of files out myself this morning. I turned them in properly, in accordance with Bureau protocols."

"This office is authorized for open storage," he said half-heartedly.

"Only when you are in it," I countered. I held up a pair of files. "I know for a fact these are in relation to a case you were working on two weeks ago."

"They're all open cases, Amelia. The Bureau's not actually good at closing cases. I don't think we even have a protocol for it."

I sniffed. "This entire office is a five hundred cubic foot practice dangerous to security. The way your Bureau picks and chooses what to be lax about confounds me daily."

Walsh shifted uncomfortably in his seat. "You're referring to your request to attend college, aren't you?"

"Shall I infer from your guilty expression that my request has been denied?" I asked. I tried to keep my own face as neutral as my voice. I kept it pointed at the drawer, because I didn't trust myself not to let my frustration show. As if I didn't already know the answer, known it as soon as he stopped by my dorm that morning, but I'd learned long ago it was polite to ask.

"I know that there's no point in being anything but completely honest with you, Amelia," Walsh said. He sounded defeated. "The new deputy AD didn't even consider it."

I wrapped both hands over the lip of the cabinet's topmost drawer, gripping it until my knuckles turned white. I slowly slid the drawer back into the cabinet, then turned around and leaned against it. I folded my arms across my chest. I wouldn't look at him.

"You could still try to soften the blow, you know," I said, my voice just above a whisper.

"I'm… I'm sorry, Amelia."

Walsh rose from his chair, holding out a hand to comfort me, but pulling it back just before he touched my shoulder. The memory of the girl appeared in his mind again. He slipped around the desk and sat on its edge, hands clasped between his knees.

"I'm sorry," he said again. "I'm still figuring this out. It's hard to tell how I should talk to you, hard to remember how old—how young—you really are."

I didn't respond. I tried to collect myself, pushing a stray hair out of my face and tucking it behind my ear. A normal gesture made by normal girls. I'd known when I first made the request that it was probably going to be denied. There had been changes over the last three years, fallout from the incident with Agent Pickman, but at its core, the Bureau was still the same. I'd been trying to make a point more than genuinely wanting to further my education. Still, the rejection hurt, especially when it was so out-of-hand.

"Let me guess," I said, once I had calmed enough to speak. "It would present too great of a security concern."

"On numerous levels, Amelia, not the least of which is your personal safety."

I snorted. Nothing the Bureau had ever done suggested that it

36

prioritized my safety above anyone else's.

"There are also the logistical concerns. Bureau support, for starters. I'm the primary agent assigned to your care, but I'm also an active investigator. I can't watch over you constantly during six to eight hours of classes."

"So who says you'd have to?"

"The deputy AD, for one."

I supposed I should have seen that coming.

"Number two, you don't even have a high school diploma, no transcripts, not even a record of enrollment…"

"And whose fault is that? Fake them. The Bureau's faked practically all my identifying documentation as it is."

"That was only as a precautionary measure," Walsh said with a sigh. "They didn't intend to actually have to ever use it."

"This is ridiculous. You know I've had an education. I've had tutors—"

"And the Bureau is willing to keep providing them if you want continuing education."

"On Bureau-approved topics! Not a real degree, not choosing what I want to study!"

"Well, the Bureau is footing the bill, and it thinks it should have a say in what it's paying for," Walsh said, exasperated, while thinking that the Bureau was also afraid of just what I might choose to study unsupervised. "Look, Amelia, I'm on your side. I made the exact same arguments to the deputy AD. He wouldn't even listen to me. When I tried to appeal his decision, I was dismissed by his secretary. His secretary."

I stood stock still in silence. I knew he was telling me the truth. I didn't want to believe it, but what choice did I have? It's not as if he could lie to me. He had pushed for me, as hard as he could… or so he told himself. He had at least made an effort on my behalf. Pickman or

Carlisle wouldn't have done even that much. Not that it changed the outcome one iota.

I pushed off the cabinet and turned to face him. I wanted to look him in the eye when I played the one card I had left.

"It's September. I turn eighteen in December, you know. I'll legally be an adult. The Bureau won't be able to stop me from leaving then. I'll be able to make my own way."

Walsh met my eyes. I could see the sadness in them, mixed with shame. He didn't respond at first. Not a word. I could see the question in his mind, though.

He swallowed, wincing at the words he was trying to say. "Amelia…"

Do you really believe that's true? he thought.

Tears smarted at the corners of my eyes. I closed them and tried my best to keep them at bay. I wouldn't give them that. Not that.

"So that's how it is, huh?" I whispered.

It was another thing I'd suspected but had somehow convinced myself wasn't true. The slight measure of hope that kept me going through the bad times was that someday I would be an adult. I'd done nothing wrong, or rather, nothing that a reasonable person wouldn't consider self-defense under the circumstances. The Bureau had no reason to keep me locked away from the world. But they had. What childhood I'd been permitted had been stretches of isolation and neglect, punctuated by experiments and interrogations. The limited freedoms I'd been granted recently were treated like a gift. Something I should be grateful for, and something that could be taken away whenever they wanted.

I'd endured by convincing myself the Bureau could only have that power because I was a child. When I was an adult, they would have to let me have a real life. Outside of the Bureau's grasp. Outside of its protocols. Outside of its walls.

I felt a twinge in my upper arm, the ghost of pain from years ago. I slid my other hand up my arm to rest over the marks that were no longer visible. I should have known better by now.

"Amelia, please," Walsh said, his voice low and sad. "This is what I wanted to talk to you about. Will you sit down?"

"Yes, Agent Walsh," I said, sullen. "I should know better than to think I have any choice of my own, shouldn't I?"

He didn't rise to the bait, just waited for me to sit down. He pulled a handkerchief out of his jacket and offered it to me. When I didn't accept, he set it down on the corner of the desk, within my reach.

"You're right," he said softly. "You know you're right, and so do I. You're going to be an adult soon. You deserve a chance at a real life, to be more than a, a…"

"A prisoner? A lab rat?" I asked fiercely.

Walsh flinched but didn't dispute that. "I believe certain elements within the Bureau also see you as some sort of early warning alarm. But you're far more than that, Amelia, and we both know it. You're a person, one with tremendous potential. If we could help you harness it… that's how I was able to convince the deputy AD to give you the instructor assignment. You know the material better than some agents who've spent their adult lives looking into it."

And wouldn't the Bureau like to know how that is?

(Wouldn't I like to know?)

"So you're saying I could be of use to the Bureau?" I said, my voice flat as the desk he sat on.

"That's how I had to pitch it to the higher-ups, yes," Walsh admitted. "I've almost got them seeing it as a return on their investment, and that they'll get more if they invest more."

He opened a drawer in his desk, pulled out a small black purse and held it out for me. "This is yours. Think of it as an early birthday present from the Bureau."

I looked at it. Really looked at it. There was a wallet inside with a checkbook and a few bills, a booklet of bus passes, a Maryland state ID card, and a pair of clearance passes, one blue and one orange. And a small paperback book by Isaac Asimov.

"What's this?" I asked, shaking the purse at him.

"Freedom," he said with a grin. "Limited freedom, I know, but you are still a teenager. I've convinced the Bureau that it's worthwhile and safe to give you a town pass. You have money, after all, and things I'm sure you'd like to spend it on. You'll have some limits, of course. No more than twenty miles from the campus, and your curfew is six p.m. Just for now, obviously. If we show them that this works, I can argue for increased privileges."

I set the purse in my lap. What he was offering was tantalizing, but I could tell there was a hidden catch. There had to be. "But? Are you really willing to spend your evenings chaperoning me through town?"

"No. Not unless you want me to," he said, grinning more widely. "I actually have things I would like to do, at least on the evenings I have off. And you're misunderstanding me. You won't have a chaperone. You're being allowed out on your own."

My eyes widened. I couldn't believe that was really what he meant. In seventeen years, I had never been outside Bureau property on my own. Not without my handler or a group of armed guards. What Walsh was offering…

"So what is the catch? I can believe you're doing this out of a sense of decency." Or obligation, misguided as either would be. "What is the Bureau getting out of this?"

"Hopefully? Cooperation. Right now, I have them convinced that things are going well, because they are, obviously. But, we don't want any more incidents, do we? I think this is a better way to avoid them in the future. We let you have your space, you stay calm, and maybe in the future, you'll think about what it is you're really good at, and who you want to do it for. And so will the Bureau."

He stood and stretched out his hand again. This time, he did put it on my shoulder.

"If this goes really well, we can talk about college later. Maybe as early as next year. Sound fair?"

No. Nothing about this sounded fair to me. But what other choice did I have?

06

When I left the campus late that afternoon, my shoulders were drawn so tightly together I could barely move my neck. The fear in my chest clutched at my heart, which wanted to pound through my ribcage. My lungs could only take in short breaths before forcing them back out. As I approached the main gate, I spied the pair of armed guards at the end of the drive. That they were soldiers was obvious from their drab green uniforms and general bearing; that they were ready to kill any intruder was apparent from both their rifles and their vigilant attitudes.

The one standing outside the small white booth beside the road turned slightly toward me as I neared his post. I tensed, anticipating trouble, but the only change to his expression was a slight lift of the eyebrows. He was mildly curious what a girl was doing here, especially so long after hours, but his alertness didn't rise, nor did his hand move toward the rifle slung over his shoulder. He turned to face me full-on when I stopped just over an arm's length away, holding out both my state ID and blue access badge. I was permitted here, I was trying to say. I belonged. Please, do not attack me.

The soldier cocked his head to one side, momentarily looking like a confused owl. I swallowed my nervous laughter and stretched out my arm to put my identification closer to him. Somewhat hesitantly, he took them from me and flipped them over, staring first at the cards and then at me, wondering what he was supposed to do with either of us.

"My name is Amelia Temple," I said. "I'm going out. To town."

"Okay?" the soldier said.

"I have permission to do so."

"Good for you?" he said, looking to his partner in the booth for support. "Most folks do?"

"Then, I may leave?"

"Sure, miss," the other guard said, leaning out through the booth's window. He had a lopsided smile on his ruddy face. "Our job's more to keep folks out than in."

"Yeah, you're thinking this is more like Ashville State Penitentiary," the first guard said. "That's the next county over."

"You can tell it's not 'cause the food's better."

"So are the hours."

"And the lawns."

"Also, the state pen's guarded by the Department of Public Safety," the first guard said, handing my identification back. "And you don't need to show that on the way out."

"Just when you want to come back through the other way," the second guard said.

"I... I see. Thank you," I said.

I put my identification away and nodded to them before walking to the gate. I cringed just a bit as I passed through, but nothing happened. No alarms, no dogs, no bullets. The two soldiers watched me with a mix of curiosity and concern but did nothing to obstruct me.

I was outside the campus! For the first time in my life, I was on my own!

I had no idea what to do with my newfound freedom.

The nearest town was Chatham Hills. I'd been there twice with Agent Walsh in the past few months, buying furnishings and other items he had deemed necessary for me. I didn't know it very well, other than that it was quiet. A handful of Bureau employees lived there, though most took the train in from suburbs further out. There was a bus stop not far from campus, and by the time I realized I had decided where to go, I was sitting patiently on the bench.

The bus ride was pleasant and uneventful. The driver accepted my pass without comment; I had steeled myself to explain why I was out and where I was going, but he had no interest in me except as another fare. The other passengers took little note of me; a few looked up just to see who was getting on the bus, then went back to their reading or quiet conversations. For a moment, a touch of giddiness made my head swim, and I had to grab hold of the nearest seat back to steady myself. Knees wobbly, I took the first open seat up front and settled in, watching the campus slide past the window as the bus resumed its route.

A part of me wanted to listen in on the other passengers, to find out who they were, where they were going. To just hear what they were talking about, or whatever they were reading that was so interesting. I decided not to. They had done me the courtesy of ignoring me, and I felt I owed it to them to do the same. Instead, I looked ahead to Chatham Hills, trying to come up with a list of things I wanted to do in town.

It was harder than it should have been, because when we were halfway there, I realized I didn't really know what anyone *did* in town.

I still hadn't figured it out by the time the bus reached the first in-town stop. I simply didn't know Chatham Hills. To me, it was a collection of buildings without context. This first trip would have to be about exploring, I decided. With no real reason to wait, I decided to get off at the first stop and have a look around.

I don't know what I expected to find, or where I might have ended up if left entirely to my own devices. Some place to eat, perhaps? Or a clothing store? Possibly I would've browsed the Woolworth's on Main Street for an hour or so before returning to the campus. I suppose I'll never know; I can see an awful lot that most people can't, but even I can't see the roads not taken. The road I *did* take began the moment I stepped off the bus and felt something… unusual.

It was a sensation at the back of my mind. Not a sound or voice, not even a feeling or a desire. The closest I could describe it was as a faint pull drawing me away from the bus stop, but that wasn't right, either. Does water feel a pull when it flows downhill? I don't think so. That's just the way it has to go. I realized I had to go up the street, a couple of blocks farther into town. I barely registered the stores I passed, ignoring their signs and displays in favor of that eerie sensation. I passed a few people on the street—a couple pushing a baby carriage, an older woman with an armful of groceries, a young man snapping his fingers to a beat only he could hear—all heading the opposite direction, all oblivious to whatever was drawing me in. I wasn't surprised. At this point in my life, I was used to being the only one to sense something.

The slope of the weird psychic gravity reached its nadir at a used bookstore off from the center of downtown Chatham Hills. I paused at the door to read the wooden sign hanging above it: Orr's Used Books, Est. 1926. Then I stepped through the door. The eerie sensation didn't cease, exactly, but became omnipresent. It was all around me, but I no longer felt a need to go anywhere in particular.

I stopped and stared as the door closed behind me, now utterly disoriented. My head swam. It felt almost like I had whiplash; I'd been so focused on where I was going, as if I was being pulled along by a rubber band that had just snapped back. My confusion certainly did nothing to impress the silver-haired woman behind the front counter, who looked up at the jingle of the door's bell to see me gaping at the dozens of bookshelves filling the dimly lit store.

"If you're lost, they have maps at the gas station two blocks down," she said, barely holding back her irritation.

"I… I'm not lost. Sorry," I stammered. "I've just, um… never been out before. Here, before! Your bookstore is nice."

She looked around the room, then back at me. Cobwebs draped across every corner, the ruins of lost arachnid civilizations. The dust layering some of the shelves had geological strata. The handful of reading chairs scattered through the stores were worn and half-collapsed, the promise of protruding springs lurking in each seat. Not the sort of place that invited customers. Because the owner—Maxine Orr, that was the woman's name—didn't keep it to sell books. So why run a bookstore? I couldn't tell, and I was reluctant to look deeper.

Maxine snorted and returned to her book, a dog-eared copy of the *Prose Edda*.

"You want to look around, go ahead, but if you're not gonna buy, you might as well turn 'round and go to the Arcadia," she said. "I hear they've got some new teenagers in cars flick. That might be more your speed."

"I've… I've never been to the movies," I said, taking a couple of steps toward her. "I don't think I'm interested in teenagers driving cars."

"Hmph. Maybe you've got more taste than you look like you have," Maxine said. "Go on, then, have a look. No smoking in the stacks."

"I don't smoke."

"Good for you. Filthy habit," Maxine said, as she lit a cigarette. She waved it at me, sending curls of smoke wafting through the dusty air. "Forget the Reds, these things'll kill us all someday. Mark my words."

"Yes," I said, more to have something to say than anything.

I clutched my purse to my chest and began navigating the miniature labyrinth of shelves. If there was an organization to the store's layout, it was idiosyncratic to such a degree that only Maxine could make sense of it. Histories were shelved cheek to jowl with romances and boy's adventure tales. The top three shelves of one stack were filled with worn weird fiction paperbacks, the middle two with biographies, and the last with cookbooks. One entire shelf on another case was full of westerns by Zane Grey, except for the last book, a thick, leather-bound tome. *What is that about?* It had no dust jacket and the letters embossed on the spine were almost entirely worn off. When I flipped through the pages, I saw drawings of continents I didn't recognize. The sticker on the front cover said fifty cents. I figured that was worth the price of curiosity, tucked it under my arm, and went back to browsing.

After some cursory glances through the stacks, nothing else leapt out at me. At the far end of the shop, a staircase rose to the second floor. There were more books there, at least in half of the space. There were also, I realized, three people up there. I hadn't noticed them before, and I wasn't quite sure why. That, more than anything else, put me on edge.

I suppose I wasn't looking for anyone else, I said to myself. *Who would expect to find another customer in a place like this, let alone three?*

The thought hardly mollified me, but I pushed it away. The three people up there sounded like they were close to my age, and I was struck by an intense need to meet them. That pull was nearly as strong as the one that led me here, but this didn't come from the back of my mind.

I made my way up the stairs as quietly as I could, which, thanks to years of practice, was very quiet indeed. I'd become good at being unobtrusive. I told myself that I didn't want to disturb the strangers' conversation, but truthfully, I was scared. I wanted the opportunity to hide or flee if it turned out they were less than welcoming.

The stairs led up to a short hallway stretching the length of the store's short wall. Doors flanked either side. The one on the left, going to the back of the store, was locked; behind it was a small apartment or something, possibly where Maxine lived. The door on the right was ajar, leading into the additional shelving space I had seen. The three strangers stood together next to a bookcase, two boys and a girl, all only a couple of years older than me. One of the boys was tall, with dark hair just long enough to be rebellious without drawing too much comment. Other girls would probably consider him handsome, I guessed. He was showing the others a thick book; I could almost reach out and touch his excitement. He was the leader of the trio, or at least he believed he was. His name was Lucas, Lucas Dowling.

The other boy, shorter and less confident, kept wringing his hands or fiddling with the arms of his glasses. There was something permanently rumpled about him, even though his shirt and trousers were recently pressed; it was if he was hunched over himself on the inside. His feelings for Lucas were a confused bundle of contradictory emotions I couldn't get a handle on, and I don't think he could either. Ralph Connor, though Lucas called him Ralphie, which he hated. I couldn't understand why he wanted to be Lucas' friend, and I didn't think he understood either.

It was the girl, though, who drew my attention. Her hair was long and blonde, with a touch of red. My first impression of her was "girlfriend", but I quickly realized that no, that was what the boys wanted. She just wanted to keep Ralph out of trouble. She was aloof, as if she was floating above them. Her expression was bored, but she paid keen attention to what Lucas was saying. Or rather, to what he was saying *behind* his words. That was intriguing. I'd learned to do that myself.

Her name was Lucille. Lucille Sweeney. She was very pretty.

I wanted to hang back and observe them more. I wasn't ready to introduce myself, not yet. I didn't know what to say, how their dynamic would change if I joined them. These were the first people my age I'd encountered, or close enough. How likely was it that they would want to know me? Wasn't it more probable that they'd be offended by my presence, that they'd find me intrusive? What use was I to them, really? It would be better to turn around and go back downstairs. That's what I was going to do. I'd pay for my book and return to the bus stop and wait for the bus to take me back to where I belonged.

Only the stairs weren't very well maintained, and when I turned to go, the step beneath my foot let out a loud creak. It sounded like a tree cracking in half, and for a moment I feared I would fall right through the stairs.

"Who's that?" Lucas called. "Maxie, is that you?"

I cringed, but it was too late now. They were already turning toward the door. I took in a deep breath and climbed to the top of the stairs, plastering an attempt at a smile on my face as I walked through the open door.

"Don't mind me!" I said. "Just browsing!"

All three stared at me. Ralph looked utterly lost and confused, while Lucille was simply curious as to who else was here. Lucas, on the other hand, radiated thinly disguised hostility at the unexpected intruder. He tucked the book under his arm the moment he saw my eyes drift toward it.

"Who are you? What do you want?" he demanded.

"Knock it off, Lucas," Lucille said, rolling her eyes. "She's obviously a customer. This *is* supposedly a bookstore."

Lucas wasn't mollified, though he was somewhat embarrassed at Lucille's criticism. He still found my presence unwelcome but was now more concerned about losing face in front of her. He stood a little straighter and turned so that his back was mostly to me.

"Just so long as she stays out of the way," he said.

"Stop being rude," Lucille said, giving his shoulder a slight shove. "Just because you rent a space up here doesn't mean you can chase the customers out."

"Um, Lucille's r-right," Ralph said. "I, ah, don't th-think Miss Orr would appreciate the l-lost business. If you m-make her mad…"

Lucas looked at Ralph as if he was a complete idiot. Lucille shook her head and decided to completely ignore the boys. She gave me a dazzling smile and took a couple of steps toward me. My heart started to pound. I wanted to shrink into the corner. I wanted her to come closer.

"What is it you're looking for?" Lucille asked. "Maybe we can help you find it? This place is kind of a maze."

"I, ah, I noticed," I said.

I could feel the heat rising in my cheeks. Lucille stood very close now. She was almost my height with heels on. Her clothing was immaculate—a bright blue skirt and white blouse, with a matching blue scarf tying back her hair. She wore a light scent; it smelled faintly of roses. I wondered what I must look like to her. I looked outside of myself. I saw a tall young woman with messy hair, wearing a drab gray dress, her arms folded protectively across her chest. There was nothing impressive about me at all. I doubted she would have even looked twice if she passed me on the street. If Lucas hadn't started out being immediately hostile, she probably wouldn't have been so nice.

Well, that was certainly a weird thing to be grateful for.

While I was thinking, Lucille had noticed the book in my arms. "Looks like you found something interesting. May I see it?"

"Oh… it's just an old book," I said, fumbling to hold it out for her to see. "Kind of a weird one, actually."

Despite himself, Lucas had been paying attention to our conversation and grew increasingly irritated that his audience had wandered off. When he saw Lucille looking at the book, he dropped the pretense. Before I realized what he was doing, Lucas darted forward and snatched the book out of my hands.

"Hey!"

"Lucas!" Lucille said. "I said quit it!"

Lucas ignored us both. He opened the book and started flipping through the pages. His lips twisted into a sneer.

"What sort of pulp trash is this?" he said. "This looks like it belongs in one of those weird fantasy magazines you waste your money on, Ralphie."

My shock at his rudeness was quickly buried beneath a rising indignation at his presumption. My hands were trying to curl into claws, and my left arm twitched. I tucked my hands behind my back before anyone could notice. Fortunately, Lucas was too wrapped up in his mockery, while Lucille and Ralph were in turns irate and mortified at his behavior.

"I-I don't think you're b-being very p-polite, Lucas," Ralph said.

"You're being more than just impolite, you jerk!" Lucille said, smacking Lucas on the arm. "Give it back. Now!"

"Yes. It's mine. Or it will be, after I pay for it," I said. I forced one hand to unclench and held it out expectantly. "Give it back, please. Or I'll be forced to speak to the owner about your ridiculous behavior."

Lucas laughed. "I'm a regular customer here. You're just a random passerby. Who do you think she's going to side with?"

"Not you, if you keep trying to drive off her customers," Lucille said.

I had serious doubts as to whether Miss Orr genuinely relied much on customers, and Lucas was equally unconvinced. Fortunately, Ralph appeared to know Lucas' real currency.

"Y-you know Miss Orr hates being d-disturbed, Lucas," he said. "If-if she thinks you're causing t-trouble in the store, she m-might stop letting us use her space."

That got Lucas' attention. His contempt turned to resentment, mixed with a touch of fear. Grumbling, he thrust the book into my hand. He then folded his free arm across his chest and rested his hand possessively on his own heavy book. He wanted to tell me off now, make me go away, but his fear of upsetting Miss Orr or Lucille was holding him back. I wasn't interested in probing further. Something about him was so unpleasant, I wanted no part of it. It was like an oily film that stuck to anything it touched. I couldn't have been the only one who noticed it, could I? Ralph was... not unaware of it, exactly, but seemed willing to dismiss it for whatever reason. Lucille... I could tell she didn't like him. Or did she? I very much hoped that she didn't, but she obviously had some sort of relationship with him. With them both.

"Thank you," I said sharply and turned to Lucille. "And thank you as well."

That was said more sincerely. Lucille smiled, and I had to stop myself from giggling. I was blushing again.

"You're more than welcome," she said. "I'm sorry about this. I'm afraid Lucas hasn't been told 'no' often enough to learn how to deal with it."

She offered me her hand. "All of this trouble and none of us have even bothered to introduce ourselves yet. I'm Lucille. The nice quiet one is Ralph, and the absolute pill over there is Lucas."

I tucked the book under my arm and took Lucille's hand. Her fingers were warm and smooth. "I'm Amelia. Amelia Temple."

"It's very nice to meet you, Amelia. Isn't it, boys?"

"Y-yes. Very nice," Ralph said.

Lucas glared at me and grunted something that might have been a "yes" and was more likely a "no". I got the distinct impression that this wasn't over, even when he turned his back to me and began aggressively searching through the books on the shelf behind him. He couldn't insult me further, not with Lucille standing there, so he was trying to dismiss me. My arm started to twitch again, faster this time. It was getting hard to hold on to my book. I let go of Lucille's hand and put my own over my upper arm. I could feel the flesh rippling beneath it.

If I didn't calm down, things were going to get very bad.

Lucille saw my rising agitation but mistook its source. "Are you okay, Amelia? I know Lucas is a jerk, but you don't need to take it so hard."

"I'm… I'm not upset. It's just, ah, a muscle cramp. I'm a little dehydrated, I think."

"Why don't we go take care of that? I'm thirsty, too, and getting a little tired of the company here to boot," she said. "No offense, Ralph."

"Oh, uh, none taken, Lucille."

"Whatever, Lucille," Lucas said to the books, peevish.

"Come on, I know a great place to grab a bite," Lucille said.

She put a hand on my arm—the one not experiencing morphological difficulties, fortunately—and gently led me out of the room. I decided to allow myself to be led; I wanted nothing more to do with those boys, and spending time alone with Lucille sounded more pleasant than what I'd intended when I came to town. Much more pleasant. Still, I had the presence of mind to remember one thing I had to take care of.

"I have to pay for my book," I said as we went down the stairs.

The last thing I wanted to do was leave it behind now. I wasn't going to let another overbearing man win against me.

07

Lucille assured me that the place she was taking me was only a few blocks away. We walked arm-in arm; on the way out the door, I felt a moment of boldness and slipped my good arm through hers, and she didn't pull away. By the time we got to our destination, we were laughing and talking like old friends. Well, she was doing most of the talking. I wasn't sure what to add to the conversation, and I didn't understand more than half of what she was talking about—mostly people I'd never met and movies I'd never seen. I didn't mind. It was pleasant just to hear her talk, to feel the warmth of her arm against mine. I found myself laughing not because I understood her jokes, but because I was so happy.

The "great place" turned out to be a diner. I understood that for Lucille, it was something of a comfortable establishment, a very no-frills sort of eatery. To me, it was the fanciest place I'd ever seen. The spotless counters and floors, shining chrome appliances, and neon lights in the signage made the place seem almost like another world. I squeezed Lucille's arm excitedly as we walked through the doors.

"This place looks amazing!" I said.

She gave me a puzzled look but smiled. "I'm glad you like it. I always try to eat here when I come to town. The folks who run it are terrific."

The diner was laid out around an L-shaped counter, with the base facing the door. The long end wrapped around the diner's right side, parallel to a row of wide, red-cushioned booths under windows facing the street. Three of the booths were empty, but Lucille led me to the counter.

"You don't want to sit over there?" I asked.

"No, I always sit at the counter," she said. "I like talking to Gloria."

Gloria was the young woman on the other side of the counter. Her dark skin made a lovely contrast with her peach-colored dress. She was a bit older than me and a bit younger than Lucille. This was her family's diner; though she wanted to be more than a waitress, she also wanted to help her family, and she loved talking to her regulars. Sure enough, when she recognized who had come in, she came off all smiles. She pulled a menu out from under the counter and handed it to me. Lucille had no need for one.

"Your usual, hon?" Gloria asked.

"One of these days I'm going to surprise you and order from the menu," Lucille said.

"Mm-hmm," Gloria said, giving Lucille a knowing look. "And how about you, honey? Care to try the blue plate special? It's meatloaf today, with mashed potatoes, peas and carrots."

"Um, okay," I said. It sounded as good as any other option. "May I still look through the menu, though?"

"You can look through anything you like, so long as you're paying," Gloria said with a wink. "What would you like to drink, hon? Comes with the special."

"I think a couple of Coca-Colas would be fine," Lucille said.

"I know what *you* want, Luci. I'm asking your friend."

"I'm sure she'd like a cola too. Right, Amelia?"

"Ah, that sounds fine," I said. To tell the truth, I would have preferred tea, but it was easier to go along with the force of Lucille's personality. It extended well beyond her, like great golden rose-scented wings.

Gloria set a pair of glass bottles in front of us. She turned to give our orders to the cook and then leaned against the counter to keep chatting. Lucille—*Luci*—took a long drink from her bottle. I pulled mine closer to me and looked through the menu while we waited for our food to arrive. Most of the offerings were familiar—one didn't prepare her own meals for the past five years without becoming well-acquainted with sandwiches and hot dogs—but the list of blue-plate specials drew my eye. A different item every day—meatloaf today but southern fried chicken tomorrow and crab cakes the next, all served with what the menu described as a "generous portion of fixings". There was something unmistakably comforting about it. I felt an ache deep inside that I couldn't explain.

I set the menu aside, hoping to banish that feeling, and focused on the bottle of Coke. The droplets of water sparkled in the bright fluorescent lights of the diner, casting tiny rainbows across everything. Lucille didn't seem to notice, but I was used to that sort of thing. She set her bottle down, making a satisfied noise. Then began the part I'd been dreading.

"So, Amelia, do you live around here?"

"Um…"

Yes, really pretty girl I just met and want to think I'm nice and normal, I live nearby, I thought. *I live in a secure building operated by what I'm only mostly sure is a secretive government agency, and this is the first time they've let me out without a visible handler holding my leash. It's a lot less fun than it sounds, actually.*

Instead, I said, "I don't live in Chatham Hills, but I live nearby. I just wanted to see, you know, a larger town."

"It isn't that, really," Luci said with a laugh. "Chatham Hills is a pretty sleepy burg. If you want fun, you ought to come with me to Baltimore some time."

Baltimore was well outside my prescribed limits, but I smiled and nodded.

"Are you going to school around here? The dynamic duo and I attend Del Sombra U, over in Regina."

I was suddenly intensely jealous of her, but I didn't dare let it show. Luci liked me so far, and I didn't want to give her any reason to change her mind or ask more questions with uncomfortable answers.

"Not yet. I'm looking at colleges to apply for next year. What do you think of Del Sombra? Is that where you met—well, I would say 'friends', but from what I saw, I'm not so sure."

Luci laughed. "Neither am I. Ralph and I are friends. We grew up together, and freshman year it felt like we were the only ones we knew at college. Then he met Lucas in class. They're both physics majors, taking some intense courses, and they started palling around together."

She took another sip of her Coke. "Honestly, I only spend time with Lucas to keep Ralph out of trouble. Don't get me wrong, Lucas is harmless. He's just intense. I think he's trying to drag Ralph along on some secret project of his."

"Secret project?" I said.

Luci and Gloria shared a look. There was something underneath there, a shared suspicion, but they didn't want to talk about it in front of me. That smarted, but I reminded myself that I had just met them.

"Messing around with radios or something," Luci said. She rolled her eyes. "Boys. I don't think they ever grow up."

I tried to laugh along with her, to sound like I knew what she meant. "Yeah. So what are you studying?"

"I'm majoring in English. They say it's a gimme degree, but you know those B.S. program types. They don't respect anything that doesn't need a slide rule."

She stood up straight and tried to adopt an air of fake sophistication, looking down her nose at me. Her voice took on a close approximation of Lucas' slight sneer. "Seriously, Lucille, what can anyone do with an *English* degree? It's a waste of time and money. It's not like you're *building* anything."

I snickered a bit. It was the expected thing to do. Also, I'd already decided I didn't like Lucas, so mocking him had to be a little funny.

"How stuck up," I said.

"Tell me about it. At least he's learned to stop suggesting I'm really just after my 'M.R.S.' degree," she said. She shook her head with contempt. "As if I were the sort of person to plan my life around some man."

"What are you planning?" I asked, trying to ignore my heart beating a little faster. I placed my hand a bit closer to hers. I wasn't sure what I was doing, or why, but it felt nice.

"I'd like to be a journalist. You know, like Nellie Bly?" she said. Her eyes flashed with excitement, and she leaned in a little closer. "Go out, find stories, uncover corruption and criminals, dig for the truth, and tell the world."

"That sounds like a lot of fun, actually."

"Doesn't it? Much better than being someone's housewife," she said.

"Some people seem to enjoy it," Gloria said, somewhat reproachfully.

"Oh, come on, your mother's not just a housewife," Luci said. "We both know she's the one really running the family business."

Gloria shrugged, but her smile showed she agreed. She wasn't chiding Luci that seriously. The thought of being stuck cooking and cleaning at home didn't appeal to her either.

"What about you, Gloria?" I asked.

Gloria turned to look at the kitchen. The cook, who I realized was her older brother, happily worked on our meals. It held little appeal to her. "I'm helping out around here like always, but next year I'm looking at going to Hampton."

"You're not going to go to the same school as Luci?" I said.

Luci blushed, while Gloria just laughed. Kind of. There wasn't any humor in it.

"Del Sombra doesn't have a whole lot of interest in integrating," Gloria said. "They only just started letting women in. *Colored* women come in as help."

My brow furrowed, and I started to ask why. Then I thought about the Bureau and the people who worked there. The agents were all white men, the handful of secretaries all white women. Mrs. Chisholm, Miss Valerie, all the women who worked in the cafeteria or on the cleaning staff were colored.

I thought about the bus ride into town. A sign hung over the last three rows: *This Part Of The Bus For Colored Race*. There weren't any such signs in this diner, but the twenty other patrons had separated themselves by skin color, apparently voluntarily. Our little trio was the only mixed group, and now I realized no few of the white patrons had been sneaking Luci and I ugly looks. I hadn't noticed because I was used to that, but Luci had. She deliberately ignored them, but they stoked a flame of resentment inside her.

I hadn't thought about it, because neither did anyone else. They all took it for granted that things were supposed to work that way. And therefore, so had I.

"That's horrible," I said quietly.

"It absolutely is," Luci said vehemently. "You belong at Del Sombra as much as any of us. I still think you should apply. Make them deny you and then take them to court!"

"The Lane Diner doesn't bring in enough to afford that kind of lawyer," Gloria said with a sad smile, "and Mom and Pops don't want that kind of attention."

Luci grimaced and dropped the subject. I could see the contours of an old argument there. Moreover, I could see that Gloria wasn't interested in going to Del Sombra or the Hampton Institute, for that matter. It was her way out. She wanted something more, but not something she could get at another school. She wasn't sure what that was yet. I felt a sudden kinship with her. I'd wanted to go to college as a way out from the Bureau, but beyond that I didn't have any plans, as Luci suddenly reminded me.

She downed the rest of her drink and set the bottle down, then turned to me. "How about you? What do you want to do?"

My mind raced, trying to come up with something to say. Luci leaned close to me, looking so interested in what I was going to say next that I couldn't help but tell the truth.

"I haven't thought about what I want to do with my life," I said. "I've been doing academic work, sort of, but I don't know that it's my passion. It's just something to do for now."

I must have looked very sad saying that, because Luci's eyes came all over with concern, and she placed her hand over mine. "Don't worry about that. We all find ourselves doing things we don't really want to do at this age. I've been doing clerical work over the summers to pay for college, but I'm not going to stay a secretary. You won't be stuck in what you're doing forever, either. You'll figure it out."

She patted my hand and smiled when I clasped her fingers. She said, "Right now, you have all the time in the world."

Gloria turned to the window to get our plates and set them in front of us. "Well, don't you two look like a couple of gal pals?"

Luci and I held each other's gaze for a bit, then broke into laughter. Gloria watched us with a look of puzzled amusement, then pushed our plates toward us when we finally stopped giggling. Business was light at the moment, so Gloria sat with us and chatted while we ate. She and Luci actually did most of the chatting while I listened; I was still a little lost by their conversation and didn't want to make a fool of myself. More importantly, the meatloaf was *delicious*. I understood that it was supposed to be a simple, inexpensive dish, but it was made with such care that it practically dripped with flavor. I had to stop myself from rushing through the whole thing in a couple of minutes, and every few bites I interrupted them to comment on how good it was. By the time I pushed my plate away, Gloria was beaming and insisting I had to come back again to try the other specials. I promised that I would with gusto.

"Told you this place was the best," Luci said. She pushed her empty plate away. "Ready to go, Amelia?"

I wasn't. Not yet. Leaving meant having to say goodbye to both of them. I knew Luci was ready to go back to the Del Sombra campus, and I couldn't go with her. Not without the Bureau discovering I'd gone out of bounds, and I knew they'd find out. There was always an agent on duty after hours, and checking on me was one of their responsibilities. If I didn't answer when they knocked on the door at 8 p.m., there would be trouble. The leash might have been loosened, but they still held it.

Instead of leaving, I started looking for desserts, and something halfway down the menu jumped out at me.

"Actually, could I get an ice cream float?"

I had a sudden memory, one I hadn't bothered to handle in a long time. At seven years old, Agent Simmons drove me south, away from the old Bureau building, the one in Massachusetts that had to be abandoned. He had only been my handler for a few months, after the incident. Not the one that meant the Bureau building had to be abandoned, the one before that. The one that *had* been my fault. Sort of.

No, I was innocent of this one. Maybe the only person who was.

It was a long drive, and it was getting dark. Agent Simmons didn't know much about me, just that I was a young child who needed looking after and that I was probably tired, hungry, and scared. One of the three was true, so we stopped at a diner in Pennsylvania, and he bought me a burger and fries and it smelled like heaven must smell like if only there was such a place. I ate every bite, and he laughed that a small fry like me could eat so quickly and asked where I was putting it all. Right then I knew I could like him and trust him because he didn't know what he was saying and that was fine by me. Once we both finished our burgers, he bought me an ice cream float and if I thought the burger was amazing, I didn't know anything yet and I loved it so much I made him take a sip and he laughed and played along and I hoped he would take care of me forever.

Four months later, Agent Simmons was dead. And that really had nothing to do with me at all.

"Honey? Are you okay?" Gloria asked.

"Sorry. I'm sorry," I said, swiping at my face and trying to laugh. "Just a little dust in my eye, I think."

08

~◆~

Luci had talked about going to the movies, but Gloria insisted that wasn't fair at all since she wouldn't be off-shift for a couple of hours. Waiting was no good, either. It turned out Luci also had a curfew, which made me feel a little better. A little more normal. We all agreed to put it off until the weekend. Gloria would have Saturday off, so we decided to meet for lunch. Somewhere different, Gloria insisted. The Lanes appreciated how much we liked the place, but she was getting bored with her brother's cooking.

Luci and Gloria each gave me their phone numbers and warned me the lines were likely to be busy if I called. Luci shared a phone with the rest of her dorm room on campus, and Gloria was on a party line with four other houses on her street. Then they looked at me expectantly.

"I don't have a phone, actually," I said. "Well! I do! Ha ha! Of course I do, it's just that… service is out for now. We don't know when it'll be fixed. I've been using a pay phone down the corner from where I live."

"That's perfectly understandable," Gloria said.

"Yeah. You said you were from a smaller town, right?" Luci said. "I bet utilities out there are a little rough."

"So small it's not even a real town," I said, now being perfectly truthful. "I'll give you both a call when it gets fixed, okay?"

Luci walked with me to the bus stop. After leaving Lucas and Ralph to whatever they were doing, she would have to take the bus back too, though on a different line. When I sounded concerned, she responded that she wasn't too bothered about it.

"Lucas isn't much of a gear head, but he's still overly proud of that car," she said with a dismissive toss of her hair. "Especially the back seat. I'm all too happy to stay out of it."

I sat silently for a minute, choosing my words with care. "Is he… unsafe? I can tell you don't really care for him, but…"

"Am I that obvious?" she asked, wrinkling her nose happily before becoming serious. "No. I don't like him one bit. He's got this weird pull to him, though, and it's caught Ralph somehow. I don't like that either, but someone has to keep Ralph out of trouble."

"What if that gets you into trouble?" I had found Lucas to be much more unsettling that she did, though I couldn't put my finger on why. It wasn't his interest in Luci, I was sure. Ralph was slightly smitten with her as well, but he seemed nice, if a bit… wet. No, this was something else. Something familiar in a way I couldn't quite describe.

"Don't worry. I'm not involved in whatever Frankenstein those two are whipping up in the bookstore's spare room," she said, laughing. "I don't think they're going to get in trouble with the law or anything like that. Lucas is a pill, but he has too much to lose, like his family's support and reputation. I just worry whatever silly game they're playing is going to ruin Ralph's grades. He's on a scholarship."

"Maybe we can come up with something else to occupy him?" I asked, trying to figure out what normal college students did for fun. "Like a book club?"

"Maybe we could start a bowling team," Luci said. She was teasing, though she appreciated my trying to help. "Don't worry about him, that's my job. I'm sure it'll turn out all right in the end."

"Famous last words," I said.

I wanted to say more, but my bus pulled up. Luci stood to give me a hug, which I held for as long as I dared, and said she'd see me on Saturday.

That, at least, was something to look forward to. I found myself making plans the entire bus ride back to the campus. Wondering how the day would go, imagining conversations with my new friends, deciding what we would do next time. Figuring out how to explain my situation to them without telling them things I shouldn't, or just plain didn't want them to know about me.

That last bit was harder, and finally I stopped trying. I sat in silence for the rest of the bus ride, clutching my book to my chest until it was time to get off.

A different pair of guards stood watch when I went through the gate. These looked at me no less curiously than the men they'd relieved, but now I felt a little more confident. I simply produced my identification cards as I approached and held them out for inspection. The guard in the booth looked at them suspiciously—it was an unusual time for someone to be coming in, credentialed or not—but after consulting his thick access list, he could find no reason to turn me away. So he didn't. He waved me through, and after I crossed the gate, I ceased to exist for the two guards.

It was a little odd making my way through the building so late in the day. It was close to sunset, and well after the working day for all but a skeleton crew of agents and the most dedicated of investigators. The building was dark, lit only by the emergency lights, and my footsteps echoed eerily through the empty halls. At least, I suppose others would have found it eerie. I actually enjoyed the solitude of having the building all to myself, and the freedom to go where I pleased. Previously, once everyone had begun leaving for the day, I tended to remain in my dorm. It wasn't so much that I was explicitly discouraged from wandering around—at least, not anymore. For the first seven years of my life, the door between my dormitory area and the rest of the old building had been locked after hours. Then the incident occurred, and the Bureau suddenly began worrying about emergency exits. For the next seven years, they'd simply left a guard outside the dorm area in this building. Then everyone started to feel uncomfortable about that, and it simply became understood that I would stay on my side of the door when no one was around unless I absolutely needed something. It had always been easy to comply; there was nothing I thought I wanted in the building. At least, nothing I thought I could get to without being caught.

I exercised my newfound freedom by simply walking back through the orange zone and up to my dorm, feeling at once pleased and awkward. I'd made new friends! New friends who didn't think I was weird. Well, new friends who didn't know how weird I was.

It would occur to the Bureau later that this was a mistake, but at the moment, I wasn't worrying about that.

I didn't have much time to think about my new friends during the next week, though. The indoctrination class ate up more of my time. After the first day's introductory lecture, we began diving into individual investigations, analyzing the data recovered (not much) and trying to make educated guesses as to what was really found and what it implied (provoking arguments lasting for hours). I ended up leaving the material checked out for several hours after class concluded, just so I could prepare. I was generally aware of most of the investigations and their subjects, but I had little actual background on many of them.

Not that more background *helped*. Each investigation was a collage of individual incidents—weird sightings, Fortean phenomena, and a few genuinely frightening moments—all of which refused to coalesce into a coherent image. This was still helpful in its own way, of course. I wanted to emphasize just how little the Bureau really knew about the things it investigated. This proved frustrating to the prospective agents, who desperately hoped for some kind of answer buried in the data.

It all came to a head on Thursday, when we turned to the strange case of Subject 05, otherwise known as the Beowawe Event.

Beowawe was a small town in northeastern Nevada. The Leonids were particularly spectacular in 1901, and Beowawe had a good view of them. While stargazing, an amateur astronomer named Douglas Puck found his attention instead drawn to a series of strange flashing lights above the mountains. A few days later, workers in the nearby Albright Mine started unearthing unusual mineral formations. According to reports, the ore appeared to be "rotting" and gave off a pungent odor. None of the samples survived to the present day and neither did photographs, if any existed. Some sort of evidence must have reached the locals, because after hearing about the ore, Puck grew obsessed with proving a connection between it and his curious light show.

(It is worth noting at this juncture that no one else reported such a display, so the only evidence for that sighting is in what remains of Puck's private journal.)

After the mine was (then only temporarily) shut down, Puck surreptitiously set up shop in the foreman's office and began exploring. His notes describe a series of unusual rock formations within the shafts, formations that didn't match any of the descriptions given by workers interviewed after the fact. He also described hearing a strange noise like "metallic bees", which later analysts speculated was some form of radio static.

A week later, the mine collapsed. No one ever confirmed whether Puck was in it at the time, but he was never seen again. Curiously, investigators found what was left of his journal at the foreman's desk.

"When this hit the Bureau's desks thirty years later, the mineral anomalies were collectively designated Subject 05," I said in conclusion. "Other mines in the area were unaffected by the 'mineral rot', and the phenomenon has not recurred there or elsewhere. At least, not so far as we know."

"So, where the hell did it *come from*, then?" Morris asked. "Did it ride down on one of those meteors?"

"Meteor*ites*," Dawes said. "If they land, they're meteorites."

"Let me ask you something, Stan," Morris said. "Does the nitpicking thing actually pull in the dames? Oh, 'scuse me, 'the ladies'?"

"*Gentlemen*," I said, trying to head off the budding testosterone-fueled argument. "That's not a bad hypothesis, Mister Morris, but there were no reports of a meteorite within a hundred miles of Beowawe during the event's timeframe. It may not even have had anything to do with the meteor shower. The Leonids have been seen all over the world for decades, after all. The timing may have simply been a coincidence."

Morris ran a hand through his hair in frustration. "Then how did that crap *get* here?"

I frowned, trying to hide my discomfort. Something about the tone of the question set my teeth on edge. I shuffled the papers spread across the lectern, trying not to look like I was struggling to formulate a good response. Unfortunately, I didn't have one.

"We don't really know for certain, not yet," I said, "so the only answer is 'it's complicated'."

Most of the agents looked disappointed, not that I could blame them. Uncertainty did not lead to closed cases. I wondered how they would handle learning that the Bureau had never actually closed a case.

"Consider a thunderstorm," I said. "We know the weather is the result of elements—heat, wind, moisture—combining. When you have just the right amount of each, you get rain. Add in a buildup of charged particles, and you get lightning. Then, under the right conditions, you get a lightning strike.

"If there was a thunderstorm outside right now, we could probably make a good guess as to where lightning would *probably* strike, but we would have no way of predicting what would be struck with any certainty, nor even if there definitely would be a ground strike."

Dawes stroked his chin thoughtfully. "In other words, these incursions are the end result of a complex interplay of factors."

"Exactly."

"Has anyone ever figured out how to replicate them?"

"That's... I..." I stumbled over the answer, not sure what to say or how to say it. Yes, obviously the Bureau had been studying this, under controlled conditions of exceeding strictness. Which might explain why they'd never had any success. That was a specific division within the Bureau, however, and the agents involved were hand-picked to a degree that made the Bureau's general recruitment guidelines look lax. No one below the assistant director was even supposed to know who was in that group. I'd carefully hidden the fact that I did.

"Remember that this area of study is still in its infancy and also highly dangerous," I finally said. "Whether anyone has tried to replicate an incursion, I can't say. Actual proof of that can be hard to come by. The exact factors, and to what degree, are exceedingly complicated and no doubt highly esoteric—they would have to be, or we would see extranormal events more often. The Bureau genuinely has not identified what those factors were in any of the incidents it investigated. I can tell you that it would look suspiciously on any attempts to replicate an event, and if you wonder why, go back and read your notes on the Richmond Incident."

I left the conference room feeling deeply unsatisfied. I kept mulling over Dawes' last question. Was it possible to replicate the conditions that allowed an ultraterrestrial incursion into our fragment of the universe? Of course. In theory. It was theoretically possible to engineer a rainstorm as well, though the methods there were far better known and yet far from one hundred percent successful.

I didn't have much time to mull it over, however. When I left the conference room that day, Agent Walsh was waiting in the hallway. A look of concern hung over his face like a thundercloud.

"Amelia," he said. "Could you come with me, please?" Despite his tone, it wasn't a question.

I fell into step behind Agent Walsh, following him through the orange zone and to his office. Another agent waited inside, arms folded across his desk as he leaned against the doorframe. My heart sank as I recognized him.

"Thomas," Walsh said when he reached the door. "Do you mind?"

Agent Thomas didn't smile. I didn't think he could. He smirked and stepped out of the way, taking two steps back into my handler's office. Walsh's jaw tightened, but he didn't say anything. He simply walked into his office and took a seat behind his desk. Thomas leaned against the filing cabinet, turning his gaze to me.

So they both wanted to talk to me. Wonderful.

Despite our differences, Agent Walsh and I had developed something of a rapport. I didn't trust him, exactly—I didn't trust anyone at the Bureau—but we had at least a positive relationship. Agent Thomas, on the other hand... something about him set off an alarm in my head. He always looked at me as if he knew something I didn't, but I couldn't read him well enough to figure out what it was. He was of a different sort. The sort that would have been behind the incident that closed the original offices in Massachusetts, had he been part of the Bureau a decade ago. I knew he was part of the Specials Division, but only because Agent Walsh knew that.

I'd tried looking into Agent Thomas' mind before. All I got was the mental equivalent of radio static. Not blankness, just this incoherent mess blocking his thoughts from my view. I didn't think he knew I could see it, but it frightened me just the same. He was unpredictable, unknowable.

But he didn't like me, I knew that much.

"Sorry to butt in on your side project, Pat," Agent Thomas said to Walsh, "but the AD figured you could use a little more oversight for this."

Agent Walsh grimaced. A half-dozen retorts flew across his mind, but none of them reached his mouth. Instead, he looked at me.

"Amelia," he said. "We have some concerns."

I saw right away what he was trying to say, and my mouth drew into a tight line. My fists balled up on their own, and I tucked them behind my back before the men could see. I tried to keep my voice as level as possible. I didn't succeed.

"This is about my friends," I said. "You're going to try to keep me away from them."

Walsh flinched. Agent Thomas looked at him with a bit of contempt but didn't say anything. Walsh dropped his eyes to a stack of manila folders on his desk. Each one was marked with my friends' names. And Lucas Dowling's.

"That's putting it a bit bluntly, Amelia," he said.

"Really? Because you were about to ask whether I wanted to be hanging around 'people like that'."

"It's a valid question, kid," Agent Thomas said.

"That's ridiculous!"

"Amelia, please," Walsh said. "If you would hear me out for a few minutes."

Agent Thomas rolled his eyes. "You're too soft on the kid, Pat. Who's in charge here, you or *her*?"

I cut my eyes to Agent Thomas, glaring at him. "What exactly do you mean?"

Walsh turned in his chair, giving the other agent a cool look. "Yes, Agent Thomas. What do you mean? Because I believe Bureau protocol is quite clear on this matter."

Agent Thomas sneered at us both. "This is ridiculous."

"I didn't ask for your opinion," Walsh said. "Or your presence."

"Too bad. You're getting 'em both," Thomas said. "You've been too soft on Temple from the start, and it's showing. Lay down the law so we can go to lunch."

Walsh looked at me when he responded. "I'm not 'laying down' anything. But a red flag or two has popped up, and I want to discuss it with you. I won't lie—there are elements in the Bureau who are already reconsidering the expanded privileges you've been granted."

We both looked at Agent Thomas, who rolled his eyes.

"What I want," Walsh continued, "is to be able to reassure them that there aren't any problems brewing. Can you help me with that?"

I glared at the stack of folders indignantly. "You've been prying into my friends' lives."

Walsh gave me an impatient look and waved the file marked with Luci's name at me. It looked rather slim. "Do you know how long it takes to run a proper background search? It's only been a couple of days."

"Oh."

"We pulled their student records from Del Sombra. Except for Miss Lane. We just asked the local police department for her arrest record."

72

Ignoring my horrified look, he showed me the slimmest of the four files. "You'll probably be pleased to know she doesn't have one."

"I would expect not!"

"We should have the arrest records for the other three by the end of the week. If there are any. Cooperation with local police departments can take time. And it's not me, it's another division entirely. They don't know why they're looking into these kids. Don't act so surprised, Amelia. Do you think we'd really let just anyone have access to you?"

"Trying to protect me from bad influences?" I asked nastily.

"Trying to protect you from people who might hurt you," he said, refusing to rise to my bait. "Regardless of what you think of the Bureau's treatment of you, we do have your best interests at heart."

"And to keep away bad influences," Agent Thomas said. "Show her the Sweeney girl's file, Pat."

"Sweeney? *Lucille?*" I asked, aghast.

"She's a… I don't want to say 'troublemaker', but we did get some of her past history," Agent Walsh said. "Did you know she was raised by her mother?" He and Thomas shared a look. Volumes passed in that glance. "No man in the picture at all."

Sounds lucky, I thought. "So?"

"Her father's still alive, living in Colorado," Agent Thomas said. "'Miss' Sweeney has some… let's call 'em *convictions*. She may have passed some of them down to her daughter."

"You need to be careful what sort of friends you're making," Walsh said.

I know exactly *what kind of friend I'm making*, I thought.

What I said was, "Luci's a good person. She's nice and caring. She isn't the sort of person who'd get me into trouble."

"You can't possibly know that, Amelia," Walsh said. "You've known her for less than a week. You've interacted with her *once*. You don't know anything about her."

I know that she smells like roses and her face looks like the sun coming up when she smiles, I thought. *I know she stood up for me when Lucas was being a jerk. I know if she were here, she'd be giving you a piece of her mind.*

"I won't get to know her if I'm not allowed to see her," I said. "She's my friend. Or at least, she wants to be. Am I not allowed to have friends?"

"The Bureau does not see that as necessary to provide," Agent Thomas said.

I slapped my hand on the desk. Agent Thomas, all six feet and one inch of him, drew back and raised a hand to his jacket. Where he kept his service pistol. Walsh looked at him in alarm, raising an open hand. I ignored them.

"The *Bureau* is the one keeping me here! The *Bureau* is the one that raised me! No one asked the *Bureau* to do that. The *Bureau* just decided to! What right does the *Bureau* have to determine what is and isn't necessary?"

Agent Thomas moved his hand to his tie, adjusting it and trying to assume an air of authority. "Are you asking for a copy of the executive order creating the Bureau, or are you speaking rhetorically?"

"Does saying that make you feel clever?"

"*Enough*, Amelia," Agent Walsh said.

He stood and glared down at me, and I suddenly feared that I had pushed him too far. What if he decided to revoke my off-campus privileges? What if they started locking me in my dorm again?

What if he pushes me too far? a part of me wondered

"If you want to be treated like an adult, you need to *act like it*," he said. "Right now, you're acting like a child who's been told 'no'."

"I *am* a child, and I *have* been told 'no'," I muttered.

"I'm an adult, and I get told 'no' all the time," he said. "Just recently,

I put in for some time off. It was denied. Do you think I appreciated that?"

"No," I said, more surprised than anything. I had no idea he had tried to take a vacation. How had he kept that from me?

"Do you want to know why it was denied?" he asked.

That he couldn't keep from me. "Because of your duties as my handler."

"Exactly. I have too much responsibility right now."

He sat down heavily, turning his attention back to his paperwork and letting me stew on that. I was short on sympathy for Walsh's plight. It might not have been fair, but when had life ever been fair to me? Why should it be fair for anyone else?

"Despite what you seem to think, you haven't been told 'no' yet. The Bureau does not find it necessary to provide you with companionship," Walsh said, giving Agent Thomas a cold look, "but it doesn't find it necessary to deny it, either. At least, not yet."

"The Bureau reserves the right to revisit that decision," Agent Thomas said.

"But only if necessary," Walsh said. "None of your new friends seem like bad kids, exactly, although Dowling's professors have some choice words about his attitude. And the Connor boy could do to focus more on his liberal arts classes."

"And there's everything to do with Sweeney's political ideas."

"Which we don't actually have confirmed yet," Walsh said. His tone was growing more cross. He'd already resented Agent Thomas' intrusion into his duties, and the other agent's attitude wasn't changing his mind. "Did she say anything to you that seemed odd? Inappropriate?"

"No," I said. "We talked about college and Gloria's family. *Normal* things."

Of course, that wasn't entirely true. We'd also talked about segregation, and how ugly it was. To my dismay, I realized that this was one of the "political convictions" Agent Walsh was concerned about. I couldn't tell what Agent Thomas would think about it, but it wasn't hard to guess. I'd seen the way he interacted with the support staff. I understood that this wasn't the time to mention that, though. Walsh wanted to hear there was nothing to worry about, so that's what I told him. It made me sick, but the two white men controlling my future weren't likely to be sympathetic.

"That's good," Agent Walsh said. "Nothing about the Bureau, correct?"

"Of course not," I said. "I wouldn't even know what to say."

The two agents visibly relaxed. Was that their biggest concern? Whether I was keeping their secrets? They might have just started with that and saved me a lot of frustration.

"I'm not sure what to tell them about me," I said. "About where I live or what I do."

"Nothing," Agent Thomas snapped. "You tell them absolutely nothing."

Agent Walsh took a deep breath, trying to control his frustration with his colleague. "We've developed a cover story, if you're willing to hear me out."

I pulled the chair over to his desk and sat down. It was a small enough concession to keep my friends. "I'm listening."

The cover story Walsh had cooked up had just enough of a ring of truth to make it work. I was an orphan (true, so far as I knew) living as a ward of the state (also true, technically) in a small, state-run facility near Chatham Hills (probably true?). I couldn't accept visitors, but due to my age, I was allowed a certain measure of freedom outside of "school hours". I wasn't happy about having to be honest about how old I really was—Lucille and Gloria were two years older than me and had assumed I was the same age as them—but Walsh insisted it would make things easier. The less they had to fabricate, the better it would hang together. I had to concede he was probably right.

As a concession for my cooperation, or possibly a small payment for my silence, I would be allowed the use of a semi-public phone in a disused office within the orange zone. One of the duty personnel would pose as a social worker during certain hours in the event of an outside call. It wasn't perfect, but it was something.

Just not something like a normal life.

09

Saturday came, eventually, and found me in Chatham Hills with my new friends. We met up at Hanners Square, near the heart of downtown, and tried to decide where to go next. At least, Luci and Gloria did. Still having no more an idea of where in town was a good place to visit than I did of the moon, I was content to let them deliberate and agree with whatever they decided to do.

I was less content with how I looked next to them. Luci wore a robin's-egg blue cardigan over a light yellow dress, Gloria an orange sweater and long black skirt. I had simply selected at random one of the half-dozen near-identical gray dresses that some man at the Bureau had purchased for me. My friends both looked incredibly stylish; I looked utterly drab in comparison, a boring tag-along to two dynamic women-about-town.

To their credit, Luci and Gloria had simply assumed that fashion wasn't my thing, until Luci caught me glancing wistfully at her outfit.

"What's wrong, Amelia?" she asked.

"Oh! Um, nothing…" I stammered, trying quickly to change the subject. "I was just thinking about… something."

Very *clever, Amelia*, I thought, inwardly kicking myself. *That's* certain *to throw her off the scent.*

"I don't mean to pry, hon," Luci said, "but I'm going to. It looks like something's bothering you. It's okay, you can tell us."

"You really ought to," Gloria said with a smile. "She's not going to let up until you get whatever it is off your chest."

"You're making me sound like a busybody," Luci said, tossing her head to the side and sniffing faux-dismissively.

"Isn't that your career goal?" Gloria asked.

"Being a journalist is so much more than being a busybody, and also stop trying to distract me. I'm being a concerned friend."

Luci put a tender hand on my arm, and my heart skipped a beat.

"I'm not being too nosy, am I?" she asked, her brilliant blue eyes wide with compassion. "If I am, you can go ahead and tell me off. I won't mind."

"She will. She completely will," Gloria said. "But she'll also drop it."

"I'm going to say something unladylike at you, Glory," Luci said, smirking.

"Four brothers, remember? You think you can come up with anything I ain't heard before, college girl?"

"Don't say 'ain't', it ain't sophisticated," Luci said. "And stop distracting me. Amelia's about to spill it."

"I am?" I was. I did. "It's silly, really…"

I plucked at the fabric of my dress. It was coarse. Not uncomfortable, exactly, just cheap. Cheap and drab.

Luci, fortunately, understood what I was trying to say immediately. "Oh, honey. There's nothing wrong with the way you're dressed. I never thought anything of it. I just thought that was, you know, your *style*."

She wasn't being entirely truthful, but I dismissed the little lie as a kindness. It's not as if I wanted to hear her say how boring she thought

I looked at first glance.

"I don't think I have a style, actually," I said. "I've never... they always just picked out clothes for us."

Gloria's brow creased slightly with concern. "You mean your parents?"

I bit my lip and quietly shook my head. A little tear pricked at the corner of my eye. That wasn't me faking.

Luci took my hand. "Say no more. You can pick out your *own* clothes now. Change of plans, Gloria?"

"Change of plans," Gloria said, nodding firmly.

And that was how we ended up at Farley's department store instead of the Arcadia Theater, trying on dresses, laughing, and generally having a fine time. I had pointed out the Woolworths on Main Street—it was closer, after all—but Gloria had looked the other way. It came down to Luci to quietly explain that most of the stores in town were as segregated as her university. Gloria was likely to be refused service at Woolworths, but Farley's was in the part of town where the colored families lived.

The world outside the Bureau campus was shaping up to be much worse than I'd imagined, but I went along with my new friends.

Luci and I drew some odd looks as we made our way through the store, but I was used to that. Luci less so, but she took it in stride. She understood a lot more than I did, or at least she thought so. She would rather be the stared-at girl than her friend, and at least she had the advantage of knowing *she* wasn't going to be refused service over her skin color.

The girls at the shop were friendly enough, and not just in the interest of customer service, and the three of us quickly settled into a routine. One of us would dig through the racks and pull something out for another girl, and the third would insist they at least try it on, come on, it'll look *perfect* on you, and then the second girl would come out of the dressing room and either agree or roll her eyes at the others, and then it'd be her turn at the racks. It all felt so wonderfully normal.

Obviously, it couldn't last.

None of us had the money to buy everything we wanted, so once we narrowed it down to a pair of outfits apiece, we left the store. It was nearly noon by the time we were done, and everyone was hungry. This time, however, Luci and Gloria knew exactly where they wanted to go. I thought we might go to the diner for lunch, but the other two took me to a small restaurant a couple of blocks east of the diner. And much closer to Orr's Used Books.

I realized why we'd picked this place when I picked up a knot of nerves, anxiety and second thoughts in a back corner of the restaurant. Ralph Connor sat there, poking at a plate of fries. Luci pretended not to see him, although I could tell they knew he was there before we even came through the door. They were expecting him. I wanted to ask why, but I wasn't quite sure how.

Instead, I asked, "Why did we come here? The diner's not far away."

Gloria and Luci exchanged a look.

"We're not eating here," Gloria said with a tight smile.

"Definitely not," Luci said. "We're just here to see someone. Then we'll eat."

"You two go on ahead," Gloria said. "I'll be over by that newsstand."

I was confused for a moment. Then I noticed the sign on the restaurant's big picture window. *Whites Only*. Which wasn't true at all. There were several colored people in the building, working in the kitchen.

Luci flashed Gloria a guilty look. "It'll only be a minute."

"It's fine," Gloria said, even though it wasn't. "It's the best way to catch him."

"Catch him at what?" I looked between the two of them, expecting an explanation.

Luci was hesitant. "The best way to catch him to… talk. You know. Make sure he's doing okay."

There was more behind what she was saying. I could see it in both of their minds. Something about whatever he was doing with Lucas. Luci's thoughts were tinged with worry, Gloria's with suspicion. I wanted to look further, but something about that made me feel guilty. I'd never felt any compunction about probing through Agent Walsh's thoughts, or Pickman's, or anyone else's at the Bureau. Luci and Gloria, however, had been kind to me. Even if they never knew, it would be a betrayal of their trust.

"All right," I said. "Let's go talk to your friend."

Ralph was sitting with his back to the door, so he jumped in his seat when Luci cheerfully called his name. He turned around so quickly he almost fell out of his chair, but he smiled awkwardly when he saw Luci. The smile faltered a bit when he recognized me.

"L-Lucille! Hello!" he said. Then he looked at me. "Um, hello…?"

"Amelia," I said. "We met at the bookstore the other day. It's nice to see you again, Ralph."

"L-likewise," he said. He wasn't entirely unconvincing, either. "I, um, w-wasn't expecting to meet you again."

"I wouldn't let Lucas drive her off." Luci gave my hand a quick squeeze that sent my heart beating faster. "Speaking of Tall-Jerk-and-Handsome-I-Guess, I'm surprised to see you here without him."

"W-we're meeting up after lunch," Ralph said. "Lucas d-doesn't like eating here. In t-town, I mean." He dropped his voice to a conspiratorial whisper. "He thinks all the food in town is terrible."

I took a bit of offense at that. I didn't have any great attachment to Chatham Hills, but Lucas' casual contempt made me like the town that much more. I was tempted to recommend the Lane Diner, but did I want to inflict Lucas Dowling on Gloria's family? No, I did not.

"Lucas is entitled to his opinion," Luci said, in a tone that made it perfectly clear he wasn't. "You're meeting up with him? Still working on that mysterious project instead of, say, your history paper?"

Ralph looked away, guiltily. That paper was due this coming Monday, and here it was Saturday and half-written. He had every intention of finishing it, or so he had told himself. After he finished his work with Lucas.

I was beginning to understand Luci's need to meddle.

Ralph looked back to Luci, then to me. He wasn't sure what he was allowed to tell her. He was definitely sure he couldn't say anything to me. Lucas Dowling loomed heavy in his thoughts, as if the boy were looking over his shoulder. Lucas wasn't there, however, and Ralph needed friends other than him. Not that Lucas Dowling was anything like a friend to him.

"It's fine, Ralph," I said. "I like you. You're nice. You can talk in front of me."

He hesitated for a moment, unable to decide whether I was putting him on. Luci smiled and said, "You're right. Go on, Ralph. I mean, it's not like it's a secret or anything, right?"

"Yes. Luci told me all about you and Lucas and your side project. It sounds really interesting!"

Ralph fidgeted a bit—they really hadn't told Luci much, or at least he hadn't—but he wanted to share what they had with her. To impress her. Myself, not so much—I was just Luci's weird new friend—but he was already starting to come to the conclusion we wanted him to reach.

"Since you already know… L-Lucas and I are onto something pretty n-neat. We think the th-theory is s-solid, but we're working on the application. It's kind of untrodden ground, actually. We're making an awful lot of progress, but there's still more work to do."

"What *are* you working on?" I asked.

"It's k-kind of hard to explain..." he said.

Mainly because he didn't fully understand it. Something about additional dimensions of space, I could see that much, but Lucas had given him the information in dribs and drabs. That seemed like a poor way to run an experiment to me, but a good way for Lucas Dowling to be able to claim all the credit.

Luci was itching to know what they were doing. I couldn't quite understand why—one didn't have to be a mind reader to see she thought the whole endeavor was foolish—but I could see she was angling for a way to get inside their laboratory. And he'd just given her an opening.

"If it's so hard to explain, why don't you just show us?" she asked, smiling winsomely.

"I d-don't know. L-Lucas is pretty firm about n-not letting anyone see it unt-til it's ready."

Lucas didn't want anyone to see it at all, in fact. He'd said as much to Ralph many times. I could see snatches of what I could only describe as rants, about so-called experts and busybodies who wouldn't understand. No wonder they were working in the back room of a bookstore miles from their university. Ralph didn't understand his "partner" and his obsession with secrecy. And Luci's opinion meant the world to him. I could feel how badly he wanted to share his work with her, his only friend from childhood.

So I reached in and *touched* that want.

There won't be any harm, I thought to him. *What you're doing is fascinating, and Luci will be so impressed by it.*

I didn't know what I was doing. I didn't know I was doing it. And honestly, I wasn't sure that I'd done anything at all, except I saw Ralph's mind *change* in front of me.

"W-well, I s-suppose there w-wouldn't be any harm," he said. "I m-mean, it *is* a really fascinating experiment. *I* think so, anyway."

"No harm at all," I said.

"Won't take more than an hour, right?" Luci said with a chipper bounce. "We can catch lunch afterward. So long as you're on board, Amelia."

"Wouldn't miss it," I said, although I kept my eyes on Ralph.

10

Lucas was waiting for us outside the left-hand door on the bookstore's second floor. He looked pointedly at an old-fashioned pocket watch cradled in his left hand. When the four of us tromped upstairs, he finally deigned to look up from the timepiece.

"Ah, Ralphie. Took you long enough," he said, looking disdainfully at Gloria and me. "I see you brought a menagerie."

"You and Ralph seem so proud of your little experiment," Luci said with a charming but frosty smile. "We thought you'd like to show it off for us. Isn't that right, Ralph?"

"Uh… r-right. That's right," Ralph said. He had thought no such thing, but nodded along, already convincing himself. "I m-mean, it w-would be g-great for Luci to understand what w-we're doing."

"How very droll." Lucas snapped his watch shut. "I suppose. Perhaps it will get Lucille off our backs. Let's get started."

He opened the door and gestured for us to follow him inside. I slipped behind Lucille, with Gloria last to follow. As I crossed into the room, something in my head… flickered. I'd originally perceived the room as an empty space, like an unused storage room. Instead, I found a private, one-room apartment hastily converted into an amateur laboratory. The furniture had been pushed to the side or cleared out entirely, leaving shapes covered in white sheets. In place of furnishings, the room held a trio of brass armatures, a large metal sheet propped against the far wall (and blocking the room's sole window), and a chalkboard half-covered in equations.

Nothing about the scene was particularly troubling, if one ignored Lucas Dowling's odious presence, but the fact that I couldn't see any of it until I stepped into the room set my heart racing. For a moment I felt adrift, lost in the space between four simple walls, an uncarpeted floor and dingy ceiling. Luci kept an eye on Lucas as he made Ralph wheel the chalkboard to the middle of the room, so she didn't notice anything amiss with me. Gloria, however, must have seen something in my face, because I felt a slight touch on my shoulder. I turned to see her brown eyes full of concern for me.

"Amelia? Is everything okay?" she whispered.

I put my hand over hers and gave her fingers a light squeeze. "Just a headache. A little one," I said, trying to smile.

Lucas, of course, took no notice of any of us. He erased a portion of the chalkboard and drew a rather familiar diagram: a three-dimensional representation of 4-D space-time. Almost the same one I'd shown my class a week ago, if somewhat simpler. And sloppier. The coincidence caused my hand to twitch, but I tried to dismiss it. The two boys were math majors, after all. Extra dimensions came with the specialty.

"They probably never covered this in those poetry classes you take, Lucille," Lucas said, "but this is a rough representation of the universe's shape. Einstein's equations describe, and please understand that I'm vastly oversimplifying this—"

"You're too kind," Luci said dryly.

Lucas paused but decided not to retort. This time. "Ahem. I'm oversimplifying this, but basically space is curved. Not just curved but *contoured*. What we call gravity is basically a series of troughs and divots that massive objects create in space."

He went on like this for some time, and he was right. It was an oversimplification. More importantly, it was mistaken. Partially.

"Your math is off," I said.

Lucas' head snapped around. He was in the middle of describing one of the equations. "I beg your pardon?"

"Your math is off," I said. "That doesn't describe what you think it does. Like that, it doesn't describe *anything*."

Lucas' open mouth slowly formed into a sneer. My interruption had thrown off his thought processes, and he was struggling to switch gears. I didn't wait for him to finish formulating his snide comeback. I walked up to the board and wiped out the offending equation with my hand, then wrote in the correct figures.

"There. *That's* how to properly describe how space works in six dimensions. What you wrote was… well, it looked like someone just playing around with a slide rule."

Lucas drew himself up to his full height and raised one arrogant finger to say something, but before he could get a word out, Ralph coughed politely behind him.

"A-actually, um, I th-think she's r-right."

A mixture of hurt and indignation crawled across Lucas' face. He turned to glare at Ralph, who took a halting step back and shrugged apologetically. Lucas rounded back on me, glaring imperiously down his nose.

"How could *you* possibly know anything about multidimensional mathematics?" he demanded. "You aren't a Del Sombra student. What university are you attending? Have you even *been* to college?"

I slowly put the chalk down and placed a hand on my hip. Eyes narrowed, I glared at him through my eyelashes. When I spoke, my tone nearly lowered the temperature in the room.

"I have had *excellent* tutors."

Lucas' mind was a red snarl of awful words and injured pride. I saw everything he wanted to say fighting it out as he tried to come up with the perfect way to put me back in my place, held back only by his fear of losing face in front of Luci and of his own suspected inferiority. Something else was there too, something I couldn't quite reach, but it was ugly. Ugly and infuriating and suffused with unearned superiority. It was everything I was sick of putting up with, and I decided in that moment I wasn't going to. I reached in to grab that barely buried fear, and I *pulled* on it.

You're absolutely right, I thought. *You really* are *just dabbling in something you barely understand. You'll never get this right. You don't even know what you're doing.*

Lucas flinched and took a stumbling step backward, mumbling something under his breath. It might have been an apology, or even a "thank you". It wasn't, but it could have been. His face flushed a bright red. Luci covered her mouth to hide a snicker, while Gloria shook her head.

"It's not a big deal, hon," she said. "Everyone makes mistakes."

Lucas turned his glare to her, but the retort he was going to make died in his throat when Gloria raised an eyebrow at him. He coughed uncomfortably and ran a hand through his hair, trying to recover the air of respectable authority he'd thought he was projecting. He only made himself look like more of a self-important twit, but I supposed it was preferable to petulance.

"So, Lucas," Luci said, trying to drag the afternoon back on track, or at least toward a conclusion, "this has been a very entertaining tutoring session in a class I'm not actually interested in taking, but I was sort of wondering if you were *going* anywhere with all of this."

Lucas coughed once. "Yes. I am. Of course I am. Ralphie?"

Ralph rolled his eyes at the name but went to fetch one of the armatures and a box of components, primarily a selection of glass lenses and telescoping struts. He set the armature up in front of the chalkboard while Lucas watched off to one side, arms folded across his chest. Ralph began fiddling with the device while Lucas gave instructions and the occasional snide remark. We stepped back to give them space, forming a small circle. Luci stood with her hands on her hips, being performatively bored, but Gloria paid close attention. After a few minutes, the boys produced something like the unnatural offspring of a table lamp and a camera, mounted on a gimbal.

"As Amanda here so helpfully pointed out," Lucas said, nodding vaguely in my direction, "*this* equation describes the way space-time is shaped in six dimensions."

I rolled my eyes. Luci was about to say something, but I shook my head and waved her off. The insult was petty and not worth our attention.

"While this is, of course, perfectly coherent to the mathematician, it's a bit opaque to the less-educated masses. Thus, I have, with Ralphie's assistance, developed a way to *demonstrate* that bend.

"This device simply produces a focused beam of light. When configured *just* right, we should be able to project that light and see the way higher dimensions cause it to bend."

Luci looked skeptical. "We've all used flashlights before. You're telling me you're whipping up a flashlight big enough to light Dimension X in the attic of a used bookstore, and that's why Ralph's failing History 101."

"I'm n-not *failing* yet, Lucille," Ralph said sheepishly. No one took any notice.

"I recognize that to you art studies' types, it must seem like 'higher' dimensions are, in fact, much farther away," Lucas said, his lips curled into an infuriating sneer, "but in actuality, we're talking about direction, not distance. The sixth dimension is simply at an angle we can't naturally perceive. We're going to correct that."

"Once we f-finish building the rest of the equipment," Ralph said.

Lucas scowled at him, then turned back to us. "Yes, after that."

Lucille sighed. "And how much longer is that going to take? You're going to have mid-terms soon, Ralph."

"I-it's nearly ready!"

"Ready in time for you to study?" Lucille asked, glaring at Lucas. "How much of his time is this going to eat up?"

"I was hoping to make progress on assembling the apparatus," Lucas said, disgruntled, "not listen to another lecture about how Ralphie spends his free time. It will be ready soon. Very soon indeed."

Gloria took little notice of their argument. Instead, she studied the equations scrawled across the chalkboard. Committing them to memory, in fact. I could sense an underlying disappointment, though— she expected to find something else, although she wasn't entirely sure what.

Lucas wasn't telling us the whole truth. His experiment had something to do with multidimensional geometry, that much was obvious, but the purpose of his equipment? What he'd told us was nonsense. Luci had picked up that much without even being able to see him formulate the falsehood in his mind. But why lie about it in the first place?

"If you're so concerned about the amount of Ralphie's time this is taking up," Lucas said, ushering Luci toward the door, "perhaps you should leave so we can get back to work?"

"Perhaps I should," Luci said, letting herself be led away. "Thank you so much for the *very* informative afternoon, Lucas."

Lucas didn't rise to her bait. Instead, he looked over his shoulder at Gloria and me. "I assume you're leaving too?"

"Of course," Gloria said. "I'd hate to take up more of your time."

"Th-thanks for p-playing along!" Ralph called after us.

Lucille managed to keep quiet all the way through the bookstore, though her mind whirled with everything she wanted to say. She finally let it out once the door closed behind us.

"What an odious little twerp!" she said. "Amelia, Gloria, I'm so sorry you had to put up with that. I don't know why Ralph does. I don't know why *I* do."

"I've known young men like him before," Gloria said, choosing her words with care. "Usually before the world knocks the cocky out of them."

"It's going to take a pretty hard knock for that idiot," Luci said. "A wrecking ball."

She and Gloria shared a look. Despite what they'd said upstairs, I could tell they were very interested in what Lucas was up to, and didn't believe his explanation any more than I did.

"So…" I said, picking my words with care, "he's lying, right?"

Gloria nodded. "Like a snake."

"I'd like to know why. That felt like a waste of time," Luci said. Then she laughed. "I suppose it was worth it to see someone prove that jackass wrong. The look on his face!"

"I really thought he was going to say something rude to you, Amelia," Gloria said.

"He was, for a moment," I said. "I guess he changed his mind."

"He's a coward, deep down," Luci said firmly. "Boys like him always are. So full of themselves when they're on top, then running away the first time they get knocked down."

That's not quite right, I thought. *What about when they get into a corner?*

I didn't disagree with her out loud, though. "Maybe he'll learn some humility from this."

"I doubt it," Luci said. "And I don't know any more about what he and Ralph are doing instead of attending their general education classes. Taking apart telescopes and sticking them on rods? This is what Ralph's risking his GPA over?"

I felt a flash of nameless fear from Gloria. I caught a snatch of a drawing, something sinuous and shadowy. She looked up at the bookstore's second floor. Inside, Lucas and Ralph were up to something. Something I couldn't see; now that I was outside, the bookstore's back room appeared as empty to me as it had before.

This was about more than Ralph's grades, but I didn't know how to ask what my friends were afraid they were doing.

"That's enough worrying for one day," Luci said. "We were going to the Arcadia, weren't we?"

"I'm game for whatever you want to do," I said, though my thoughts never left the bookstore.

11

Days passed, and my misgivings about Lucas' experiment hadn't gone away. I couldn't understand what I found so troubling. Was I responding to his attitude? It certainly wasn't the sort of thing to inspire love, although I had to admit it had at least earned him a degree of Ralph's loyalty, somehow.

What it came down to, I finally decided, was that I didn't trust Lucas Dowling. Something was inherently fishy about him. I knew, and Luci and Gloria knew, that he was hiding something, although I couldn't possibly prove it, nor understand why. Not without seeing more. So I waited and brooded on it and tried to come up with some way of learning more about their experiment.

On Wednesday, I dreamed.

It was dark and cold. I sat in the middle of my bed, skinny legs drawn up against my narrow chest, thin arms hugging my knees. There was something going on outside the door, something I couldn't hear, but it scared me. Men were angry. Were they angry at me? They usually were. Especially after what happened to Agent Carlisle.

For a moment, I didn't realize I was dreaming. Everything was familiar but too big. My bed was huge, my one room that was the whole of my world was gigantic, the door that kept me locked away from the others cyclopean. Then I realized I was right the first time. I wasn't dreaming. This was a memory. I was seven years old again, and everything was about to go bad.

I slid off my bed and crept to the door. I tried to *see* what was going on, but it was unclear. Back then, I hadn't yet learned to see outside myself very well. Too young to understand, I pushed my dark hair out of my face, as if it was blocking my view—it was getting long again, the way I liked it, but I knew the men would force a haircut on me soon. I crouched down and put my ear against the door. I heard men running through the halls and shouting. Not outside my door, fortunately. Farther in. Where the other one was kept.

I wasn't supposed to know about the other one, of course. Neither were most of the other men. He was a secret, like me. They hadn't yet realized how hard it was to keep secrets from me, though. They had brought him in a little over a year ago and put him in one of the other empty rooms on the third floor, across the building from me. One of the men had joked about the Bureau starting a menagerie, not knowing I could hear him.

I had imagined another young child, like me. Someone else the Bureau had found—"rescued", they always said they had "rescued" me—and taken in for study. Someone my age, I hoped, who would play with me and talk to me. Someone to sit with me during all the tests and examinations. Someone who would understand what it was like.

I never asked if I could meet him. Even at that age, I knew better.

There was another loud noise—a scream—down the hallway. A shape ran toward my door. I scooted backward quickly, just before the door flew open. One of the men stood in the doorway. It wasn't Agent Simmons, the new one. It was a man I'd never seen before. His name suddenly came to me. Agent Carl Matthews, and he was terrified. Not of me; he was scared of me, but he was used to that. He was terrified of what was happening down the hall. Terrified of what was happening to the other men.

"The kid's still here!" he shouted to another man I couldn't see.

"Forget about that!" the other man shouted back. "We need to evacuate this floor!"

"We need to evacuate the damn building!" Matthews said.

He looked down at me, curled up on the bare floorboards. I stared back, shivering. He looked down the hall, where the other man was. I tried to focus; the other man was running away, toward the stairs at the north end of the building. Matthews said an ugly word under his breath, then stepped into the room. I gasped and scrambled backward, pressing my back against the wall. No one ever came into my room. Not at night, not ever.

"Cut it out, kid!" he said, reaching out to grab me.

I screamed and flung my arm in front of my face, fingers spread wide. He jerked back, eyes wide and full of fear. He waited for something to happen. He didn't know what.

We waited for far too long, staring. Waiting. Both terrified, both alone in the dark.

"Come on, kid," he said after a moment. He reached out again, slowly, but this time his palm was up. He was holding his hand out for me.

"I can't leave you in here," he said. "We gotta go."

I didn't move at first. "Where's Agent Simmons?"

"Simmons?" His brow furrowed. He was trying to think. "I don't know. Downstairs, I hope. Or out of the building. Like we need to be."

A scream sounded from outside. We both flinched. Then it was cut short.

"Kid," he said. "I can't wait forever."

Agent Matthews was afraid. Of me, and of something worse than me. But he was still waiting for me. Not for much longer. But he was here now.

"Okay." I took his hand.

Matthews hauled me to my feet and ran. When we took off through the door, he pulled so hard he almost yanked my arm out of its socket. My short little legs could barely keep up with him, but for all his concern, he wasn't going to slow down for me. So I ran faster.

The hallway ran along the building's east side before taking a sharp turn to the left. At the north end, a single door opened onto a stairwell that led all the way to the ground floor. It was barely thirty yards from my room to the stairs. Easy enough, Matthews thought. Just get to the stairs and we'd all be safe. Only something else had reached the door first.

Lines of charred wood and plaster were spreading across the walls, floor, and ceiling like vines... or veins. The char coiled over the surface of the door in a feathery spiral. A body lay in the midst of the tangle of charred lines, reaching out for the door. Probably the second man. He didn't look burnt. More like mummified. There was no extra heat in the hallway, and I couldn't smell smoke. Instead, the air was filled with a sticky-sweet smell.

"What's happening?" I asked.

"I don't know," Mathews said.

They let it out, he thought.

"Let what out?" I asked. "Is it the other child?"

The char continued to spread. It turned the corner and stretched toward us. Faster.

"The other way. Back the other way!" Matthews shouted.

I didn't know where he was trying to go. There was another hallway that ran west, just before the double doors at the other end of this hall, but it went farther into the building and dead-ended in a set of offices and a restroom. I wasn't sure what was beyond the double doors. I'd never been allowed that far. Whenever I tried to focus through them, my head felt fuzzy.

Behind us, we heard the harsh crackle of wood and plaster splintering. The hallway buckled under the strain of whatever was happening to it. The sticky-sweet smell grew stronger, and I could hear a low hiss just under the cracking, the sound of a radio tuned to nothing. I got a funny feeling in the pit of my stomach, like I was standing still while the floor fell out from under me.

Agent Matthews tried to shoulder his way through the double doors, but they barely budged. He said another ugly word and slapped his hand against one of the doors. Locked. I turned away while he rummaged through his pocket for the key. The walls behind us sagged inward, while the floorboards buckled up. It was as if a giant hand had reached down and squeezed them tight. The lines of char had grown thicker, spreading out smaller fingers across every surface. Where they were thickest, little strands of something dark and green sprouted. Whatever was happening was only a couple of feet away now, spreading faster.

"Jesus!" Matthews glanced over his shoulder. "Don't look, kid!"

The doors unlocked with a loud click, and Matthews grabbed me by the shoulder. He threw me across the doorway, and it was like a knife had been driven through my head. I clutched the sides of my head and screamed, falling to the floor with my knees against my chest but away from the spreading thing. Agent Matthews wasn't so lucky.

He should have gone first. In the time he wasted getting me to safety, the spreading thing reached his foot. Something burned its way up his leg, freezing him to the floor. Whatever it was doing was agonizing; I could see the pain on his face, hear it in his mind. He dug for something in his jacket pocket as the thing came closer. Not his gun. A scrap of paper. I couldn't make out what was written on it, but he held it out like a badge. He hoped that would stop it.

He was wrong.

I struggled to my knees, my mind a red haze of pain, and *looked* at the thing for the first time. Something else was spreading, above-behind-beyond the marks it scorched into everything. The shadows of its passage. It was like a mass of tree branches or thorn vines but not made of wood. Not made of any substance I recognized. One of the branches climbed up Agent Matthews' leg and wrapped around his body, burning him, changing him. He screamed once, then collapsed. Just shriveled, charred flesh wrapped around corroded bone, the only smell that sticky-sweet stench.

Something grew on top of him now, from a direction no one else could see.

The branches loomed closer, searching for me, and I kicked against the floor to push backward, but they stopped at the doorway. They couldn't come through. Something like a spider-web of lightning draped across the door, blocking their path. The branches grew thicker, crumbling the walls around them, but on this side of the door I was safe. The lightning came from strange symbols written around the door frame, a bunch of interlocking circles wrapping around the door. I'd never seen them before, but then I hadn't been on this side of the door in years.

I pulled myself up on my knees and watched whatever it was grow.

Agent Simmons and three other men found me there an hour later. The others wanted to know how I'd made it into the "clean space", but Simmons hushed them. He was just glad I was okay. He picked me up and carried me away while the others started setting up... something. It made my head hurt to look at it, so I hid my face against Simmons' coat.

I woke with my face buried against my pillow. Tears ran down my face. I tried to tell myself I didn't know why I'd dreamed about that night. That I didn't know why I didn't make the dream change.

People aren't good at lying to me. Not even me.

12

In the days that followed, I tried to push that afternoon out of my head. I had my class and the Bureau's intransigence to deal with, not to mention my growing friendship with Lucille and Gloria. I had no need for Lucas Dowling and his arrogance squatting in my forebrain. I succeeded. Almost.

I would go for hours at a time, thinking about investigations or meal plans, my aggravations with Agent Walsh or the gold of the sun on Lucille's hair. Then suddenly I would remember what he said to Gloria and me, and my lips would curl. Or I'd recall part of his ridiculous experiment and try to puzzle out what he thought he was doing. Or I'd see that sneer hanging on his arrogant face. Whatever it was, no matter where I was or what I was doing, it seized my attention. I couldn't force the thoughts away. Usually it would take someone else, layering intrusion on intrusion.

I didn't realize it at the time, but I wasn't the only one fixated on Lucas' experiment, which actually pulled me out of my anger one day. I sat in my dorm, brooding on Lucas' shoddy grasp of extradimensional mathematics and inability to admit it, for approximately one hour and sixteen minutes. I was so wrapped in my thoughts that I didn't recognize someone was nearby until they were right outside my door, hand poised to knock. I gathered myself and waited for the sound. It didn't come. Brow furrowed, I drummed my fingers against my thighs and watched my visitor, one of the office girls on the first floor, repeatedly almost muster the courage to rap her knuckles on the door before cringing and stepping back. Stephanie wasn't sure what would happen if she disturbed me. She wasn't sure she was even supposed to *be* in the orange zone, but one of the agents had sent her up with a message for me. Now she was stuck. She'd get scolded if she returned without delivering the message, and she might get eaten if she actually tried. I wondered whether it was worth talking to Agent Walsh—again—about the stories the other agents spread about me.

Under normal circumstances, I probably would have taken pity on her. I hoped. Right now, I wasn't in the mood. I pushed off the couch, stalked across the narrow room, and yanked the door open just before Stephanie tried to knock again. She let out a little squeak of fright and jumped back while I glared at her out of the gloom in my dorm.

"What do you want, Stephanie Baines?"

Stephanie's soft hazel eyes nearly bugged out of her face as her red-lined mouth formed a perfect O. She held a piece of notepaper clenched in one trembling hand, and I realized that must be whatever message she was supposed to bring me. If I reached out to snatch it from her, though, I'd probably give her a heart attack. Her heart already beat so quickly I worried she'd faint.

I sighed and found a measure of pity inside, after all. "Is that a message for me? Is that why you're here?"

"Uh… ah, y-yes."

Stephanie tried to compose herself as she wondered how to address me. All she accomplished was cringing in a completely different way.

I rolled my eyes. "'Amelia' will be fine. Or 'Miss Temple', if you feel like being formal. Just not, and I want to make this very clear, 'that thing on the top floor'."

She flinched again. She hadn't been going to call me that at all, it was just something she'd heard from the wonderful agents downstairs, but it had been rolling through her mind the whole way up here. That, as much as me, was what she was afraid of—that she'd blurt that out instead of my name.

Plucking words out of her mind was a handy parlor trick, but it wasn't going to end this charade any quicker. Fortunately, I had another trick up my sleeve now. The one I'd used on Lucas a few days ago. I leaned against the door jamb and peered inside her head. Pushing through the sharp thorns of her fear, I saw a surprisingly firm sense of self-possession. She was no steely field agent, but she was normally pretty level-headed when she wasn't being forced far outside her comfort zone by a pushy agent who thought he was too good to play mail boy. I anchored myself in the middle of that sense of sensibility and sort of *pushed* the fear down. Like sweeping dirt under a rug, only nothing like that at all. Metaphor is inherently suspect.

It worked. The trembling stopped, and Stephanie's eyelids lowered a touch. Her mouth closed, then formed a winsome smile. She had dimples. They were very cute.

It was an act, the same act she gave the agents when she needed their attention, but it was more useful than fear. Stephanie held out the paper to me. "You received a phone call earlier from a Miss Gloria Lane. She asked if you could meet her at the public library in town this afternoon. She left a phone number, if you need to call her back."

I thanked her and took the paper. I'd gotten bits and pieces of that through her panic, but it was useful to have the whole message in one go, in the order Gloria had said it in.

"Did Gloria say anything else? Like why she wanted to see me?"

"I couldn't say... Miss Temple," Stephanie said. "I didn't take the call, Agent Bell did. All I know is what he wrote down there."

"Mm. Well, I guess I'll find out when I get there," I said. "Thank you, Miss Baines. I appreciate you bringing this to me. And I apologize if I scared you earlier."

"Oh, you didn't scare me," Stephanie said cheerily. "I don't spook easy. You can't, if you work in this place. Right?"

It was a lie, but it was kindly meant, so I let it go. I smiled and wished Stephanie a good day before closing the door. On the other side of the wall, she let out a sigh of relief before walking out of the orange zone as quickly as her heels could take her. I paid her no more mind once she passed through the dormitory's outer door, instead re-reading Gloria's message. Or rather, Agent Bell's reproduction of Gloria's message. I couldn't summon Bell's face to mind, which meant I had probably never met him and barely knew of him, if at all. There could have been more to Gloria's message and Bell had just left it out in favor of one sentence and a phone number, but I couldn't say for certain whether he was the type. I'd have to wait a few hours to find out.

As it turned out, there was quite a bit more that Gloria had wanted to pass on. She just hadn't been willing to tell it to a stranger over the phone. It would be months before I was ready to decide whether that turned out to be a smart decision. It could have saved us a lot of trouble that autumn—in exchange for a completely different kind of trouble.

The Chatham Hills Public Library was a wide red-and-beige brick building in what I would later learn was the neoclassical style. It sat back from Morrison Street at the end of a short green lawn dominated by a very incongruous statue of a gaunt, wild-haired woman. Her arms were spread and her head thrown back, as if she was singing. Or screaming. The sun, starting to creep behind the roof, threw shadows across the lawn. It looked like the shadow of the woman was reaching out for me.

The shadows shivered. I told myself it was the wind rustling the short trees against the building's face. I tried to believe it.

What was this place? This sleepy little town on the river where the Bureau had chosen to hide its secrets? How many more oddities were hidden here?

I thought about giving the statue a wide berth as I crossed the lawn but decided that was foolish. She stood on a short granite pedestal in the center of the walk; avoiding her would mean crossing the grass and possibly looking like a fool. After all, it was only a statue.

I stopped in front of her before passing. From afar, I had thought she was carved from granite or something similar, but no. The woman was carved from some sort of blueish gray stone I did not recognize, something with a lightly mottled texture. Gingerly, I put my hand on hers; the stone was cool to the touch, which I supposed wasn't surprising considering the time of year. I looked up at her face, turned to the sky with an unreadable expression of rage or ecstasy. I tried not to think of my mother.

A brass placard was affixed to her pedestal. It read "The Genius of Wisdom" and thanked the Chambers Foundation for Higher Learning for donating the statue in 1929. The sculptor was not credited. An unfamiliar symbol was inscribed next to the foundation's name—a circle with a cross inside surrounded by three narrow ellipses, each marking the point of an equilateral triangle. The astrological symbol for Earth… or was it meant to be a sun cross?

I thought about the pull I'd felt from Orr's Used Books that first day in town. Now there was this statue; I couldn't *feel* anything from it, but there was something unearthly about it. I looked from the statue to the public library, scanning the brick façade for unusual designs. Had the Bureau chosen to locate its headquarters here for reasons other than relative remoteness?

I found nothing unusual outside the building. Inside was another matter. The library was unsurprisingly dusty and poorly lit. Strange statues stood at the corners of the large vaulted central room, facing inward. I supposed they looked like angels to anyone who didn't examine them too closely—and other than me, who could?—but there was something nearly insectile in the shape of their faces, the bulge of their eyes. Their lower bodies were hidden beneath trailing robes, but I could see the hint of legs beneath them. More legs than the usual complement, I thought.

It occurred to me that the first thing angels usually said was to not be afraid. There was probably a good reason for that. And for them to be facing inward, not outward.

Gloria waited for me in the back, at a table near a door marked "Archives". She had a small stack of books in front of her and a pair of notepads. She already had a copious number of notes scribbled on one of the pads. The other, I gathered, was waiting for me.

I wasn't trying to be especially quiet, but Gloria didn't notice my approach until I stood over her. She felt a sudden jolt of fear when my shadow fell across the table, but she controlled her response well. Gloria slowly lifted her head, rolling her eyes up until they met mine. When she realized it was me, her face relaxed into a warm smile.

"It's about time you got here, hon," she said. "I've been here for about an hour."

"I can tell," I said, pulling out the chair across from her. "And that's not fair, you actually live around here."

"I live on the other side of town."

"Still closer than me. So, why was it you wanted to meet me here?

Not that I mind. I like spending time with you."

"Miss Amelia, you're like to make me blush," Gloria said, smiling wider for a moment. Then her face fell, becoming deadly serious. "Listen, you remember the other day? With those two boys above the bookstore?"

Ha. Better to ask whether I could get them out of my head.

"Yes, I believe so," I said. "The ones with the half-baked experiment?"

"I've been wondering about that," Gloria said. "Luci, too. Actually, we've been wondering about them for a while now."

I let out a little sigh of relief. Gloria had finally given me an opening to talk about my, and their, misgivings.

"Me too, actually," I said. "They're lying about whatever they're up to, or at least Lucas Dowling is."

Gloria nodded. "Luci and I think we kind of have an idea. Well, half of an idea. And we figured maybe you'd like to help us puzzle out the other half. You're pretty smart and, well, Luci likes you an awful lot."

My heart fluttered at that. I tried to keep my voice steady. "Where is Luci? Is she joining us?"

Gloria shifted in her seat. "She's supposed to be meeting us in a bit. She wanted to check something out first."

A thrill ran through my breast and down my limbs, making my fingers and toes tingle. My mouth curved up into a little smile. Gloria noticed it and smirked a bit. I couldn't quite tell why, though I could pick up her quiet approval behind a bit of apprehension.

"You're worried about something?" I asked.

"Those two boys... never mind that for now," she said, misunderstanding what I meant. "Sit down so I can catch you up before Luci gets here."

I slipped into the seat across from her. Gloria looked around, as if she was afraid someone might be watching, then leaned in close. She beckoned for me to do the same, then dropped her voice to a whisper.

"My family's lived in this area for a while now. Long enough to hear some stories... and to be a part of some of them. I don't know if you'll believe this one—Luci didn't at first, either—but I promise it's true."

I smiled in what I hoped was a reassuring way. "You'd be surprised what I can believe."

Gloria ducked her head for a moment and curved her lips into a slight smile. "Grandma on my mother's side moved here in the twenties. Momma's older brother Matthew got a job working for a local... honestly, I don't quite know what to call them. A charity or a private club or something."

"Don't tell me, let me guess," I said. I flashed back to the statue outside. "The Chambers Foundation?"

She gave me a wry smile. It didn't meet her eyes, nor her forebrain. "You've been paying attention to the local scenery. No, the Chambers Foundation didn't come until a few years later, but I think there's a connection."

That connection being a gentleman named Maxwell Thorpe, a board member on the Foundation at the time the statue outside had been donated, as well as a member of the private gentleman's club that had employed Uncle Matthew as a hired hand. I got all that within moments as Gloria composed her thoughts, flipping through her notes and pulling two more books from her stack. One was an old town registry, the other a collection of minutes from the city council dated 1920 to 1922. The club, understatedly named the "Apollonian Society for Illumination", had been instrumental in getting the town to fund an observatory on Banks Hill, outside the eastern town limit. I was entirely unaware of any such observatory existing, mainly because it didn't anymore, except as a ruin. There had been an incident in 1925, a scientific experiment gone wrong. The club disbanded as a result, under what Gloria's melodramatic notes called "dubious circumstances". Thorpe and what looked like a handful of remaining members started the Chambers Foundation a few years later.

It was maddening, sitting and pretending to listen as Gloria laid this out over the course of an hour. No fewer than three times, I wanted to interrupt her and tell her I already understood and could we move on, but that would have led to questions I wasn't ready to answer. Also, it would have been rude. Gloria wasn't the sort of person I wanted to be rude to. She was too kind and too clever, and besides, she wouldn't abide it.

"So, this incident at the observatory," I said, once she had finally gotten to the end, "what was it, exactly? A fire?"

"Eventually. But it started as a lot more." She pulled a yellowed piece of paper out of her notes, folded over lengthwise. She hesitated before she opened it. She caught her lower lip between her teeth, and her eyes trembled.

"This... you're probably going to think I'm fooling," she said. "I promise, I'm not making this up. Maybe my uncle was..."

I reached out my hand and paused for just a moment, my fingers inches from her skin. She looked at me, eyes full of concern. I took a breath and brushed my fingers lightly against the back of her hand, in what I hoped was a reassuring gesture.

She had reason to doubt me or anyone. I could already see what she was going to show me. No one else would believe her.

"It's all right," I said. "Whatever it is, show me. I'll believe it."

She nodded and unfolded the paper. It was a sloppy pencil sketch of a strange, bulbous column of *something*. Something tall and slender, topped with a cap that dripped with long tendrils. Something that looked an awful lot like it belonged in the Bureau's archives.

Dread gripping my heart, I picked up the paper and stared at it while

Gloria explained. "Uncle Maxwell drew that after Doctor Thorpe dragged him out to what was left of the observatory to clean up. I still remember the stories he told late at night, if he'd had at least three drinks and Momma wasn't around to hush him. He said that thing was sticking up in the middle of the room. Singing, he said, though he couldn't ever describe the song."

"Probably because he couldn't hear it with his ears," I said. At least I thought I was the one who said it. The words seemed to come from a long ways away.

Gloria frowned. "What was that?"

I shuddered and dropped the paper. "Nothing. I don't know what that was... or what *that* was. But you think there's a connection to Lucas' experiment."

Gloria opened her mouth to explain, but before she could, I turned and looked behind us. Luci opened the library's outer door and stepped inside, letting in a draft of early autumn air swirling around her summer sun. She saw me watching her and gave a slight wave, with a friendly smile for Gloria. She had a manila envelope tucked under one arm.

"Sorry I'm late," she said when she reached our table, sounding slightly out of breath.

"I'm used to it," Gloria said, smirking. "Besides, it gave me time to catch Amelia up."

"Pictures take time to develop," Lucille said.

She set the envelope on the table before sitting next to me. I found myself shifting my chair a little closer to hers. Gloria said something, but I didn't really notice it. Lucille's presence filled my attention, like a rose-scented light glowing warmly beside me. A few stray red-gold hairs slipped free of her ponytail and brushed against her cheek, still tinged bright pink from the chill. Her green dress slipped softly around her shoulders as she slid open the envelope and tipped out four glossy photographs. I barely registered the images as her slender fingers delicately fanned them out across the table.

At the edge of my obsession, Gloria picked up the first of the photographs. Her eyebrows shot up. She flipped the photo around.

"Lucille Sweeney, what have you been up to this afternoon?" she asked. From her tone, the question was at once curiosity and a warning.

Luci shrugged nonchalantly, a slight satisfied smile quirking her coral lips. "Just doing some investigating, same as you."

Gloria looked at me. "Amelia, talk some sense into this girl."

"Huh?" I snapped myself out of my reverie as best I could with its cause still sitting too close beside me. Gloria showed me the photo. It took me a moment to realize what Gloria found so important; at first glance, Lucille had snapped a photo of several ears of corn propped up on a simple wooden tray. Then I looked closer. Just beyond them, and off to the right, stood a pair of men. One was young and the other older, standing on the sidewalk in front of a dilapidated brownstone. The older man had his back to the camera, but I thought I could just make out the younger man's face. Between the distance and lack of focus, it was difficult. I took the picture from Gloria's unresisting fingers and peered closer.

And then the world *shifted* around me.

13

In the space between one heartbeat and the next, the air around me dropped to a freezing cold… if it was air at all. A blazing green light flared, blinding my entire sensorium. I felt my body fall out of the chair, or maybe leap, but when awareness returned, I stood firmly on my feet.

The dusty bookshelves around me had fallen away, and the harsh lamps of the library were replaced by the bright autumn sun. I was surrounded by rows of wooden stalls laden with produce. There was still a table in front of me, but instead of books and notepaper, it was piled with artfully arranged bundles of yellow corn. Lucille was still on my left, wearing a completely different dress, blue not green, but across the table I didn't see Gloria. The two men across the street carried on a muted conversation. One of them was a senior, probably in his fifties or sixties, and the other much, much younger. Lucas Dowling couldn't have been more than twenty-one, after all.

The green light had faded, but everything around me had a slightly blurry look, as if I was staring through a smudged window. The colors were slightly off, and the sounds just muted enough to notice, as if I were standing in another room and had a regular person's hearing, maybe. The chill had gone away, but my skin felt tight, as if my whole body was a garment a size too small.

Dozens of people milled around us, but they took no notice of my sudden appearance. Nor did Luci, who had just lowered her camera. She chatted amiably with an older woman in a gingham dress, Ellie Wayne.

"They really are so charming," Luci said, gesturing to the bundles fanned out in threes and fours, wrapped in bows of dried husks.

"Perfect for Thanksgiving decorations," Mrs. Wayne said.

"Absolutely," Luci agreed, paying half attention. Her eyes followed the two men across the street, though her mouth was well able to carry on the conversation. "Not enough people decorate for Thanksgiving."

"That's what I told Amos. He says corn's just for eating, but I say we had a blessed harvest, enough to feed the whole town if we wanted, but they're all going to buy from different farmers, and that means a surplus…"

Mrs. Wayne was more than capable of carrying on like this for quite some time, which I'm sure was working to Lucille's advantage as she pretended to take notes for a newspaper article she was never going to write, but I had no interest in it whatsoever. I only had the vaguest idea of what Thanksgiving even was, but it was surely less important than whatever Lucas was talking about. Or how I'd gotten here.

"Luci, what's going on?" I asked.

Luci paused in the middle of a question and turned to her right. She looked right through me, puzzlement written across her pretty brow.

"What's wrong, dearie?" Mrs. Wayne asked.

"Oh, nothing," Luci said with a shake of her head, before turning back to Mrs. Wayne. "I thought I heard someone call my name, that's all."

"You did…" I started, but I let the words trail off.

The town clock tower was two blocks away, close enough for me to see without adjusting my focus. The hands read 11:35. It had been a little bit after three p.m. when Luci joined us at the library.

"What did I just do?" I said to no one in particular.

Luci had turned back to the corn display, though she was actually looking at Lucas and the older man again. I raised a hand to tap her shoulder but pulled it back before my fingers brushed her skin. Instead, I slapped my hand against the table. I half expected it to pass right through, but my hand hit the wood with a muffled smack that made my palm sting. Neither of the women next to me took any notice. Curious, I reached out to the bundle closest to me and rested a finger on the tip of the tallest ear. I gave it a flick, and to my surprise it toppled right over and landed on the sandy ground.

"Oh, bless it!" Mrs. Wayne said, apologizing as she scooted between Luci and me. "Sorry, honey. Some of 'em are a little unbalanced."

"Aren't we all," Luci said under her breath as she snuck another look at Lucas and his older friend.

They were shaking hands. It looked like they were probably finishing up whatever they were talking about. Luci quickly thanked Mrs. Wayne for giving her an interview and promised to send her a copy of the school newspaper when it was published—which I supposed wasn't technically a lie—and hurried over to another booth with a different vantage. She was hoping to get a better shot of the older man before he left.

I had ideas of my own in that regard, at least now that I had my bearings. While Luci wasted time trying to find a good position to surreptitiously snap another photo, I shifted my attention away from her and across the street. It was more difficult than I thought. Even with the oddities affecting my perception, I found myself drawn back to her. To the way the sunlight played through her hair, the way her dress clung to her figure, the way she pushed out her lower lip in frustration as she tried to line up a good shot. I wanted to slip my hand into her hand, to rest my head against hers more than I wanted to know what Lucas was doing, or even how I came to be here at this time.

And I completely missed the last words Lucas and the other man said to each other.

The two turned away from each other, Lucas heading down the block to where his car was parked, the older man to the other side of the brownstone. I swore under my breath (not that anyone would hear if I shouted the foulest word I knew, apparently) and forced my attention away from Luci and across the street. I decided to ignore Lucas, as I already knew who he was, and follow the other man to his destination.

Instead, I snapped back to where I was, in the middle of a farmer's market four hours ago.

What in the world? I thought.

Confused, I tried again. The other man had already disappeared around the corner of the building, but before my perception even reached the far sidewalk, I felt a rush of vertigo and fell back to where I was standing. I tried to focus on Lucas instead, who I could dimly perceive was getting into his car. No luck. I tried to look the other direction entirely, to the storefronts on the opposite side of the market. Again, my perception swam, and I found myself focused exactly on where I was standing.

A spike of irritation slashed through me. I knew there were limits to my perception, but they had steadily diminished as I had gotten older. They were measured in miles, not mere yards, but here I was, able to see no further than the limit of my bare eyes.

"No wonder people invented cameras and things," I said to Luci, who of course didn't respond. "How can you all *live* like this?"

Lucille, meanwhile, had much the same idea as me. When the two separated, she ducked behind a tall display so that Lucas wouldn't see her, then started walking purposefully toward the brownstone. As she crossed the street, I felt a tug. It wasn't like the weird gravity of Orr's Used Books, or even like the pull I realized was my growing attraction to her. It was like a compulsion to follow her, as if a line I couldn't see had me tethered to her. More out of curiosity than anything, I tried to ignore it. I folded my arms across my chest and watched her walk away, willing myself not to follow.

Something around me hiccupped and I was standing behind her.

"I'm not sure what rules are governing whatever's going on," I said to her, "and not knowing is beginning to make me cross."

Luci glanced over her shoulder, again looking through me, then turned her attention back to hiding in the alley behind the unkempt hedge lining the brownstone's not-inconsiderable rear lawn. I thought she was being reckless, but there didn't seem to be anyone around at the moment. I muttered that she ought to hurry up and do whatever it was she was going to do so we could get out of here.

She had shown up at the library four hours later, though, so I supposed that she hadn't gotten caught. That was sort of a relief.

The other man had gone into the brownstone, or so I presumed. He was nowhere to be seen, but there was a servant's entrance in the back of the building. Most likely he used that. It was difficult to say for certain. I couldn't see inside at all. At first, I thought it might be from whatever was keeping my focus centered on Luci—a side effect of my method of traveling here, presumably—but I could at least see into some of the back spaces. There were two storage rooms and a utility closet, piled with dust and debris, and a well-worn trail of footprints leading from the servant's entrance and into the building proper. Past that, I couldn't see at all. It was similar to trying to peer into the back room at Orr's Used Books, except here all I got was static.

Like when I tried to look into Agent Thomas' mind. That was certainly interesting.

Luci crept around the alley side, occasionally stopping to take pictures of the brownstone's upper floor windows. I had no idea what she was trying to capture, but even through the haze surrounding us, I could feel her frustration. The evidence wasn't out in the open for anyone to stumble upon, which was the point, obviously. To uncover the truth, she'd have to dig deeper.

In other words, she was working herself up to doing something reckless.

Luci moved farther along the hedge, toward the neighboring house. Her eye was on a particular window on the brownstone's northeast corner. She thought it looked slightly ajar enough to jimmy open and slither through. The only complications were that the older man was still inside, and a policeman was approaching.

Luci wasn't aware of that last part.

I didn't know whether he was a simple beat patrolman or if some upright citizen had notified him of the beautiful girl sneaking around this alley, but either way, he strode down the sidewalk toward us. The alley was largely clear of debris and obstructions; the only dumpster was too far to reach without running, drawing even more attention to her. The officer would see Luci as soon as he got within a few yards of the alley.

"But he didn't. Obviously," I mumbled.

Talking to myself now. A good sign.

I reached out again to touch Luci, to tap her on the shoulder, but again thought better of it. Instead, I grabbed a branch of hedge just above her head and shook it. Luci frowned and glanced to her right,

wondering why the hedge was shaking in the absence of a breeze. The question fell from her mind, and the irritation from her face, when she saw the policeman. She crouched down lower and scrambled to her left, farther into the alley. She was trying to find a place to hide before he saw her, but after a look around the alley, she quickly came to the same conclusion I had. There was no place to go, nowhere to hide, and no time to come up with a convincing story for skulking around an alley in the better part of town, alone.

Luci tried to press herself into the hedge, but to no avail. She got her body about halfway through, back-first, before getting tangled in the branches. They scratched at her hair and dress, and she only managed to get herself further stuck trying to free herself stealthily. The resulting racket of course drew the attention of the policeman, who stopped in his walk to peer across the back lawn at us.

"Here we go," I muttered.

The policeman crouched a bit, hoping to hide himself, and crept toward the mouth of the alley. His plan was to get into position to see whoever was skulking about back here before bursting out and catching them. Which was, admittedly, a better plan than whatever Luci was up to this afternoon. Fortunately, she couldn't see him approaching, or else her panicked struggles might get even more unmistakable.

I couldn't leave Luci's side—and wouldn't even if I could—but Officer Plumm was close enough for me to pick up his thoughts even through the strange green haze. His suspicions weren't high at the moment; he thought it was just a couple of kids messing around where they shouldn't be and wanted to shoo them off. His attempts at stealth were a mix of caution and mischief. All to the good. Hopefully that would make this a little easier.

As Plumm got into position at the hedge's street-side corner, I stepped forward. He peeked around the hedge and looked straight at me. He couldn't see me, of course, but I made sure he could feel my presence where it mattered.

You don't see anything, I thought. *There's no young woman there. Probably just a breeze or something. Nothing to worry about.*

Plumm hesitated, trying to peer past me. Luci was pressed into the hedge, eyes staring wide, feet kicked out and heels digging into the gravel, trying to guess where the policeman was. And behind us, something small and wiry rustled through a small pile of cardboard.

The policeman straightened up and laughed when the scrawny calico stepped out of the trash and meowed. He walked up the alley, stopping a few feet away from her. And from us. Luci stared out of the hedge in horror as Plumm crouched back down.

Or it was the cat, I thought with an irritated shrug. *That works, too.*

"Hey there, puss," Plumm said, stretching out a hand to her. "Was that you making all that noise?"

The calico looked up at him suspiciously. She crouched down low, ears flattened. I saw her hackles raise. I looked into her mind. It was bright and direct, and there were flashes of sharp pain associated with tall apes like Plumm. Boots and bottles and such.

It's okay, I thought to her. *This one will be kind.*

You will be kind, I thought to him. *And her name isn't "Puss". It's a complex set of smells you can't replicate, but you can at least try to come up with something decent to call her.*

The calico stretched out her head to sniff at his outstretched fingers, then slowly crept toward him. Plumm waited until she was close enough without him taking a step, then scooped her into his arms. She stiffened for just a moment, then settled against his chest and purred.

"You haven't been committing any crimes, have you, Missy?" he said softly.

Actually, she had murdered no less than twelve small rodents within the past six hours and eaten exactly one of them, but I supposed that was legal for a feline.

"She's a stray, and the last of her litter," I said. "She doesn't have anyone to belong with anymore. Why don't you take her somewhere warm and feed her?"

"How'd you like to go back to the station house and get a bowl of milk, Missy?" he said.

"Not milk," I said, rolling my eyes. "Milk is bad for cats, actually."

"Or some nice fish instead?"

"I suppose that'll do."

Officer Plumm tucked the calico under one arm and carried her away. As he left, she remained in his arms but crawled up his chest to peer over his shoulder. At me. Her green eyes locked with mine for a moment, and she let out a soft mew.

"It's fine, Missy. Just a few blocks," Officer Plum said, as he turned onto the sidewalk and away from us.

I closed my eyes and let out a breath. "Well, that went better than it had to."

Behind me, Luci was staring in utter shock. She leaned forward a bit, trying to get a good view of the retreating policeman without being seen. As if she was hidden at all.

I smiled softly at the sight of her. "Oh, Luci."

I knelt down to help her untangle herself from the hedge, pulling away branches and unsticking them from the fabric of her dress. I kept my hands as far from her body as possible but couldn't help but stroke one finger against her soft cheek where it had been scratched. I felt a strange tickle, sort of like electricity, and wasn't sure if it was a genuine sensation or of a piece with the way she made my heart beat faster.

Luci stood, brushing stray leaves from her dress. She picked up her camera from the part of the hedge where she'd tried to stash it and slung it over her shoulder. She stared back at the brownstone, still curious, but now more wary.

"Uh uh," I said. "Don't even think about it."

"I suppose it's not a good idea right now," Luci said. "I already almost got caught once today."

"Exactly," I said. "I can't begin to explain what happened today, which is probably a bad sign. Can we go now?"

"Yeah, let's get out of here," Luci said absently. Her words weren't addressed to me. At least, not consciously.

I took her hand and felt the world *shift* again.

14

"*A*melia."

The not-green light crawled at the edges of my awareness. I felt cold all over. Not a chill, but the utter absence of heat. And gravity. And any other reference point.

"Amelia."

Reality spun around me on more axes than I could count. Weight and light slammed into me, forcing the breath out of my lungs. Which I fortunately didn't need. Probably.

"Amelia!"

I felt Luci's hand on my shoulder. Gloria's hand covered mine. I didn't experience the electric tingle I'd felt when I touched Luci's check moments and hours ago. I felt the resolute certainty of *now*. I was in the Chatham Hills public library at 4:16 pm, September 18, 1954. I was with my friends. We were discussing the pictures I had watched Luci take four hours ago.

"I'm fine," I said. I pressed my palms against the hardwood table, finding comfort in its reassuring solidity. "I just got lost for a second."

"A second? More like five," Gloria said, squeezing my wrist. She peered into my eyes, as if she could see some clue to whatever ailed me.

"What are you talking about?" I asked.

"I showed you and Gloria this photo," Luci said, holding up the photo of the two men at what she hoped was a safe distance. It must have fallen from my fingers when I did whatever it was I did. "You went blank for a second."

"Five seconds," Gloria said again.

"Five, one, what's the difference?" I pushed myself to my feet.

I put a hand to my head and turned away from the table. I'd never lost time before, not even when I slept. I was always acutely aware of my exact position in time and space. To lose that, even if only for a second... or five...

"Honey, are you okay?" Luci asked.

"I said I'm fine," I said, a little more sharply than I'd intended.

I regretted my careless tone immediately. Luci flinched, her hand flying to her chest. "Amelia?"

"Just a headache," I said again. "It'll pass. Sorry. Who is this man with Lucas Dowling?"

Gloria took the photograph from Luci. "You're sure this is Lucas? It's not that clear."

"Oh, sorry," Luci said. "I was across the street and trying not to be noticed. It's him. The other guy's a visiting professor at Del Sombra. Professor Blake, I think."

Gloria frowned and picked up her notebook. "Professor *Henry* Blake?"

"I think that's right. Could be," Luci said.

I had no idea, which did nothing to help with my disorientation. Invariably, a person's identity was at the forefront of their mind. I could pick it up as easily as I could the color of their hair, what they were wearing right now, their initial impression of me. But if this was Professor Blake, I got nothing. Not the slightest inkling of what was going on in his head. It wouldn't be the first time that had ever happened—Agent Thomas, for instance. But he was with the Specials. Surely a visiting professor of mathematics shouldn't know how to do whatever it was that made Agent Thomas' mind a blank to me.

Perhaps it was an artifact of whatever phenomenon had kept my focus centered on Luci. I hadn't picked up anything from Lucas either, had I?

Wait… yes, I had.

I ran the memory back through my mind. There was Lucas Dowling, talking to his… mentor? Teacher? I couldn't make out any of the words, but I could taste Lucas' feelings about the professor. Admiration and fear, hidden under a nasty blanket of contempt. Impressions only, nothing concrete—nothing I could take hold of—but enough to prove to me I could have read something from Professor Blake. But no. My unfocused attention slid off his mind like fingers on wet glass. Different from my experiences with Agent Thomas. With him, it was more like a screen of static around his mind. Professor Blake was simply… nothing. An absence of thought. Which wasn't possible, considering he was engaged in conversation. I had been too distracted in the moment to notice, but now it unnerved me.

I hid it well from Luci and Gloria, though. They took no notice of my distress as Gloria flipped through the pages of her notebook. She let out a little sound of victory when she finally found Blake's name in a newspaper clipping pasted to one sheet. She tapped the paper to signal her success to us.

"Here he is. Professor Henry Blake." Gloria showed us a picture of a much younger but still mature-looking version of the man who'd met with Lucas. "He was definitely a member of the Apollonian Society."

She passed the article around for Luci and me to read. Luci perused it carefully; I glanced at it, picking the details out of their minds. It was a simple article, what Luci would call a "puff piece", a term that implied the subject had paid for it. It described the club's charitable endeavors. Professor Blake and two colleagues were providing an endowment to a local private academy on the society's behalf, "to promote education and understanding of the physical sciences and mathematics." I dismissed most of it. The second photo in the article was what grabbed my attention.

It showed twenty men in two rows, all dressed for a formal occasion. The caption simply identified them as the Apollonian Society for Illumination. I recognized Thorpe at the center, just off to the left side, but it was another man near the end of the front row who made my heart stop. While the other members were smiling in a somewhat self-congratulatory fashion, his face was stern. Stern and cold. Although the photograph was black and white, I knew his eyes were a piercing blue.

The cold man, the man who had taken me from my mother, stood with the men behind Lucas Dowling's experiment.

I sucked in a sharp breath. Fortunately, Luci and Gloria didn't notice. They were more focused on the other implications of the society's activities. Gloria tapped the article, drawing my gaze back to the part about charitable endowments.

"Luci," she said, "didn't you say Ralph was attending the university on a scholarship?"

"Yeah. That's why I'm so worried about him," she said. "He's not keeping his grades up, and if he fails a class…"

I don't think his grades are really going to be a factor, I thought. "Do you know who granted it? Was it a private organization?"

Gloria nodded, glad that we were on the same page. "Like the Chambers Foundation, for instance?"

"I don't know. I don't think so," Luci said. "I think it might be through the school directly, but a private organization might have endowed it."

"Like they did with this school," I said. "Whitehead Academy. Is it still functioning?"

"Not sure if I've ever heard a school described as 'functioning' before," Gloria said with a wry smile. "No, it closed its doors about ten years ago."

"After a series of unusual accidents?" I asked.

"I think I remember some stories floating around," Gloria said. "This would have been when I was little, mind."

"Something to look into later, I suppose," I said.

"Yeah, let's stay focused," Gloria said, nodding. "What about Dowling? He a scholarship boy too?"

"No, his family's paying for his education," Luci said with a dismissive wave of her hand. "I think they're big into silver or something."

"Hmm. No Dowlings in the club, at least that I could tell," Gloria said.

"They wouldn't be, I don't think," Luci said. "He's not from this area. He told me the Dowlings moved west from New England a hundred years ago. He's the first to come back."

"Then he has some other connection," I said. "Probably as simple as Professor Blake or someone similar picking him out of a class. We're all thinking the same thing, aren't we?"

"That whatever reckless experiment my uncle had to clean up, Dowling's trying to repeat," Gloria said. "And these folks are the ones who put him up to it."

"It's a stretch," Luci said. "I mean, we don't have any *real* evidence."

"We're not trying to bring this to the authorities," I said. "But we need to know what he's doing. What he's *really* doing."

"Would your uncle remember anything, Gloria?" Luci asked.

Gloria shook her head. "I doubt it. It was a long time ago, and he's not in the best health these past few years. Some days he can't even remember names."

"Then we don't need to bother him," I said. "We have other avenues to explore. What about the observatory? Could there be any evidence left there?"

"I doubt time has been any kinder to that wrecked building," Luci said. "Besides, there's somewhere I think we should look first."

Luci held up two of her photographs, still trying to keep them a safe distance from me in case I had another "incident". They showed upper floor windows of the brownstone.

"Lucas met Blake in front of this building," she said. They had actually met off to one side, but I didn't correct her. "Supposedly it's abandoned, but it's actually gone through a couple of owners since the late 1920s."

"And who owned it then?" Gloria asked.

"The Apollonian Society for Illumination," Luci said with a grin. "Who's up for some light burglary?"

I wasn't, it turned out; at least, not yet. There was too much to plan, and I found that I'd much rather turn my attention to what I'd done that afternoon. *Time travel?* I was used to perceiving the world in dimensions most people couldn't, but to move in them as well...

Also, it was edging close to the time I'd have to catch the bus if I were to be back in time for my curfew. Although, my excursion offered tantalizing possibilities for circumventing that, if I could just get a handle on how I'd done it. In the meantime, it was a safe enough reason to beg off Luci's field trip.

"I can't stay out late," I said, "and if we want to do this, it'll have to wait until after dark. Otherwise we're just increasing our risk."

"None of us can stay out," Gloria said. When Luci tried to object, she added, "Amelia's right. This is going to take some thought and planning, Lucille. Give us a couple of days, at least."

"Why not tomorrow night?" Luci said. "We can just sneak out. I do it all the time!"

"And you worry about your friend Ralph," Gloria said under her breath. A bit louder, she added, "Will you at least accept that Amelia and I can't?"

"I suppose," Luci said, grumbling. "But I don't know how much longer we can wait. Ralph told me yesterday that Lucas has been pushing to do the experiment soon. I don't know *how* soon 'soon' is."

"It can't be within the next couple of days, then, or else Ralph would have said," Gloria pointed out.

"Besides, you said this building wasn't as abandoned as it's supposed to be," I said.

"That's a good point, Amelia," Gloria said. "What if this Professor Blake's living there? What happens if we pop in on this man while he's having dinner?"

"Okay, okay, you've made your point," Luci said. She put a hand to her chin and thought for a moment. "Okay. There's a faculty thing at Del Sombra this Wednesday. Most of the science and math departments are supposed to be there. If there's a night Blake definitely won't be there, it's Wednesday."

"'Definitely'?" Gloria asked.

"Probably, okay? Probably definitely," Luci said.

I wasn't sure about that, but I wasn't willing to let my friends go it alone, either. Luci was committed to this idea, so if she was going, I was going with her.

"All right," I said. "Wednesday night it is. Hopefully we find some useful information."

We agreed to meet at Hanners Square, where the farmer's market was held, a little after seven on Wednesday evening. We'd sneak across the street and, once we were certain the brownstone was unoccupied, we'd slip inside and look for evidence that the defunct gentlemen's club, or the modern Chambers Foundation, was involved with Lucas Dowling.

"Okay, this is a plan," Gloria said with a firm nod. "Or at least more of a plan than 'let's all head over there right now'."

"Hey!"

"I agree," I said. "We reconvene Wednesday. In the meantime, let's explore any additional avenues for research we might have, if we can do it safely. By which I mostly mean Luci."

"Hey!"

Luci folded her arms and pouted. "Why is everyone picking on me all of a sudden?"

Gloria and I laughed, and I put an arm around Luci, pulling her in for a close hug. The scent of roses tickled at my nose. Luci put her head against mine for just a moment, and I thought I heard her sigh softly. Then she broke the embrace.

I was still trying to stay out of my friends' heads, but I picked up a quick burst of longing from Luci and a note of alarm from Gloria.

Luci bid us a good evening and left. I turned to follow her, but Gloria asked me to hang back with her for just a second, saying she still had something she wanted to go over with me.

"What is it?" I asked.

Gloria waited until Luci was safely out of earshot. She opened her mouth to speak, then stopped. She glanced down at her hands resting on the table amid a pile of notes. Despite myself, I could see her trying to put the words together in her mind. Something about Luci and I alarmed her, but she didn't quite know how to say it. Especially not in public like this.

"Do you want to go somewhere else?" I asked.

"No, this is fine," she said.

She still couldn't bring herself to just come out with it, though. Her indecision was frustrating, to say the least, and it finally got the better of me.

"What is it about Luci and me that you don't like?" I said.

"I... it's not... of course I like you," she said. "I like both of you! It's just..."

"It's just *what*, Gloria?"

She put a hand to her head and sighed, giving me no better an explanation. I knew it wasn't jealousy—she was happy to have both of us as friends and happy the two of us were friends as well. There was something about Luci's closeness with me that she couldn't share, but that in itself wasn't a cause for distress, either. Her issue was tied up in that, though.

"Okay. Can you at least tell me what it is you're afraid is going to happen?"

"Amelia," she said, folding her hands. "You're sweet and sharp as a tack, but sometimes you make it really obvious that you come from a sheltered upbringing."

That stung, and I didn't mind telling her so.

"I'm sorry that I didn't have a... a mother and a father," I said, a little more loudly than I intended to. "I'm sorry I don't have anyone to tell me the... the way of the world, the way you obviously did!"

The fingers of my left hand twitched, and I hid them behind my back and clenched them into a fist to make them stop.

"I'm sorry, that's not... that was rude of me," Gloria said. "I just meant..."

"It's fine," I said, taking a deep breath. I needed to calm myself. She just said something thoughtless, not deliberately cruel. I knew the difference but hadn't expected it from her.

I could sense Gloria's regret so strongly that I practically felt it myself. That, as much as the rational need to not make a scene, helped me get a hold of myself.

"I'm just a little frustrated right now," I said, "by a lot of things. And I have to say, it's not helping that you want to warn me about something and then can't seem to say what it is."

"I understand. That's fair," she said. "It's just... this isn't the sort of thing people talk about."

I rolled my eyes. "Clearly."

Gloria winced. "Okay, I deserved that." She took a deep breath. "So, let's work up to it with a kind of analogy. When I was little, my uncle Robert fell in love with a woman. A white woman."

"Oh," I said. Then, "*Oh.*"

"Yeah. The way I understand it, my family didn't disapprove, exactly, or at least that's what they tell themselves now. Her brothers, on the other hand..."

A gulf of sorrow hung between us. I didn't dare try to cross it. Gloria's family grief was not for me.

"My daddy, he always wished he had said something different. The *right* something. The something that would have made all of it not happen that way. Don't know what that could be, exactly, but... now I finally know how he felt."

"Why?" I said. "What does this have to do with Luci and I?"

Gloria stared at me, then let out an involuntary laugh. "Lord, you really are an innocent, aren't you? Look, honey, I'm glad you and Lucille found one another, and heaven knows you two aren't the first women to find love together like you did, but you have to be careful. Most folks aren't like me. They won't approve of you two, the way they didn't approve of Uncle Robert and his gal."

I wanted to argue with her, but I could see her conviction across the forefront of her mind. Gloria believed that what she was telling me was true, and that she was trying to help us. I had to admit, she understood this society better than I did. Understood it and liked it even less.

I thought back to four years ago, when I first began insisting I was a girl. I remembered the way the Bureau reacted. It all seemed tied up in the same sort of strange ideas about men and women I'd picked up from people. I'd long known I didn't fit into their neat little boxes, but for the first time I wondered whether I'd made a mistake.

"If... if I were male," I said hesitantly, "people wouldn't have an issue with us."

"Well, Luci probably would," Gloria said with a wry smile. "I've never known her to *like* men. Not that it matters in your case, hon."

Part of me wanted to laugh, but she was right. Not that she had any reason to doubt it. The thought of going backward, of pretending to be male again just to get the approval of a society I had never even been a part of, made my skin crawl. No. Not ever.

"Thank you for the talk, Gloria," I said. "You've given me a lot to think about."

"Amelia, wait!" Gloria said.

She came out from around the table, catching my hands in hers. "I'm *not* telling you to stay away from Luci. I said that I was happy for you two and I meant it. I just want you to be careful. At least while you're in a town like this. I don't think it's right you should have to hide, but... but you do."

"Of course. See you later, Gloria."

I gave her a tight smile and squeezed her hands, then turned and walked away. Luci was waiting for me just outside the library, as I knew she was. I smiled when I saw her, putting a tender hand on her upper arm. I stood close to her, so close our noses were almost touching.

"Hey, Luci," I said, and plucked the next words right out of her mind. "Do you want to go to the movies with me tomorrow afternoon?"

"I... yes, of course," Lucie said. Her tentative smile broke into a wide grin.

"Good," I said. "Then it's a date."

15

I returned to my dorm a whirling storm of emotion. Outwardly, I slipped through the darkened hallways like a ghost, my pulse and expression held still by years of practice. Inwardly, my mood changed from moment to moment as new thoughts whipped across my mind. I was elated at my growing understanding of my feelings for Luci and the realization that she might share them. I was disturbed by Gloria's warning, upset at her presumption, and angry at the nameless, faceless strangers who might object to our relationship. I was anxious as to Lucas' experiment and my suspicions as to its true purpose.

And at the center of it all, the cold eye of my emotional storm, I was afraid of what I had done this afternoon. So afraid I could barely name it. I had moved backwards in time. Physically, or at least as something that could physically affect the world around me. No one could perceive me, and I wasn't able to use my full capabilities, but I hadn't moved from the library, only sat insensate for a handful of seconds. I'd moved through Lucille's past for nearly a half-hour in the time it took my body to blink twice.

Part of me was excited by what I'd done. This part wondered what else I could do if I really tried. If I ignored the limits the Bureau had placed on me. That I'd placed on myself.

Another part of me heard Agent Pickman's voice. That needling, nasal sneer that even in memory set my teeth on edge. So like his bloodless fingers, always poking and prodding. Scraping across my ears like his colorless nails on a blackboard.

"I know you can do more," Pickman said.

"I can't do what you're asking," I said. I hated the whine that crept into my voice, but I couldn't keep it out. "It's not possible."

"You just aren't applying yourself," Pickman sneered. "The cup is in the other room. You can see the cup."

"Yes," I said.

"Yes. The cup is upside down. The ball is underneath the cup. You can see the ball, can't you?"

"Yes," I said again, dipping my head meekly.

"Yes. I know you can," Pickman said. "Now, take the ball out of the cup."

"I can't!" I said.

For a single, terrifying moment, there was silence.

And then, "Note that the subject refuses to cooperate."

A spike of fear burst up through my chest. I knew what would come next. My body didn't hold scars, but my memory did. Aversion techniques, he called them. Many of which went undocumented in any official report until the end. When they found his private journals.

I flew up out of my seat and behind the couch, trying to hide. And I stayed right where I was sitting, hunched down, my ten-year-old self trying to make itself smaller. As if I could shrink down far enough to hide from Pickman's microscopic gaze. I wasn't in my dorm. I was surrounded by the antiseptic walls of a Bureau lab room. Number Four. Agent Pickman's private playground.

Pickman turned away from me to the array of instruments neatly arranged on the folding table that was the only furniture in the room other than my steel chair. He preferred to stand, and insisted his assistant, Dolores Grover, do the same. She was on the other side of the table, the only witness to his experiments. A glorified stenographer, she normally did little more than take notes. The real notes, and the secret ones. This was one of the times she did a little more. Very little.

When Pickman picked up the electrodes, her face went white.

"Agent Pickman," she said, "he's just a boy."

I'm not a boy, I thought.

"The subject is not a boy," Pickman said.

There was no comfort in those words.

"The mistake my predecessors made," he continued, "was in treating Subject 19 as a human child. Subject 19 is *not* a human. What the subject might be is still a matter of scientific inquiry. And if the subject will not cooperate with that inquisition…"

Pickman touched the electrodes together and pressed a button on the attached apparatus. Electricity sparked between them.

"…more extreme measures are necessary."

I cowered in my chair as he leaned in, fixing the electrodes to bare skin with medical tape. He returned to the table and reached for the knob that controlled the voltage. Dolores raised her hand to object, to push his hand away. Then she let it drop, wilting like a flower in the heat. He was her superior, after all. She was only following instructions.

Seven years ago, I hadn't understood. I was too focused on my own fear to look at her feelings. Now, I could see her own fear. Of Pickman. Of unemployment. Of worse, for her complicity in what surely could not be permissible. Or horribly, of what could be. She would carry her own scars. It wouldn't make it right, or change what was about to happen, but I decided to forgive her for her role in it.

After all, seeing her reservations, Pickman relented this time. At least as much as he was willing.

"One final chance, Subject 19," Pickman said. "The cup is upside down."

I began to cry.

"The ball is underneath the cup."

Hot tears flowed down my pale cheeks.

"Take the ball out of the cup."

"I can't!" I wailed.

"We'll begin at two hundred volts."

I screamed. Seven years ago, I cowered in my chair, my arm spasming in pain. Seven years later, I flung my arm out, rending space.

Next door, the cup and the ball and the table that held them both flew across the room. The cup shattered against the wall. The ball bounced off it and struck the agent watching it under his eye.

Pickman turned toward the adjoining wall, a sour look on his pinched face.

"What in the hell is all that racket?" he said.

The door flew open. Agent Larson all but fell through it, the ball in one hand, a fresh bruise spreading across his face.

"He did it!" Larson said. "He moved the ball!"

Silently, Pickman held out his hand for the ball. Larson dropped it into his dry palm. Pickman let it roll around in his hand, staring at it curiously. When he turned to look at me, his expression was something like pride.

"There, Miss Grover, you see? All the subject needed was a little motivation."

He handed the ball back to Larson. "Set the experiment back up."

I clasped my hands to my face and flung myself *forward*, away from Room Four, away from my ten-year-old self and my pain, my too-short hair and my ill-fitting trousers, away from Pickman and Dolores and fear.

Again, my mind was awhirl with thoughts. I remembered that day, of course. One of the only successful experiments in months of attempts spread out across years. I had thought that Agent Larson had felt some sort of pity for me, that he'd knocked the experiment over himself in a vain attempt to get Pickman to stop. It made no sense, but at the time it was the only explanation that almost did.

But no. The experiment had succeeded, after a fashion. I had moved the ball. Just seven years later.

I hadn't seen myself back then. Was I too distracted? My awareness, my senses, were still developing at that time. Maybe I simply had not known what to look for.

But now…

Now I was adrift. Nowhere around me were the sterile walls of the lab or the drab but comforting walls of my dorm. There were no floorboards beneath my feet. There was nothing. Only a distant discordant music, like an armful of chimes flung down a stairwell, and a riot of strange colors twisting and turning at the edge of my awareness. The same colors I'd seen in the night sky the moment of my birth.

I tried to reach out and find purchase, something to focus on, to hold, to give me gravity and velocity, a point against which to reference myself, but there was nothing. It wasn't a void. A void implied space, length and width and depth, and I couldn't tell if there was any around me. I was frozen.

No. Not frozen. I could feel my heart beating. Once. Twice. Again. Again.

There was direction, a single direction I knew I could move through. Forward in time. My heart beat out a tempo, marking time as I moved forward at eighty-four beats per minute. It was something. I closed my eyes—an even more useless gesture for me than normal—and focused on the sound. On the motion.

And then I heard my heartbeat again.

I was in my dorm room, in the dark, but not as I had left it. What furniture I had was overturned. I could smell smoke in the air and hear not too distant alarms.

I stood in front of myself.

"Yes," I said. "It's about time."

I was older. How much older I couldn't tell—my body had aged at a strange rate and then stopped—but certainly more than a matter of months. I was clearly dressed to travel and to do so unrecognized. I wore a long coat over a sensible yet unremarkable dress. A floral scarf hid my hair and dark glasses my eyes.

"When am I?" I asked.

"Further along in my timeline," I said.

"*How* much further? Am I... where am I going?"

I shook my head.

"That isn't important right now."

I balled my fists in frustration. I could feel my mind... months from now? Years? If I focused, I thought I could reach myself. It was the same mind, wasn't it? One entity in two points in time. My body stretched across dimensions of space and time. Looping back, touching down now... on myself at age ten, sitting in the metal chair... at minutes old, watching my mother recede in the distance... at however far in the future, watching my consternation...

My mind recoiled, and I drew farther away.

"No," I said.

I stamped my foot, trying to exorcise my fear and confusion. The floorboards shivered.

"Why *not?*" I asked.

"Because I was scared. Because I didn't. Why didn't I stop Pickman when I was ten?"

"Because…"

Because I remembered how it felt when I finally did reach into Gregory Pickman's mind. When in my untutored fury, I tore it apart. When I felt his pain and fear and sense of violation. Not a hundredth of what he had visited on me, but it made me feel sick and horrible. And worst of all, satisfied.

"Because I couldn't," I said, the words falling pitifully from my mouth.

"Because I did it when I was fourteen," I said.

I shook my head. "No, that's not… I couldn't."

"I could. I did. And I was then. I could have done it better. I could do it even better now. But I won't. Because I didn't."

I turned away and put my hands to my head. "I'm not making a whole lot of sense."

My lips quirked up in a slight smile. "Yes, I thought the same thing at the time."

I walked to the kitchen counter, where a thin layer of dust had settled. I curled my lip at the untidiness. I wasn't bothered by it. I ran a finger through the dust, sketching out two intersecting lines. I recognized x- and y- axes, though Luci would probably see a crossroads.

I put my finger at the point of intersection and drew a line straight up through the air. Z-, for depth. Then I drew a fourth line at right angles to the other three.

"That's very simplified," I said.

I smiled wider. "I have no idea yet."

I placed my finger at a point in the air. "Say this is me in 1954." I then traced a loop back along the fourth axis. "Say this is me in 1946." I then traced a series of wide loops and whorls until I reached a point far forward along the fourth axis. "Say this is me in 2054."

I blinked. "Am I in 2054?"

My smile gentled. "No. Well, possibly. I haven't seen yet."

I stepped away, clasping my hands behind my back. "Time's arrow travels in one direction. Unlike most people, I can move in more directions, but my own timeline still travels relentlessly along. I can't undo events. I wish…"

My voice faltered.

"I wish I could," I whispered.

I stood silently for a moment. I wasn't sure what to say. I had so many questions and clearly so few answers.

"Most people," I said eventually. "*Am* I a person?"

I looked down at my shoes. Sensible, meant for walking in. "Many people don't think so. Fewer, now."

I took a deep breath. "Luci and Gloria think I am. I hold on to that."

I let out an exasperated sigh.

"I understand. I want to understand. I will. When I do, I'm here."

I furrowed my brow and thought that through. "I see. I think. I still exist as a single point in time, despite everything I can do."

"Not despite," I said. I stepped closer to myself, raising my hand palm out. "It's a choice."

I looked at myself, not quite understanding. Then I stepped forward. Hesitantly, I raised my hand to my own. My fingertips touched. I didn't feel the electric tingle when I touched Luci's face in the past. I felt a sense of vertigo as the world tipped around me. And then I saw everything. All of me, in one single, awesome vision. It was terrifying. It was beautiful.

I broke contact. I doubled over, trying to catch a breath I was now definitely sure my body didn't need. I sat on the floor, hugging my knees.

"Why? Why did I choose this?"

I knelt down and smiled.

"Because on September 19, 1954, at 2:30 in the afternoon, Lucille Sweeney is waiting for me at the Arcadia. And she's worth it."

Lucille was waiting at the Arcadia, and she was worth it. She had already bought tickets, so I offered to pay for the popcorn. After a token protest, she accepted with a very odd smile. She carried the strangest sense of satisfaction all the way into the theater. I couldn't quite put my finger on it but splitting the cost with me like that made her very happy. Like it was a date.

Oh my word, I was on a date!

The theater was about half-full, so we took seats near the back. No one sat behind us for several rows, which gave us a sense of privacy in the dark. We nestled together in our seats, sharing popcorn and watching flying saucers do terrible things to American cityscapes. Every so often, Lucille would shrink in delighted fear and cower into my shoulder. The first time this happened, I looked at her in alarm until I realized that she was actually enjoying herself. After that, I just enjoyed the feeling of her head against mine.

"Isn't this great?" she said at one point, her whispering voice tickling at my ear.

"Well, the science is a little dodgy," I whispered back.

Lucille grabbed a piece of popcorn and tossed it at my nose. I caught it as it rolled off and popped it in her mouth.

"I meant this," she said as she crunched. "Just you and me, out together."

"This is pretty great," I said. "I've... never had a friend like you before."

I'd never had a friend at all, but of course I wasn't about to tell her that. She looked at me as if she understood all the same. I wondered what it was she thought she understood about me, but I didn't want to pry. Especially not now.

She reached out with one hand, running a gentle finger along my bare forearm. My skin tingled where she touched it.

"I have… sort of," she said quietly. "But not like you. It's… well, you know."

She looked over at me, her eyes shining and happy. To my surprise, she was thinking about how difficult it was to be different. To be weird.

"There's nothing weird about you," I said.

Lucille stared at me for just a second, then gave me the biggest smile I'd ever seen. Her hand slid across my arm to slip into mine. Our fingers intertwined, and my heart beat faster. I gave her hand a small squeeze, and she sighed happily. She leaned forward, her lips parting. I didn't need to see into her mind to see that she wanted to kiss me. I could see it in her soft eyes.

Then her eyes flicked to the side. There was another couple sitting a dozen seats away, a man and a woman about her age. What if they saw?

I rested my forehead against hers, comforting her with my warmth.

"Later," she whispered. A warning and a promise.

On the screen, half of California was on fire, but we barely noticed.

I was a little disappointed when the credits finally rolled and the lights came up. Not in the movie, it was tops (and now I thought I knew where Agent Morris had gotten his odd idea about meteorites), but in the fact that it was over. Now this quiet moment of intimacy had to end. Lucille felt it too. She looked at me and dropped her eyes, biting her lower lip. Slowly, reluctantly, she disentangled her fingers from mine and pushed herself up from her seat. I did the same, following her out into the aisle.

We walked side-by-side out of the theater, trying to stay as close to one another as we could. Lucille, brave as she was, feared what would happen if other people knew about us. That left me confused and a little hurt inside, but I had to trust that she knew better than I did. At least in some areas.

When we stepped out into the last light of day, Lucille turned to me and gave me the most tender smile, I melted a little inside.

She reached out and brushed her fingertips against my arm. "Can you... would you like to come back to the college with me?"

I wanted to say yes. Every part of me yearned to say yes. But I said no.

"I'm sorry. I have a curfew. I wish I could."

"Oh. So do I," Lucille said, looking away so I couldn't see the disappointment in her eyes. Or so she thought. It stabbed at my heart. She wanted me to invite her over instead, but that was also impossible.

"I wish I could ask the same of you," I said, dropping my eyes, "but I'm afraid they're very strict where I live."

"No visitors? Not even other girls?"

"No."

"That's awful. You should live somewhere else."

I laughed bitterly. "I wish I could. It's hard to explain."

"I understand. Though I wish you would. You're so mysterious sometimes."

I gave her a tight smile. There was really no answer to that.

"So, when *can* we see each other again? I'd like to spend more time with you. Just you. Not with the others."

I ducked my head and let the smile become real. "I'd like that, too."

"This Saturday? If Lucas Dowling doesn't blow up the world first?"

I nodded so quickly I thought my hair would fly loose. Luci grabbed my hand to squeeze it, and by impulse I pulled her into the doorway beside us. I looked around *everywhere*. There was no one to see us. I bent forward and kissed her. It was only a second, but it seemed to last forever.

When Luci pulled away, she let out a surprised laugh. Her eyes were dancing.

"Amelia Temple!" she whispered, delighted and scandalized at the same time. "What if someone saw?"

"There's no one around," I said. "Trust me."

Lucille slipped her arm through mine. "I do."

We walked together to the bus stop. Well, I was nearly floating. I was grateful to have her arm around mine, or I might have floated away entirely. Something that seemed to be a far more literal possibility than ever before.

I wanted to turn back, to feel our first kiss again and again. It was a shame I could never do it a better way, but to be there again... but I didn't. I stayed in this moment with her.

And a good thing, because she and Gloria would need me present for what came after.

16

Getting to where I was needed would prove tricky, though. When we set the time and date for the brownstone break-in (to call it what it was), I knew it was well after my Bureau-imposed curfew. Sneaking out after the agent on duty got around to conducting a brief bed-check wouldn't be difficult, despite what the Bureau thought, but Chatham Hills was miles from the Bureau campus. Not too far by bus, but its last stop was at five-thirty in the evening. Commandeering a vehicle was out of the question; leaving aside the fact that I had no idea how to drive, the logistics added complication upon complication.

No, the solution was clearly to leave before the bus stopped running. Which would require careful timing.

The Bureau's close of business was a strict five p.m. A few people always stayed behind—a handful of duty personnel, one or two late-night candle-burners—but most of the agents left when the shop closed up. No one but staff took the bus, car ownership being a source of economic pride for these post-war heroes. I just had to wait for enough of them to filter out to have a clear path out the front gate.

Then I had to deal with the agent meant to be watching over me.

I settled into my couch and relaxed, letting my focus expand away from this self. My senses slowly spread across the campus, taking in the four floors of the main building, the warehouse to its west, and the row of outbuildings on the north side holding the experimental labs and armory. I drifted, taking in the movement of lives through the structure. I watched the agents and staff trickling out in twos and threes, packing up their desks and punching their time clocks. With my focus spread this wide, I couldn't make out individual identities, nor perceive their minds as anything but a vague collection of feelings, but right now I didn't need to. I just needed to see the way the building emptied.

At five-twelve, I deemed that enough people had departed. I could trace a clear path from my dorm, through the orange zone, and out to the staff exit. If I moved quickly, I would encounter no one and only have to deal with one agent on the first floor. Provided the one assumption I'd made would hold true.

I pulled my awareness back until I was a single self again, while trying to maintain enough distance that I could still take in most of the building. Details were fuzzy, for lack of a better word, particularly at the edges of my awareness, but I was sure I could still perceive everyone remaining in the building. I slipped out of my dorm and away from the orange zone, taking a disused stairwell down to the second floor. I ducked across the hall to the darkened cafeteria, closing the door quietly behind me moments before a pair of agents turned the corner. I quickly crossed the room to the far door. The agent on duty was sitting with his feet up in an office down the hall from that side of the cafeteria. But he wasn't alone.

I stopped just before opening the cafeteria door. Agent Thomas was in the hall, aggressively leaning against the office door frame. Somehow, I hadn't noticed him until now. Granted, I'd been giving my surroundings only cursory looks, searching for movement rather than details. Was that how he'd escaped my notice? Or was it tied to the reason I couldn't see inside his mind?

In a panic, I threw my focus his way. Suddenly he and the duty agent resolved into focus. Agent Michael Fitzgerald was in no mood for Thomas' presence but lacked the will to tell him to leave. Thomas, on the other hand, was his usual frustrating blank.

At least I could still hear him. Not that one would want to.

"Settling in for the night, Fitz?" he said.

"Just for the moment, Thomas," Fitzgerald said. "Taking a few minutes to catch up on paperwork."

"So I see," Thomas said.

He snatched a magazine off the top of Fitzgerald's desk and smirked. The cover showed a photo of a giggling blonde woman. Fitzgerald flushed and tried to stammer out a response, but Thomas laughed nastily.

"Hell, Fitz, I don't care," Thomas said, throwing the magazine into Fitzgerald's lap. "Just make sure you look up from the pictures to check on the menagerie. Especially Temple. It's starting to get ideas. Make sure at light's out, it's in its cell and *stays there*."

Fitzgerald shifted uncomfortably in his chair.

"Come on, Thomas, she's just a kid. Kind of weird, but she's no trouble."

"A lot of agents thought that," Thomas said. "Now one of 'em is in the loony bin, one's in the ground, and the last can't walk. Temple's *dangerous*, and we need to keep it on a short leash. The Bureau's given it too many liberties already. We can't have it thinking it can wander around loose. Understand?"

"Okay, okay. I'll make sure she stays put," Fitzgerald said. "Shame, though. She's kind of a looker, from the right angle."

My cheeks burned red. My fingers twitched, and I had to press them flat against the door to make them stay.

Thomas snorted. "You're kidding me, right? How long have you been here?"

"About two years."

"So you don't know," Thomas said. He let out another nasty laugh and shook his head. "Trust me. There's more to that one than meets the eye."

Agent Thomas tapped a knowing finger to his forehead, then turned and walked away, shaking his head and laughing. Fitzgerald and I watched him go, Fitzgerald in puzzlement, me in shame and quiet anger. It wasn't the first time I'd heard words like that, but every time it was like a knife stabbing me in the stomach. I wanted to scream at Agent Thomas. I wanted to cry. But I didn't have time for either.

At least I didn't feel guilty about what I was about to do to Agent Fitzgerald anymore. He was no better than any of the rest. Let him be complicit in my truancy. I almost hoped to get caught now.

I waited for him to pick up his girlie magazine and settle back in. I didn't have to wait long. Within a few heartbeats of the door closing behind Agent Thomas, Fitzgerald had his feet up and his magazine open. His surface thoughts were dismissive of Thomas' arrogance, and I grabbed hold of them as softly as I could. For all of Thomas' bluster, Fitzgerald still thought of me as basically harmless. He wasn't even certain what I was doing in the Bureau's custody, though he'd learned not to ask that sort of question. He'd make sure I was in my dorm because he was told to, but he had no doubt that I would be.

That's right, I thought to him. *I was in my dorm. Where else would I be? I was weird but quiet. I'd be on my couch reading or in bed asleep, just as expected. A quick check and then back to a quiet night.*

I let go of his thoughts and watched them settle into position. They all fit together nicely, because they went along with what his mind would prefer to believe. By the time Agent Fitzgerald was relieved from his shift at midnight, he would remember checking up on me and finding me right where I was supposed to be.

That taken care of, I walked to the back of the cafeteria and through the kitchen, down the staff stairwell and out the back door. Then it was on to the last hurdle before the bus stop. I was cutting it close, but a brisk walk would have me there right as the bus arrived. So long as I didn't have any more trouble.

I followed the sidewalk around the outbuildings and to the front gate. I walked nonchalantly between them, not bothering to acknowledge the guards. Head high, as if I knew exactly where I was going and that I was supposed to be going there. From the first day on, the gate guards had taken no more notice of my exit than anyone else's. Which meant, I was hoping, that they didn't know who I was. The Bureau had always kept information about me tightly controlled. I was counting on that including the gate guards.

I was right. The guards watched me pass through the gate without comment. They assumed I was just another staff member heading home for the day. And, after all, their job was to keep people out rather than in.

When I reached the road, I let out a sigh of relief and hurried to the bus stop.

When Gloria and Lucille arrived at Hanners Square, I was already waiting. The stalls and booths from the previous Saturday were gone, so the square stood empty, fenced on two sides by wooden benches and short hedges. Nowhere to hide, in other words, but the girls didn't see me when they first arrived. They walked right past me, in fact, chatting amiably as if they were simply out for an evening walk. They stopped beneath a lamppost, Gloria looking up and down the street while Lucille checked her watch.

"Where on earth is Amelia?" Luci asked.

"Right here," I said, stepping into the pool of light.

Luci yelped and jumped straight up. I took a surprised step back, clasping my hands together in front of me and ducking my head apologetically. Luci bent forward to grab the lamppost for support and clapped her other hand over her mouth. She gave me a look over her shoulder.

"Sorry, dear," I said sheepishly.

Gloria had a hand over her face, alarmed and amused in equal measure.

"Where did you come from?" Luci asked.

That's a matter of some debate, I almost said before I caught myself. What I actually said was, "I've been waiting here for you two."

I hadn't been sure whether a lone young woman loitering about Hanners Square after dark would look suspicious, so I'd simply hidden. Better than I'd thought, apparently.

"Well, we're here now," Gloria said. "So long as Luci doesn't die of fright, we should be ready to do this."

Luci stuck her tongue out at Gloria, who smiled back innocently. I took a step forward, then remembered that I wasn't supposed to know where we were going.

"Lead on, Luci," I said.

She nodded. "It's up that street."

We fell into step behind her. The brownstone was as I remembered it, though it now lurked forebodingly in the dark. Lights were on in most of the houses up the street, but the former home of the Apollonian Society for Illumination was utterly dark. Hopefully that was a good sign, even if it didn't look like one.

Luci led us to the alley. After a quick look around to make sure the coast was clear, she darted up the back walk to the servant's entrance. Gloria and I shared a look before following more cautiously.

Luci tried the doorknob and said an awful word. "Locked."

"Well, what did you expect?" Gloria asked.

"Pretty much that," Luci said.

Luci had a small bag slung over her shoulder. She reached in and pulled out a small black pouch holding a half-dozen thin, crooked pieces of metal. Gloria whistled quietly, eyebrows slowly rising.

"Honey, what are you doing with those?" she asked.

"Getting us inside," Luci said.

She picked the lock with a few seconds of well-practiced work that, annoyingly, seemed to validate at least some of the Bureau's concerns about our relationship. Giving us a wink, she pushed the door open. It felt like it should have opened with a rusty creak, revealing a dark space hung with cobwebs and unspeakable stains. Instead, it slid open smoothly on suspiciously well-oiled hinges. I already knew what was here—a short hallway with utility rooms on either side. What lay beyond was the mystery.

Luci flourished her hand at the open door. "Shall we?"

She didn't wait for a response. Luci stepped smartly inside, followed shortly by Gloria. I took up the rear, wincing at a momentary headache that stabbed across my forehead the moment I crossed the threshold.

I looked at the inner doorway. Behind the peeling wallpaper, someone had scribbled a series of unusual markings. They were a set of circles scratched deep into the plaster, connected by a knot of overlapping loops and spirals drawn in chalk. They reminded me uncomfortably of the markings on the walls separating the orange zone from the rest of the Bureau's old Massachusetts headquarters. Only these were old and faded, and in many places, water damage had obliterated some of the chalk marks.

I put a hand up to the wall, carefully, as if it was a stove burner that might be hot. When my fingers touched the wall, though, I felt no pain.

Curious, I thought.

"What are you doing, hon?" Gloria asked.

She and Luci were behind me, already poking through the storage rooms I'd dismissed. Luci's face and hands were streaked with old dust.

I stuck my hand into a tear in the wallpaper and peeled it back, revealing more of the markings. "Look what I found," I said. When she saw what I was doing, Gloria came to help, and we shortly had the whole scrawl exposed. It ran across the entire top of the doorframe and partway down both sides.

Luci set her bag on the floor and pulled out her camera and a large flash bulb. "All right. Hold still."

"Oh, no," Gloria said, taking me by the hand and pulling me away. "I'd like to implicate myself as little as possible tonight."

Luci rolled her eyes but waited until we were well out of frame before snapping three photos of the marks.

"What do you think they mean?" she said. "They look kind of like music, don't they?"

"I was thinking more like an equation," Gloria said.

"Or like a sentence diagram," Luci said.

She lowered the camera and approached the wall, running a hand along the marks gently, to avoid smearing them.

"Like... okay, this is like the central thought," she said, tracing a line that connected most of the symbols. "And these smaller lines, they modify it."

"Modify it how?" I asked.

We were all silent for a moment.

"That's a very good question," Gloria said.

"Maybe it's a motto," Luci said, her tone uncertain. "Like 'Home Sweet Home'."

"'Don't Forget Your Coat'," Gloria said.

Weird Things Stay Out, I thought.

They looked at me expectantly, and I realized they were waiting for me to join in.

"Um, 'Have a Nice Day'?" I said.

Gloria and Luci laughed. None of us really found it funny, though.

"It's nothing like that, is it?" Luci said.

I shook my head. I wished I could have explained why I was so certain, but it would have led to even more awkward questions.

"I expect there are more markings like that throughout the house," I said. "Let's look around."

The short hall led past more utility rooms—a kitchen, a laundry— and then into the main part of the house. The part I couldn't see. As we approached the door, I felt as nervous as Gloria and Lucille. I had no idea what would be behind that door. It was like having a huge blind spot right in front of my face. Behind me, there was the back of the house, the yard, the alleyway, a row of empty shops. Houses on one side, full of families turning in for the night. Hanners Square on the other, waiting for people to come and make it alive again. Cold sky above me, eventually stretching up to the void of space, and well-packed earth below. Before me, nothing but uncertainty, tinged by something like static.

I couldn't bring myself to touch the doorknob. Fortunately, Luci had no such qualms. How could she be so brave, living in such constant uncertainty? How could she and Gloria stand never knowing what was on the other side of a door, what another person was thinking? How could they stand to wait to discover things?

As it turned out, what was behind the door was pain.

Also a large den. Luci and Gloria went through the door without difficulty, scanning the rich furniture and paintings. I felt a searing pain flare across my head the moment I stepped through the door. I screamed and doubled over, clutching my head. Dimly, I heard Gloria cry out my name, while Luci dropped to her knees to wrap her arms around me. It felt as if my mind had been set ablaze, flames licking along my nerves. The pain spread down my spine, along my arms, further...

There were more glyphs above this door. I could see them beneath the wallpaper now, through the white-hot glare of my agony. Above the door, running along the walls where they met the ceiling and down them where they joined, tracing out an invisible fence to keep me out. A barbed-wire fence.

I lashed out blindly. The wall buckled above the doorway, lathe splintering, plaster cracking, sending pictures flying off the walls and Luci and Gloria ducking for cover. Cracks broke the chalk marks causing my agony.

Elsewhere, alarms were going off, but I wouldn't learn about that until much later.

17

*fell forward, panting for breath, tears streaming down my face.
Luci took me into her arms and pressed her cheek to my forehead,
murmuring words of comfort. Gloria knelt and took my hand.

"Amelia, are you okay?" she whispered.

"She's burning up," Luci said.

"I'm fine," I said weakly. "Just a headache."

I squeezed Gloria's hand, then leaned my head back to give Luci a
quick kiss. I tried to sit up, but Luci's embrace held me firmly in her lap.
I put my hand on her arm and patted her gently, trying to reassure her.

"I'm fine, really," I said, my voice a little stronger this time. "The pain
has passed. You can let me up now."

"What happens if I do and you tumble right over?" Luci said,
blinking back tears.

I twisted in her lap so I could look up into her beautiful blue eyes.

"Then you'll catch me."

Despite her fears, Luci bit her lip and blushed. She didn't let me go,
but she relaxed enough to allow me to sit up. She kept one arm around
my shoulder, her hand resting above my heart, and slid her other hand

down to my hip.

Gloria gave my hand one last comforting squeeze before standing up. The damaged wall now showed the script, peeking out from behind the split wallpaper. She reached up and tore off a large strip, exposing more of the strange symbols.

"They're just like the ones over the back door," she said.

"Those didn't almost kill Amelia," Luci said, her voice brittle.

"Those were already damaged," Gloria said. "They didn't break until just now, when the wall cracked."

She looked up at the broken wall, then back down at me. She couldn't explain it, but the conclusion was unavoidable. I ducked my head and sighed. I didn't know what to say. Or what they would believe.

"You can't possibly think Amelia did that," Luci said.

"I'm not saying anything for certain," Gloria said, sounding confused rather than accusatory. "But walls don't just break on their own, even old ones. And she didn't stop screaming until it did."

"So? It didn't hurt when she went through the other door."

"Actually, it did," I said in a small voice. "It just didn't hurt nearly as bad."

"Because the writing or whatever was already broken," Gloria said.

I nodded. "Probably."

"So now we know what they are," Gloria said. "They're some kind of ward. For keeping strangers out."

"Then why did it hurt Amelia and not us?" Luci said.

"That's a good question," Gloria said. "It could just be because she was the third one through the door both times, but that's dumb."

I nodded unhappily. All of a sudden, I wasn't admiring her intelligence.

"If you wanted to keep intruders out, you'd keep all of them out," I said heavily, resigning myself to this revelation. "Why let the first two in?"

"So it's something specific," Gloria said. "Some quality you have that we don't."

"Gloria, you're scaring her!" Luci said.

"No, I'm scaring *you*," Gloria snapped. "You don't want to see it because all you *can* see is that you're in love with her."

Luci's cheeks burned. She bit back the half-dozen nasty things she wanted to say; despite her anger, she didn't want to hurt Gloria or pick a fight. And deep down, she knew Gloria was right. Instead, she turned her head while Gloria knelt again in front of me. When Gloria spoke again, her voice was gentle.

"Always knew there was something different about you," she said. "For some reason, you seemed like you weren't from around here. Growing up in an orphanage didn't explain all of it."

I laughed bitterly. So much for the Bureau's best-laid plans.

"I really am an orphan, though," I said. "At least as far as I know."

I covered Luci's hand with my own. I was afraid she would pull away, but instead she twined her fingers with mine. I could feel her heartbeat against my back, and I leaned against her, finding reassurance in her affection.

Still, now she and Gloria were looking at me expectantly, Gloria to explain and Luci to reassure her that everything was okay. I knew I was going to have to tell them something.

Part of me wanted to tell everything right now. Why not? Gloria had said it; there was something off about me. Something that didn't add up. They could tell. So would others, if they spent enough time with me. Why not admit it? I could see things they couldn't. I could move things without touching them with my hands. I could sense their thoughts. I could *change* their thoughts...

No.

"I can't explain everything," I said quietly. "Mostly because I don't know everything myself. There's a lot that's been kept from me... and if you understood what I am, you'd know how hard that is.

"But Gloria is correct. There's some quality about me that's starkly different from either of you. And those symbols, whatever they are, are somehow intended to keep that quality away. I know because I've seen them before."

"Where?" Gloria asked.

I closed my eyes and took a deep breath. "On the outside of walls meant to keep me locked away."

Luci took in a sharp breath. A single hot tear fell down my cheek. She hugged me tightly and buried her face against my neck. Gloria took my hands in hers and touched her forehead to mine.

"Oh, baby girl," she whispered.

"How could they do that to you?" Luci said.

"Because they're afraid of me," I said, as if truly understanding it for the first time. "Of what I am."

"What's that?" Gloria asked.

I shook my head. "I don't know. But it's something to do with the Apollonian Society's experiments—with Lucas Dowling's experiment."

I let go of Luci's hand and turned to pat her cheek. She still didn't recoil from my touch, and I allowed myself to feel a tiny amount of relief. I could see her fear and confusion like jagged lines pulsing in her mind. But it wasn't directed at me. It was at whoever had imprisoned me—who was likely still imprisoning me. Fear and confusion, and beneath that, a burning, affronted anger.

I was going to have to keep an eye on her.

I ran my thumb down her cheek and kissed her again. I was tender at first, but then Luci pressed her lips against mine with a passion I felt down to my toes. She cupped the back of my head with her hand and pressed her whole body against mine, filling me with love and reassurance, drawing the same from me. Trying to show me that nothing had changed, that she still cared for me just as much as she did before. I clung to that, and to her, trying to find an anchor as the world I knew threatened to fall down around me.

Behind us, Gloria coughed quietly.

"You two, uh, want to find a room or something?" she said.

Her tone was annoyed, but amusement danced in her eyes. Luci and I disentangled from one another. My cheeks flushed with embarrassment, but Luci just smiled at Gloria with an utter lack of shame. Still, she knew Gloria was right. Affirming our love could come later; right now, we had work to do. Work and explanations.

I stood and dusted off my dress. I walked to the center of the room, taking it all in now that I could focus. My awareness of the house was splintered—no doubt the result of more warding script threaded through the building—but I had a full view of this room at last. The furniture, old hardwood and deep leather seats, was overturned and strewn about, and much of it was damaged. There were deep stains in the carpet and wallpaper, and two dozen bullets embedded in the walls. The wards had rather spectacularly failed to keep out every danger, it seemed.

Against the far wall, above a small wet bar that had been damaged by what was undoubtedly a man-shaped object, was a large photograph of the society's members. Gloria had shown us a small reproduction of it in the news clipping about Professor Blake. Seeing it in person sent a shiver up my spine. The cold man stared out at me, his lined patrician face looking stoic and more than a little contemptuous. Was it just my imagination, or was there a noticeable distance between him and the men around him? Were they unwilling to get too close?

I placed a hand on my chest, trying to steady myself. With the other, I pointed him out to the others.

"That man was present the night I was born," I said.

"What do you mean?" Gloria asked.

"Just what I said. He was there when I was born," I said. "I can't explain without sounding crazy, but he took me from my mother."

I was silent for a moment. Gloria and Luci came behind me. Luci put her arm around my waist and squeezed lightly.

"I haven't seen her since," I whispered.

"Oh, honey," Luci said softly. She rested her head on my shoulder.

Gloria put her hand on my other shoulder, rubbing me with what she hoped was reassurance. But I could see the question forming in her mind. She gave me another moment of quiet before trying to ask. I didn't wait for her to speak this time.

"Yes," I said, turning my head to face her. "I haven't seen my mother since she gave birth to me. I remember that day. I don't remember anything before it, but I remember everything since."

Gloria blinked twice.

"That's…"

"Unusual, to say the least. I know," I said, laughing dryly. "It took me a while to realize that most people can't."

"I don't really remember anything before I was about four," Luci said.

"*He* took you," Gloria said. "Not the Apollonian Society."

"No. If your notes are accurate, that organization wouldn't have existed anymore," I said.

"And it looks like it ended badly," Luci said. "Our notes said it just fell apart, but…" She gestured at the room, the dusty echo of a decades-old fight. "This looks more like it was pushed."

"Yes," Gloria said. "Something destroyed the society, which is why part of it became the Chambers Foundation."

"So what happened to the rest?" I said.

"Let's look around some more," Gloria said. Then she put her arm around my waist, just above Luci's. "*Carefully*. Maybe we'll find something useful."

The two girls hugged me tight. Then we went back to work.

There was little information to be gathered from this room; it appeared to be nothing more than a den or smoking room. There were a number of other portraits and photographs. Some still hung from the walls, others had been knocked down by long-ago force or by much more recent force, in the case of the wall I'd broken. Luci paused to snap a picture of each portrait, saying we might be able to cross-reference them against something else later.

Most of the pictures depicted small expeditions the society's members had undertaken. Groups of four or five clustered around unusual apparatuses, heavily modified telescopes and theodolites and the like, in photographs labeled with the site and dates of the expedition. They had traveled to the American Southwest, the Appalachians, Alaska, and once each to the Alps and Himalayas.

"They certainly liked their mountains," Luci said.

"Except for this one," Gloria said, pulling a photograph out of its broken frame.

That expedition had been to New Mexico in 1913. The four men stood in what looked like a ruined settlement inside of a cave, though what remained of the buildings seemed to be built much too low for an adult. The doors were so low that one of the explorers would have had to crawl through it. Something about it itched at the back of my head, but I couldn't immediately draw any connection to it.

Other photographs simply showed important members of the society. Professor Blake wasn't among them, nor the cold man, but two of the portraits were identified as the society's founders. One was Maxwell Thorpe, a balding, heavy-set man with serious muttonchops. The other had been torn from the frame. The brass plate beneath it read, "Dr. Ward Stewart, Founder."

"Curiouser and curiouser," Luci said as she stowed her camera.

I was tempted to look *back*, to try to see what had happened here so long ago, but I was afraid of what might happen. The past two times, I had more of a connection to what I was seeing—either following Luci or looking back on my own timeline. Here, I had no real anchor beyond my own curiosity. I didn't know if that would be enough under normal circumstances, and these were far from that. The script running along the walls, which I was beginning to think of as a script of concealment rather than wards, was interfering with my ability to focus along spatial dimensions. I didn't want to know how it would affect my newfound ability to focus along the temporal dimension.

To put it bluntly, I was afraid of getting lost.

Instead, we chose to move farther into the building. Not that Luci or Gloria were aware of another option. Two more doors led out of the room. I couldn't determine much of what was beyond them, save that it was a single space that wrapped around this central room with more house on either side. Luci picked the door to the right as we came in, for no better reason than it was the one closest to where she was standing. She carefully turned the knob and pulled the door open. A dark hallway waited.

Luci made to step through, then stopped and looked above the frame. She pushed her fingers into a seam in the wallpaper and ripped it back. Another set of wards stood exposed.

"We're taking care of this now," she said firmly.

She pulled a cloth out of her bag and attacked the symbols, rubbing hard at the chalk until they smeared. Her desire to protect me warmed my heart, but I couldn't help feeling some trepidation.

"Um, is that really a good idea?" I said. "We're going to make it really obvious that someone's been poking around."

Gloria looked up at the mess I'd made of the rear wall and smiled wryly. "I think we're passed that now, hon."

"I don't care if anyone knows we've been here," Luci said. "I'm not letting these things hurt you again."

I folded my hands together and looked down at my feet, smiling shyly. A warm flush crept through me. Such a little thing, and yet it meant so much.

It probably would have taken only a few smudged lines to render the symbols inert, but Luci was taking no risks. She didn't stop until the warding script was a large gray smear. When she finished, she put her hands on her hips and nodded with satisfaction.

"Right!" she said. She turned to face us. "I'll go through first. Amelia, you follow me. That way either Gloria or I can catch you if something still happens."

"Okay," I said quietly.

With some trepidation, I watched Luci step into the hallway. Then I gingerly stepped forward. Steeling myself, I took one shaky step across the door. Luci and Gloria held their breath.

My heart beat once, and then I was in the hallway.

We all let out a collective sigh of relief. Then Gloria followed us into the hall. I had a moment's twinge of fear as she stepped up to the doorway—third to cross, after all—but she was as unaffected as either of us.

"Good. Hopefully there will be no more nasty surprises," Luci said.

"Let's not get ahead of ourselves," Gloria said. "We're not even to the second floor yet."

As I'd thought, this space wrapped around the den like a fat-bottomed U. The base was a large foyer, with a double staircase leading up to the second floor. The room to the side we'd entered was a long dining room, dusty and cobwebbed from years of disuse. The room on the other side of the house was a study of some kind.

The script at the crown of the walls ran along the outer walls. There were no wards on the dining room door, but we found more over every window, as well as the front door and the inside door to the first-floor study. After pausing to eliminate that ward, we entered the room.

A giant mobile of the solar system dominated the study, hanging from the center of the ceiling. The scale was necessarily hopeless, but at least some attempt had been made to represent the vast disparity in size between the sun and her children. A yellow-tinted glass globe, about the size of my head, represented the central star, while the planets were tiny colored glass spheres suspended on wires running up to elliptical tracks set in the ceiling. A wide clockwork mechanism would move the whole thing if electricity was applied to the motor.

The planets were each engraved with their astronomical symbol. Gloria frowned and walked between them, counting each planet off. She stopped at nine with a look of puzzlement.

"This can't be Pluto," she said.

"Why not?" Luci asked.

"Because Pluto wasn't discovered until five years after the society fell apart," she said.

"Maybe... maybe they discovered it sooner?" Luci said uncertainly. "And never told anyone because they didn't want to be famous for discovering a planet?"

She didn't believe it more than Gloria or me.

"Maybe they discovered *something*," I said.

Instead of the symbol for Pluto, the ninth planet was marked with a squiggly symbol none of us recognized. The other planets were smooth spheres, but this was an irregularly shaped lump of black glass. Gloria reproduced the symbol as best she could in her notebook, under the heading "Planet X".

Various astronomical charts hung from the walls. Gloria stood beneath the sun, examining the charts thoughtfully.

"I wonder if these are arranged to show where these stars are in relation to us," she said.

"That would make sense," I said.

"Do either of you recognize them?"

It was Luci's turn to smile wryly. "Del Sombra doesn't let co-eds take astronomy. It's later at night, and we're obviously distracting the boys."

"That sounds like their problem," I said.

I examined a pattern of six stars. More of the script had been written around them in a wide circle, but it looked incomplete. Something about the stars seemed familiar, although I couldn't say why.

"No," I said finally. "I don't recognize any of them."

Luci walked around the room, snapping more pictures of the charts. "If this keeps up, I'm going to run out of film," she said.

"Maybe slow down, then," Gloria said, mostly kindly. "We don't know how much of this is important."

"Exactly," Luci said. "And we don't know when or if we'll get another chance to see this stuff. I want to record as much as I can. And it isn't as if we can carry much of it out."

Gloria couldn't argue with that, although she did get Luci to promise that she got to laugh exactly once if Luci ran out of film right when we found something really critical.

We left the study to head upstairs.

18

The stairs led up to an I-shaped hallway. More of the concealment script ran up the stairs beneath the carpet, then up the corners of the adjoining walls to reach the second-floor ceiling. I grew increasingly weary of the fuzzy sensation that script was causing. My perception of the house warped and twisted as we went from room to room. It reminded me of Agent Simmons' description of a funhouse mirror. It hadn't sounded very fun then, either, though he had still promised to take me to a fair before he—

Anyway.

For all its frustrations, the second floor was mostly a bust. It mainly consisted of eight small bedrooms and two full baths, obviously for members who needed to stay a night or two. There was a large parlor on the west side, but we didn't stay long to explore it. The poker table was overturned, the liquor cabinet smashed, and as with the den downstairs, several bullets lodged in the walls. At least there were no bodies, although I could see the shadows their deaths had left on the floor. They made me shudder, and I had to hurry out of the room.

We found the society's library on the east side, or rather, its corpse.

There were six large, dust-covered bookshelves. All empty, and two overturned. The room also held several class cases, the panes smashed and their contents missing. Whoever had caused the society's downfall had thoroughly ransacked the place in its passing.

Seeing the wreckage, Luci put her hands to her head and stamped the floor in frustration.

"Gone!" she said. "It's all gone!"

"We knew that was a possibility," Gloria said, her voice far more calm than her thoughts let on. "This place is supposed to be abandoned."

"But we know it's not," Luci said. "Blake is still using it for something! I saw him!"

"We believe you," I said gently, stroking her arm. *I saw him too, after all.* "So if he has anything here, it's hidden a little better. There's still one more floor. Let's see what's up there."

That mollified her to a degree. The three of us left the library, Luci throwing one last wistful glance over her shoulder.

Two stairwells led up, one on either side of the back hallway. They met at the top of a T-shaped hallway pointed toward the south-facing front of the house. An ornate wooden door stood at the end of the hall. The symbols around it weren't hidden beneath wallpaper but inscribed directly on the bare plaster walls. There were far more than just the warding and concealment scripts we'd seen, and looking at the conglomeration of looping, whirling symbols made my senses hurt. I screwed up my eyes and grabbed Luci's shoulder to steady myself. She put an arm around my waist with a look of alarm.

"Are you okay?" she asked, holding me tightly.

I nodded. "I'm not in any pain. It's just hard to look at."

Luci's alarm slowly turned to bafflement, though she didn't let me go.

"What's hard to look at, sweetheart?" she said.

Through the haze I frowned at her and pointed to the door. "That!

The mess of script around the door."

She and Gloria followed my finger, then looked back at me. There was no recognition in their eyes.

"Hon, there's no door there. No symbols," Gloria said carefully. "It's just a blank wall."

"What are you talking about?" I said, incredulous. "The door *right there* probably weighs as much as all of us together and has an entire box of chalk's worth of scribbles around it! How do you not see it?"

Luci and Gloria shared a look. I thought they might be trying to play a stupid trick on me for some unknown reason, but in their minds, I could see that they were telling the truth. They couldn't see the door, and they were concerned that I could.

But something else was in their minds, too. Something I could barely perceive. I could only track it by the absence it left behind. It was like a stray thought, running through the front of their minds, changing them ever so slightly.

"Just look again," I said.

Luci shrugged and turned toward the door. I peered closely into her mind. The door registered for less than an eye blink. Then it was gone, erased from her mind too fast for me to catch it.

But not mine.

My chest tightened as I tried to follow it. Something in the script was affecting my friends' minds, and I couldn't do anything about it. I wanted to dig in and root it out, but was that even possible? Wouldn't I do more damage? Was it just the door? What else were they going to forget?

"Maybe it's a side effect of whatever happened to her downstairs," Gloria said.

My fear got the better of me, and I snapped at her, "Don't talk about me like I'm not here."

Gloria took a step back, eyes wide. "Sorry! Sorry!"

I sighed and put a hand over my face. "No, *I'm* sorry. It's just… Luci, would you please take a picture of the 'wall'? For me?"

Hopefully that would provide some evidence, after it was developed. Until then, I would have to deal with their skepticism. The two shared another look. Then Luci shrugged.

"Well, on the 'anything for you' scale, I guess this rates rather low," she said. "Hope this isn't my last picture, though."

It was.

I didn't feel any better after she took the picture, but I let the matter drop, much to Luci and Gloria's relief. We turned to the other doors, the ones they could actually see. There were four, two on either side of the hallway, and they picked the first on the right. After making the door safe, we went inside. And finally found what we were looking for.

It was an office, but far from disused. The small space had a roll-top desk and a wooden chair, along with a small table and a cot pushed up against one wall. A small footlocker stood against the other wall. The additional furniture packed the space so tightly that we could hardly all fit; Gloria took a seat atop the footlocker, while Luci stood in front of the desk, and I squeezed in between it and the table.

A candlestick holder sat atop the desk, greasy with recent use, next to an open box of candles. A half-eaten sandwich sat on a plate one the table. We looked at one another.

"Blake," we said in unison.

"He's been staying here," Gloria said. "Carrying on the society's work in secret, whatever it is."

"Then he'll have left evidence," Luci said.

Gloria turned her attention to a small stack of books next to the desk, while Luci and I focused on the desk proper. The roll-top wouldn't budge, however.

"Locked," Luci said. "I think I can get in."

She dug into her bag for her lockpicks again, while I looked inside the mechanism itself. It was simple enough. I put a hand to the cover, and the lock made a metallic *click*. With a grunt, I pushed the cover back.

Luci stared at me. I shrugged.

"Must have been stuck," I said.

Luci let that go when she saw what was inside. Blake had a small pile of correspondence covering his desk, most of it dating from the past year and a half. Luci picked up a handful of letters and shuffled through them. She made a face.

"No names," she said. "Look, even at the signature. Just initials."

"They're all addressed to H.B., though," I said.

"The resistance, these guys aren't," Luci said. "Let's see… most of these are from M.T. Maxwell Thorpe, obviously. These three are from R.F. This one's from M.T. but it mentions a W.S. and a G.L. These six are from L.D.—Lucas!"

We spread the letters out across the table, dropping the plate and its sandwich onto the cot to make room. Professor Blake hadn't kept his desk very organized, so we tried our best to order then by date and sender. Unfortunately, almost-certainly-Lucas couldn't seem to be bothered to date his correspondence; Luci took no small measure of offense at that. With some difficulty, we managed to place his letters within the timeline of the others, partly by context but mainly by their tone. Lucas' letters appeared to grow increasingly shrill as he demanded more and more support from Blake, support Thorpe was encouraging Blake to meter out carefully.

> H.B,
> Once again, I congratulate you on your newest pupil.
> L.D.'s eagerness to continue the society's work, however

unknowing, will certainly gratify those explorers into the unknown who remain faithful to our goals. Nonetheless, I must caution you to be more measured in satisfying all his demands.

L.D. must be encouraged to make his own discoveries whenever possible. In the first place, this will increase his desire to continue simply by feeding his pride and scientific ambition. The more he sees it as his experiment, the more he will own its results, at least in his mind.

In the second, we must hide our involvement as much as possible. I would not have the Foundation tarnished by the echoes of old conflicts. W.S.'s hounds are still sniffing around, and the results of G.L.'s recklessness is still out there, somewhere. Possibly under the control of W.S.'s faction, though that strikes me as unlikely.

Regardless, take precautions with those resources the society still possesses, namely, the remains of the 1925 Experiment and the society's library. Only give L.D. that which he cannot acquire on his own. If he objects, remind him who is master and who apprentice.

M.T.

"Self-important ass, isn't he?" Luci said.

"This is taking precautions?" Gloria said, gesturing to the pile of books.

"I doubt they suspected anyone would break in," I said.

"Are you upset that they didn't lock up better?" Luci said.

"No," Gloria admitted. "Especially not this."

She placed one of the books on the table and opened it so we could see. The pages were covered in symbols like the ones we'd seen throughout the house and the ones I'd seen at the old Bureau building. Someone had written notes in the margins, quite a few of them. Gloria quickly flipped through the pages. It was laid out like an encyclopedia or a textbook.

I glanced at the cover. It was untitled, but I could see the worn remains of a symbol tooled into the old leather. The eye in the compass.

"This has to be their primer on how they do whatever they did to this place," Gloria said. "Maybe on that experiment, too."

"Do we think Lucas has a copy?" I said. "This probably falls under the category of things Lucas couldn't get on his own."

"I don't think so," Luci said. "Here, look at this letter."

> H.B,
> I warn you again, L.D. must be controlled. He is intelligent, yes. All to the good. But he is also willful and reckless. Recall that you've already had to cover up one incident that could have drawn unwanted attention. Give him free reign and the Architect alone knows what he will do.
> Yes, you are correct that he will require some knowledge of Prospero's Keys if he is to recreate the Grand Experiment, but at this point simply handing him the books is akin to giving a book of matches to a child sitting on a keg of gunpowder. Tutor him as you need, couch the lessons in terms of extraspatial mathematics and multidimensional geometry, it is not inaccurate, but direct him along those lines we need him to follow.
> M.T.

"That's from last April. The incident Thorpe's talking about must be that fire in the shed," Luci said.

"The one that got you investigating in the first place," I said.

Luci nodded and grabbed another letter, this one from last month.

"He must have figured something out. Listen to this:

"'I quite agree with your last report. It's about time L.D.'s fumbling bore fruit. If only we had the resources to employ a dozen more like him, though preferably more controllable. L.D. may have solved the flaw that led to the 1925 Experiment's failure.'"

"One month ago... then he must be ready to actually do it," I said.

"I wonder if that's what the argument on Saturday was about," Luci said. "In Lucas' last letter, he's demanding access to some sort of specimen. And in the letter after, Thorpe's still urging caution. I wonder why?"

"Cold feet?" Gloria suggested.

"Or some other factor we don't know about," I said.

I picked up the last letter. It was three sentences long. The date was given as Saturday, September 18th.

> Go ahead and give him the sample, Henry. What's the worst that could happen? A repeat of the 1925 fiasco?
> "R.F."

Gloria frowned. "That's remarkably flippant."

"I know," I said. "Is there anything to suggest that Blake's gone ahead and given Lucas the sample he wants?"

"We don't even know what it is, let alone where Blake would keep it," Luci said. "But neither of the boys has said anything to me about running the experiment yet. I really hope that's a good sign."

"I don't like guessing," Gloria said.

"No," I said. "We need to assume Lucas will carry it out soon. Which means we need to know for sure how to stop it."

"For that, we'd need to know how it really works," Luci said. "This didn't tell us anything except that we were right all along."

"Which you love," Gloria said.

"Maybe." Luci shrugged. "But that's not helping us now."

"No," I said. "We need to go to the last place they tried this. The observatory."

I had an idea now, one that was going to be considerably risky, but that also would be the best chance of getting us to the bottom of this. Unfortunately, before I could even begin to explain, we all heard a door slam downstairs.

"What was that?" Gloria said, whispering now.

"I don't know. Could Blake be back? What time is it?" Luci said.

"Ten twenty-two," I said without thinking. "I don't think it's the professor, though."

"Why not?" Luci asked.

"Because there are two of them," I said.

I was trying to focus on the first floor. It was difficult, because my focus kept slipping, like a scratched record. One moment I was seeing the den, another I was looking down the second-floor stairwell, another I saw only static. I could make out a pair of bodies, however. They were picking through the remains of the den.

"They have to know we're here," I said.

"Then we need to go," Gloria said. Her tone brooked no disagreement, but Luci tried anyway.

"We need this evidence," she said. "This is the most important stuff we've found."

"Hurry it up, then!" Gloria said.

Luci pulled out her camera. She intended to photograph as much of Professor Blake's correspondence as she could in one or two photos. But when she pressed the button, nothing happened.

Luci said an awful word, then, "I'm out of film!"

"So what do you want me to do about it?" Gloria said.

"We don't have time to argue," I said.

I grabbed a handful of letters, trusting in quick glances and my weird intuition to guide me, and stuffed them into Luci's bag. I then grabbed up the rest and threw them back into the roll-top. I closed the lid as quietly as I could, then reached into the lock and turned the tumblers. Then I snapped the mechanism for good measure.

"Okay," I said. "Let's go."

"Wait," Gloria said.

She grabbed the encyclopedia of symbols—Prospero's Keys, I supposed—and tucked it under her arm.

"This is probably going to be more useful than anything else," she said.

"Sure. Now let's get out of here," Luci said.

The desk was set up against the office's only window. Luci grabbed hold of it and started pushing.

"Help me move this!" she said.

"Lucille! We're three floors off the ground!" Gloria said.

"And there are wards," I said, pointing to the space above the window. "Even if we could climb down without looking like burglars—"

"Which is what we are," Gloria said.

"—we won't have time to erase them so I can get through," I said. "We're going to have to go out the back door. It's the only one that's clear."

"Without getting caught?" Gloria said. "We have to hide!"

"We can't," I said. "If they know anything about this place, they'll come here first. And there's nowhere up here to hide."

I risked another glance downstairs. I had to fight off a wave of nausea as my focus skipped around the building, but I could see the shapes leaving the den. They'd be upstairs soon.

Luci saw how pale I went. She grabbed my shoulder to steady me. I slipped my arm around hers and held onto her for support.

"Amelia?"

"I'm fine," I said. "This place... it's not good for me."

"Then we need to go," Gloria said.

"Yes. Quickly," I said.

I took Luci's hand and darted down the hall, picking the stairwell on the right at random. We crept down the stairs as quietly as we could manage, but we were too slow. By the time we reached the second floor, the other two intruders were tromping up the stairs.

Luci swore quietly. She no longer saw this as an adventure. Instead, she was flashing back to a memory of a holding cell, waiting for her mother. Without looking, I put my hand around her waist and gave her a comforting squeeze. I felt no comfort myself.

Now that we were in the same space bound by concealing script, I had a full view of the other intruders. Or more accurately, the two men investigating the break-in. They were agents of the Bureau. One of them was Agent Thomas.

"Oh, no," I said.

"What is it?" Gloria whispered.

I paused, trying to explain without raising more questions. "The authorities. I think. Just wait here."

The two agents had paused at the top of the stairs. I immediately recognized the younger of the two. Nathan Poole, a prospective agent no longer, was nervous, eyes darting around and one hand continuously reaching for his service pistol. Thomas hadn't told him much, so he wasn't sure what was going on and feared the worst. Thomas was his usual mental blank space, but his body language was far more relaxed. He surveyed the space like a conqueror returning to an old battlefield.

That was interesting.

"There's no one here," Poole said.

"Won't be," Thomas said. "There's nothing here now. Or shouldn't be, anyway. We need to go upstairs."

Luci and Gloria clung to the wall, trying to make themselves smaller. Gloria hissed my name. I waved a hand for her to be quiet and concentrated on the two men. I didn't bother with Thomas. I didn't think I could grab on to anything through whatever barrier closed his mind to me. I didn't need to. Poole's jitters left him completely unguarded.

Wait, I thought. *What if they heard us? We should check the rooms.*

"Wait," Poole said. "What if they heard us? We should check the rooms."

Thomas looked skeptical, but he assented with a dismissive shrug.

"All right," he said. "Nowhere for them to go, anyway."

The two agents tackled separate rooms, Poole going to the east side, Thomas the west. Just as I'd hoped. As soon as they entered the rooms, I gave the girls a nod.

"Now!" I whispered.

Luci and Gloria slipped passed me, heading for the other stairwell as quickly as they could without making noise. As soon as they reached the stairs, I grabbed hold of the doors and slammed them shut behind the agents. Then I broke the locks.

No more point to stealth. While Thomas and Poole shouted and banged on the doors, we ran down the stairs and through the house, fleeing out the back door and into the night. I had no illusions that we'd gotten away with anything, but at least for now we were free.

19

Luci had borrowed a car from "a friend" and refused to elaborate any further. I wanted to peek and find out why she was being so evasive, but no. Luci would tell me everything when she was ready. If I wanted to have a relationship like a real person, I would have to *be* a real person. Luci had a right to her secrets. I was certainly keeping enough of them tonight.

Of course, I was going to have to share one or two of them sooner than I was ready to.

We dropped Gloria off near her house, stopping a block away to make it easier for her to sneak back in. Before getting out of the car, she asked what our next step was going to be.

"Amelia said something about the observatory," Luci said, "but I'm not sure how much help that will be. It's been almost thirty years; any evidence will be long gone."

"I know," I said, "but I just have a hunch. Trust me."

There was no easy way to explain what I was planning. I wasn't even sure how to put it into words. But Luci accepted it.

"Always," she said. "It'll be less risky than my last idea."

Let's hope so, I thought.

"Gloria?" Luci said.

"Our other options are breaking into the bookstore or Lucas' dorm room," Gloria said, "and I don't like either of those ideas. But we need to do it soon."

"Tomorrow night?" Luci said.

Gloria shook her head. "Don't want to risk sneaking out two nights in a row."

"Neither do I," I said. "But we don't have to sneak out this time. The observatory's for sure abandoned, and it's far out of town. We can go during daylight."

"Saturday, then," Luci said. "As long as you can get off work, Gloria?"

"I think I can manage," Gloria said. "I'll just say I need to go study. Momma will think I mean at the library."

"We can meet there, if it makes it a little easier," Luci said. "Okay. Saturday at nine a.m."

"It's a date," Gloria said.

She bid us a good night, stopping to give me a reassuring pat on the shoulder, and slipped out of the car. The society's primer was tucked underneath one arm. Luci watched her go with a look of concern.

"Is it really safe for her to have that?" she asked.

"I don't know," I said. "I don't think there's any harm in studying them. Maybe just in how they're used. She's certainly more cautious than some of us."

Luci stuck her tongue out at me, then asked me where she was taking me. I folded my hands in my lap and took a deep breath.

"Out of town," I said. "About fifteen miles."

Luci just nodded, though I could feel her curiosity. We drove in silence for the first few miles. I kept my face pointed at the road, but my attention was on Luci. Every twitch of her eyes, every movement of her mouth. The feelings bubbling up to the surface of her mind. In the house, she'd kissed me as if nothing was different, but how could it not be?

Was she going to reject me?

Eventually, she glanced over at me. "You're very quiet," she said, her voice soft.

"I'm usually quiet," I said.

"I know," she said with a nod, "but not like this. This is scared quiet. Waiting quiet."

"Waiting for what?"

"For me to say something ugly," she said. "Do you think I haven't sat in the passenger's seat just like that enough times?"

"I… I don't know," I said.

"Well, I have." A small, unapologetic smile crept to her lips. "And it's not fun. So I want you to stop."

"Stop being quiet?" I said, confused.

"If you like," she said. "I'd certainly love to hear whatever you have to say. Whenever you're ready to say it, which I'm guessing isn't tonight."

I ducked my head and nodded.

"Which is fine," she said. "Tonight was rough enough already."

The memory of me lying in her arms, my face screwed up in agony, flashed across her mind. Luci bit her lip and reached out to me, taking my hand to comfort herself as much as me. I rubbed my thumb against her fingers, trying to reassure her that I was okay.

"What I mean is," she continued, "I want you to stop waiting for me to yell at you. Or call you names or say that something's wrong with you. Because I'm not going to do any of that."

She risked looking away from the road long enough to meet my eyes.

"I love you. And there's *nothing* wrong with you."

I squeezed her hand tightly, tears welling in my eyes. "Thank you," I whispered.

"You don't have to thank me for loving you," she said. "It's pretty easy to do."

She slipped her hand out of mine and rested it on my thigh. After a moment, she slowly slid her hand up a few inches. Stopping with her fingers just a few spans from…

She kept her hand there, questioning. I placed my hand over hers. A warm flush, a good one, crept up through me. I wasn't sure what I wanted to say, or do, or let her do. Though even without looking, I could tell what she was offering.

Luci slid her hand up a slight bit more. I gently pressed mine against it, and she stopped. She gave my thigh a light squeeze and left her hand where it was. I ran my fingertips over the back of her hand, enjoying the smoothness of her skin.

"Not…" I said hesitantly.

"It's okay," she said. She leaned over and gave me a quick peck on the cheek. "When you're ready."

We sat in silence for the rest of the drive, but now it was a comfortable silence. The knot in my chest slowly undid itself. Or rather, Luci undid it without looking, or moving her hand from my leg. She was going to stay with me, at least for now. I made up my mind to tell her at least one thing before I said goodnight.

After too short of a time, the bus stop came into view. My heart sank a little. What would she say if I told her to keep driving past, to take me with her to Regina?

She would say yes, of course. Without a second thought. She would take me to her own dorm, much less restrictive than mine, and full of other women our age. And maybe there I would let her do more than just rest her hand on my thigh. What we would do next, I had no idea, but I knew she would come up with something. Something fanciful and impractical, but that would keep us together and free for a while.

Until the Bureau came for me.

I couldn't do that to her. I pointed to the bus stop and said, "Up there."

Luci looked at it and frowned, but she slowed the car and pulled over to the side of the road. She parked a few feet from the bus stop. She sat in her seat, her mouth a tight line, drumming her fingers on the steering wheel.

"You're not going back to an orphanage at all, are you?" she said.

I ducked my head. I couldn't speak, so I just shook my head.

"Where are you going, then?"

I was silent for a long time. Then, "I can't tell you, Luci."

"Why *not?*"

I turned to face her, my eyes brimming with tears. "Because it isn't safe for you to know."

Luci grabbed my hand. "Who are they? *What* are they? The government?"

"I don't know," I said quietly. "I think so."

"Then they can't do this to you. There are *laws*. They can't keep you prisoner!"

"I know," I said. "But technically, I don't exist. So they can do what they like for now."

"The hell they can!"

I put my hand to her cheek, trying to calm her. To still the angry thoughts and impractical plans trying to form in her mind as she lashed out at the half-imagined figures threatening me.

"You're right. They can't keep me forever, and they're realizing it," I said. "It's not as bad as it used to be. I can go outside now. During daylight hours, at least."

Saying them out loud, the words sounded weak and hollow. I could see that Luci agreed. Her anger was unabated, nor her confusion.

"Why?" she said. "Why all of this?"

"I told you earlier, when Gloria asked. Because they're afraid of me."

"Why? Should they be?"

I nodded solemnly. "Oh, yes."

I pictured Pickman's face, his expression slowly slackening from outrage to dull blankness. I thought of the way the agents jumped when I raised my voice. I thought of the wall in the society's den cracking beneath my strength.

Luci stared at me, then brushed her fingers against my cheek.

"I don't think you're scary," she said. "I think you're perfectly sweet."

I blushed and nuzzled her hand. I wrapped my fingers around hers. I could feel her pulse beating tenderly against my cheek. And I knew it was time to tell her the most important thing. It had nothing to do with why the Bureau was keeping me, but everything to do with what made me the girl I was. But the words wouldn't come. I just wanted to enjoy the softness of her skin against mine, and I wanted to tell her the truth. The conflict didn't pull; it squeezed something in my chest. Tighter and tighter. Until finally it forced the words out of my mouth.

"Luci… I need you to know. I'm a girl. But when I was born… and really, until just three years ago… they said I was a boy. They treated me like a boy. I guess I kind of looked like a boy. But I'm not and I never was."

She stared at me, her thoughts a whirl. She thought I was making it up. She thought that it couldn't be possible. She thought that she loved and trusted me and had no reason to doubt that whatever I'd tell her would be true.

"How…" she said. "If the people who raised you have locked you away for so long… why would…?"

"They tried to ignore it when I first told them. God, how they tried," I said, failing to suppress a shudder. "Finally, I pressed the issue. I pressed a *lot* of issues."

Pickman's mind in my grasp. Dolores Grover fleeing out of lab four in terror. Agents bursting through the door, guns drawn, eyes wide. Me glaring at them in triumph and fury, screaming my own name into the world.

Lucille Sweeney, looking at me in confusion and love, her hand still touching my face.

"I know that I'm strange," I said. "Stranger than you know. Stranger than I can tell you. But..."

Luci slid her finger to my lips. "I know strange. I'm a girl who loves girls."

She cupped the back of my head and kissed me, driving all my fears out of my mind. I clung to her for as long as I could until finally, she could no longer ignore her need to breathe. When she came up for air, I rested my forehead against hers, and she stroked my cheek gently.

"Whatever you are, or whatever you were, you're Amelia. My Amelia," she said. "And I love you. All of you."

Words far more easily said than understood, but I accepted them. I smiled and covered her hand with my own.

"Thank you," I whispered. "I love you, too."

"You'd better," she said, grinning mischievously. Then the smile dropped from her face. "You have to go, don't you?"

"Yes. I'm sorry," I said. "I've already been gone too long. If I'm out any longer, they're bound to know."

Luci thought about that for half a second. Then she grabbed my hand and held it tightly. "Don't go," she said. "Come with me."

"I want to," I said. "But I already thought of that. It won't work. They'll come for me."

"I don't care! We'll keep moving, we'll hide, we'll—"

"Luci," I said quietly.

She stilled but was unmollified. I thought back to myself, whenever I was. Standing with an air of finality and dressed for travel.

"Someday," I said. "But not tonight."

Luci didn't accept that, exactly, but she opened her door and walked around the car to let me out. She wrapped her arms around me, burying her face in my neck. I returned her embrace, staring over her shoulder and grateful that this time she couldn't see my tears.

"To someday, then," she whispered. "And Saturday. I'll see you Saturday, right?"

"I promise," I said. "And again and again after that."

"Okay."

With reluctance, she disentangled herself from my embrace, though a hand still touched my arm. She wanted more than anything to kiss me again, but even in the dead of night, she didn't dare, out in the open like this.

"Someday we'll find a place where you can kiss me whenever you want," I said.

She laughed bitterly. "Someday. We have a lot of 'somedays'."

"It's becoming my favorite day of the week," I said.

She touched my cheek in lieu of a kiss and said goodnight softly. I stood beneath the bus stop and watched her get back in the car and drive away. I waited until she passed outside of sight before turning for the Bureau campus. Out of a normal person's sight, that is. I kept my focus on her for as long as I could, watching her drive away, tears streaming down her cheeks, even as I walked in the other direction. I stretched my consciousness until my perception of her, and of this body, was no more clear than of dots along the black ribbon of highway. My body moved on its own, mechanically taking one step after another as I followed my love to Regina. Reaching further and further until suddenly she was gone, and the road she drove on, and the fields it cut through.

All around me was void, though I sensed the presence of the warm, wet world beneath me. Of certain values of "beneath". And something else. A presence that swam through the void. It was huge, whatever it was. It spread out in several directions, too big to encompass even at this level of perception. Here and there it stretched pieces of itself *downward*, searching for the world it sensed. Like a viper searching for heat or a predatory fish the telltale ripples of a smaller fish in the water.

I was close. A piece of it moved. It sensed me, and it reached out. I *felt* rather than saw the thought: I saw the way. Would I open?

I shut my senses tightly and plunged *down*, acting out of instinct and blind panic rather than rational thought. I only hoped that whatever it was could not follow.

I came to myself on my knees in the damp grass, panting. I was mere yards from the Bureau campus. The main building's walls were stark white through the dull gray chain-link fence. My fingers clutched at the earth for stability, digging into the soil. I looked up at the night sky, seeing nothing above me but stars.

Knowing now for certain that far more than stars were hanging up there.

20

Eventually, I picked myself up and tried to dust the dirt and wet grass from my skirt. It wouldn't be light for hours yet, but I'd spent enough time outside. No, that wasn't true at all, but the longer I was out, the harder it would be to go back in. It would raise an alarm if I wasn't safely in my dorm by the time Agent Walsh came by to check on me.

The front gate was still secured by guards, and I was less confident about my ability to return that way, especially at this time of night, than I had been about leaving. No staff came in at this hour, and I was unlikely to convince them I was an agent. Instead, I considered the fence. It was a sturdy barrier, high and topped with barbed wire, but mundane. Nothing more than steel wires strung between poles, and existing only in three dimensions.

It was risky, after what I had just seen, but necessary. I looked at the fence, then at the space around it. And I took a step *forward*.

And I was on the other side.

I didn't stop to admire the new trick, but I felt a slight sense of satisfaction as I headed for the staff entrance. It was locked, but that was already proving to be less of a deterrent for me.

Before going up to the orange zone, I wanted to stop and check on Agent Fitzgerald. I wanted to make sure he was still where he was supposed to be, and not making a sudden, unexpected bed check. He didn't strike me as being that thorough, but better safe than sorry. I didn't have to look hard to find him at his desk. Even from the cafeteria, I could hear raised voices in the hall. One of them belonged to Agent Thomas.

Back already? How? Luci and I hadn't parked for that long. I would have seen his car go past, wouldn't I?

No, it was unlikely that I'd have seen anything but her right then, but it still didn't make sense. Unless… I thought of the void above/around/between us, and the things swimming through it. Perhaps I'd been gone longer than I thought. I paused to reorient myself. I was missing almost an hour. Plenty of time for him to have driven back from Chatham Hills and arrived before me. Especially if he'd driven back at a breakneck speed. He certainly seemed angry enough.

"You're just going to sit there and tell me you didn't hear *anything?*" Thomas said.

"That's exactly what I'm saying, for the third goddamned time," Fitzgerald said. "I've been *here*. All night. Right where I'm supposed to be. Hasn't been a *peep*."

Four men were clustered around Agent Fitzgerald's desk. One was Agent Fitzgerald. Two were Agents Thomas and Poole. The fourth, to my surprise, was Agent Walsh.

"I believe him, Randall," Walsh said.

Agents Fitzgerald and Thomas stood nose to nose. Walsh stood two paces away, hands raised in a conciliatory fashion. A few steps behind him, Agent Poole stood against the wall with his arms crossed and shoulders hunched, wanting to be anywhere else.

"This idiot had *one job* tonight. One!" Thomas said, jabbing a finger into Fitzgerald's chest. "Watch the alarms! Call someone if there's a problem, *especially* one over his head. Which is just about everything, isn't it?"

Fitzgerald took hold of Thomas' wrist and pushed his hand away. "Don't poke me, Thomas. I poke back."

"Easy," Walsh said. He pushed his hands between the two men and stepped forward, forcing them apart. "Thomas, you know damn well the alarms at Site Two don't go off here. That's why you got the call from Dreamland."

Site Two? Dreamland? Those were names I'd never heard before. Site Two had to be the Apollonian Society's manor, but Dreamland? Was that another Bureau facility? Where?

I tried to dismiss the questions as soon as they bubbled up. The alarms at the brownstone had to be the more pressing concern. Why would the Bureau have alarms there, and how? They couldn't have been anything electric; I would have noticed the mechanisms.

But the Bureau must know about the scripts or had at one point. I thought about the wards breaking. A sick feeling churned in the pit of my stomach.

And I thought about the bullets imbedded in the walls and felt a chill.

"You're making excuses for him now," Thomas said, his usual sneer intensifying.

"I'm not making excuses for anyone, I'm just not trying to pick a fight," Walsh shot back. "Unless you know of some way Fitzgerald would have been alerted to an off-campus incident, I suggest you *back off.*"

That made Thomas take a step back. His mind was still closed to me, but I could see his expression. Embarrassment and surprise fought with anger—embarrassment that he'd been shown up, I guessed, and surprise that Walsh had been the one to do it. Unfortunately, his usual arrogance rallied quickly.

"What about that thing upstairs?" Thomas said. "Your little coal-mine canary. 'She' should have felt something. Isn't that the entire reason it's here?"

My heart stopped. Me. He was talking about me now.

"Amelia... Miss Temple is here so the Bureau can keep her safe," Walsh said, somehow completely believing those words. "I see no more reason she should have known about the disturbance at Site Two than Fitzgerald."

Despite my fear, I had to suppress a laugh.

"Miss Temple's been in her room since six," Fitzgerald said. "I haven't heard a peep out of her since then."

"And she's certainly fast asleep now," Walsh said.

"So wake Temple up," Thomas said. "I'll bet you anything your pet knows more than it's letting on."

No. That was the last thing I needed. But there was no way to change Agent Thomas' mind, and no way to stop him from bullying the others from going along with his whims. He was already turning away from the office, ignoring Walsh's objections.

I flew out of the cafeteria and up the stairwell to the fifth floor. I thought momentarily about trying the same trick I'd used to get back inside—three stories was a very short distance, fifth-dimensionally speaking—but I didn't dare. I didn't know what measures the Bureau might have buried in and around the orange zone. Even though I'd never seen any of the strange script here that they'd had at the Massachusetts headquarters, right now it was too great of a risk.

That was an interesting thought for another time, though.

Agent Thomas was already charging up the main stairwell by the time I reached my dorm, Agent Walsh hectoring him at his heels, Fitzgerald and Poole in tow. I slipped inside as quietly as I could, yanking my dress over my head, throwing in into my hamper and diving under my covers. I wanted to slip on a shift or something, but there was no time. I mussed up my hair and laid back, silently thankful that Luci hadn't yet gotten me into the habit of wearing cosmetics all the time. I was just feigning sleep when Agent Thomas came bursting through my front door, ignoring Agent Walsh's objections. He pounded his fist on my bedroom door.

I sat up but didn't pull the covers back. "Yes, Agent Thomas?"

"Open the door," he shouted.

I took a deep breath to steady myself, then summoned every bit of composure I had. I remembered the way Gloria had handled Lucas, and tried to mimic her poise, her cool demeanor.

"The door isn't locked, Agent Thomas," I said, my voice steady and icy with contempt. "I'm not allowed to have locks, remember?"

Agent Thomas swore and pushed the door open. I pulled my blankets up to my chin and stared at him, trying to counter his male arrogance with poise. Thomas disregarded me, stepping into my bedroom while the others had the decency to hang back. Or maybe it was just that there wasn't enough room for four adults in my small bedroom.

"You certainly look bright-eyed for three in the morning," he said.

"I'm a light sleeper," I said. "Is there a particular reason you've come barging into my bedroom, or is this just one of the typical indignities I'm supposed to endure?"

Thomas flushed angrily, but before he could say anything, Walsh clapped him on the shoulder. Walsh didn't want to come into my room, but he also didn't think he could pull Thomas out without escalating things. So he stood awkwardly on the threshold, but at least he'd managed to interrupt Thomas before he really got going.

"Amelia," Walsh said, "I'm very sorry about the intrusion. It wasn't my idea," he added, with a very pointed look at Agent Thomas. "We just need to know if you noticed any disturbances tonight."

I stared levelly at the two men invading my bedroom and arched one eyebrow. Walsh had the decency to look embarrassed, while Thomas finally noticed the way I held the blankets to my chest and my bare shoulders poking above them. He coughed uncomfortably and took a step backward.

"Assuming this can't wait until morning," I said, "could you at least give me a moment to get dressed?"

Walsh blushed. "Of course. We'll wait in the living room. Come on, Thomas."

He stood aside so Thomas could exit and stared at him until he did. Averting his eyes, he nodded toward me and quietly closed the door. In the other room, two agents watched Thomas stalk across the floor, grumbling. Walsh picked up the folding chair propped against the wall and sat down, crossing his arms and giving Thomas a bored look.

I was tempted to drag out dressing, just to annoy Thomas further, but I knew there would likely be consequences. More than that, I wanted all the men out of my dorm. I grabbed today's dress from the hamper and started to slip into it. Then I considered the robe hanging from my bathroom door. I looked myself over, at the slight curves that had slowly developed on my slender frame, and thought about the way Thomas and Walsh had reacted when they realized I was undressed beneath my blankets. To me, it was just a body—a strange one that hadn't always fit right, but just skin and bones and blood. To them, it was something completely different, and on me that difference made them blush and shift uncomfortably or avoid the subject as much as they could.

To hell with their comfort, as Luci might say. I dropped the dress back in the hamper and wrapped the bathrobe around me. I left it just open enough to hint at my nakedness without revealing anything I didn't want these men seeing. Then I called to Agent Walsh that I was ready and stepped through the door.

They looked up when I came out of my bedroom. All but Thomas quickly looked away. I ignored them all and walked to the kitchen, looking right through Agent Fitzgerald, who'd made the mistake of standing directly in front of it. I walked up to him until he flushed and stepped out of my way, grabbed my hot plate and kettle out of the cabinet, and put on a small pot of water. Thomas' face grew steadily redder, but I kept my attention on the kettle until it whistled. I pulled out one cup, a tea bag, and the sugar pot, carefully spooning out exactly two spoonfuls of sugar before pouring the hot water over the tea bag. Then I turned around and walked primly to the couch, sitting on the middle cushion and stirring my tea.

Agent Thomas stepped forward, but I turned to Agent Walsh. "So. What 'disturbance' provoked this one, and why are you asking me about it?"

Walsh started to answer, but Thomas cut him off. "He can't tell you. It's classified."

I finally deigned to acknowledge Thomas again. "So, you intend to interrogate me about an incident I'm not supposed to know anything about? How well do you expect that to go?"

Thomas' face was beet red at this point, and Walsh was beginning to be concerned—not about him, but about the explosion building inside him. Poole and Fitzgerald quickly covered their smiles, amused despite themselves, but those weren't the reactions that interested me. Their thoughts had immediately turned to the mysterious "Site Two". Poole knew nothing more than he had this evening, Fitzgerald even less. Walsh, on the other hand, had clearly been read into something and didn't like what he knew. For him, Site Two—and a "Site One" that immediately came to mind when he thought of the other—was something between an uncleared minefield and the scene of an old crime. One the Bureau somehow had a hand in. And that was somehow related to "Subject Thirteen".

The shock almost made me drop my cup. Subject 13, the thing the Bureau had found in the Richmond house in Oregon in 1935. Was that another piece of the puzzle? But that was ten years after the Apollonian Society's disastrous experiment.

Of course it was. Because they were still attempting it.

I thought back to the sketch Gloria's uncle had drawn. The photos I'd received from the Bureau's files weren't clear, but there had been descriptions. And now that I made the connection, I could see how closely they'd matched Uncle Matthew's drawing.

That's what they'd tried to do. They'd found the things floating in the other space and tried to bring one of them here. And in 1935 they'd tried again, or at least someone connected to them had. And now Lucas Dowling was going to try to do it yet again.

How to explain that to Luci and Gloria?

"Look at it!" Thomas snapped. "It knows something!"

Despite myself, I flinched. I'd been so deep in thought I'd lost control of my facial expression. Only momentarily, but that was all Thomas needed to jump to conclusions. A correct conclusion, as it turned out, but on the most spurious of reasoning. I drew in a breath to compose myself and resumed my mask of cold disdain.

"I only know that my sleep was interrupted, and I'm unhappy about that," I said. "*Whatever* happened tonight, which I've accepted you won't explain, I know nothing about. Despite what you might think, Agent Thomas, what the rumors I have to endure might claim, I *don't* have any magical knowledge of everything that goes on in the weird world you inhabit. Frankly, I don't know where you got the idea that I did."

Because Pickman's journals were supposed to be sealed, both Walsh and I thought at the same time. But the Specials had access to things they weren't supposed to. That was the whole point of them.

"I believe you, Amelia," Walsh said. "But, just for the record and to satisfy Agent Thomas' irrationality, did you experience anything unusual tonight? More intrusive dreams?"

Walsh flinched after he said that, immediately regretting using the word "more" in front of Thomas, but it was too late. Thomas didn't seem to pick up on it right away, but he would later. We'd deal with it then. Walsh believed me, and he was trying to cut this short. I almost felt grateful. A part of me wanted to tell him about the thing I'd sensed in higher space—the thing, I was now certain, that Lucas was trying to bring to Earth. Let the Bureau finish this nasty business without risking my friends.

But ultimately, the Bureau had never given me any reason to trust them. And someone had murdered the members of the Apollonian Society for Illumination. Had the Bureau existed in 1925? I had no idea, but at least some of the agents clearly knew more about this than I did.

I didn't want to risk putting Luci and Gloria in more danger. They wouldn't stop investigating if the Bureau got involved, which would inevitably pull them further into the Bureau's sights. And that might mean I would never see them again.

"I dreamt I was at the beach with my friends," I said. "I understand that's something normal girls my age enjoy."

Despite his anger, Agent Thomas let out an ugly laugh. I ignored him and shut my senses to Poole and Fitzgerald as best I could. What they were picturing was far from flattering. Agent Walsh, at least, just shrugged.

"Sounds harmless," he said. "I think we've intruded enough on Miss

Temple's time, gentlemen."

Agent Thomas looked like he wanted to argue, but Poole and Fitzgerald were in complete agreement. They moved immediately to the door. Walsh hung back, staring Thomas down until he followed them. Thomas paused at the door, glaring at the two of us.

"We'll revisit this conversation at a later date," he said.

"I'll take that into consideration," Walsh said. "Miss Temple is still *my* responsibility."

A young girl dressed all in white, laying still on a bed. A small gravestone, dated 1930–1936. A conversation I could not have with him.

I drank the rest of my tea in a large gulp and rose from the couch. I ignored the two men as I walked to the sink and washed my cup. Thomas gave one last dismissive snort before walking out, leaving the door wide open. Agent Walsh took two steps toward it, then stopped. A mix of thoughts and emotions darted across his mind, too quickly for me to sort them.

"Amelia…"

I put the cup in the dryer rack upside down and turned to face him. "Good night, Agent Walsh."

"I just want—"

"There's no point in apologizing," I said.

I went into my bedroom and closed the door behind me. I hung up my robe and climbed back into bed. After a moment, Walsh left my dorm, quietly closing the door behind him.

But I didn't sleep. There was too much to think about. I almost had all the pieces of the puzzle. I could see the shape of what was missing. And for the first time, I had an idea of where to find them.

The Bureau had always kept secrets from me, as best they could. Even when they'd given me access to sensitive materials, the files had been carefully redacted. I'd only ever received the minimum information I needed to prepare for my classes or to sit through this interrogation or that examination. They hadn't trusted me to know too much.

I hadn't trusted them in return. They still didn't know the extent of my abilities, even those who had access to Pickman's files. I'd carefully hidden the breadth of my senses. After the last incident with Pickman, I couldn't hide everything I was capable of, but most of his theories had been discredited. Or at least, no one was willing to keep testing them.

They had no way to keep me from finding things out. The greatest defense they'd had was my fear, and I was steadily overcoming that. I still had to be cautious, but I no longer had to be meek. Or compliant.

I watched and waited as the agents spread out across the building. Fitzgerald returned to his desk, trying to doze until he was relieved in the morning. Poole went straight for his car, intending to drive straight home and go back to bed; he'd likely call in sick that day. Thomas and Walsh went to Walsh's office, no doubt to have another argument before finally retreating.

But that would take them nowhere near the room I intended to visit. I slipped out of bed and back into my dress. Then I made my way downstairs.

In all honesty, I probably could have done what I intended from my bed. Space in three dimensions wasn't optional, exactly, but from my expanding perspective it was all much shorter than others thought. Still, I didn't want to risk stretching my abilities too far and too quickly. I was already in danger of walking before I could crawl. No sense in trying to run instead.

I crept through the darkened hallways, my bare feet light on the linoleum floors. I passed locked door after locked door, each an empty office. Some were merely waiting for their occupants to arrive in the morning. Others had never been used at all. They held cold chairs, bare desks, empty cabinets. More than half of the offices on the third floor, completely unused. On every floor, in fact. The Bureau had space for an organization twice its size, sitting unused. I had never considered that before.

It was another mystery for another time. I put it to the side as I followed the spiraling path to the heart of the third floor. To the Sensitive Records room.

The customer service window was shuttered. No one would be here for hours. I had plenty of time to do what was needed.

I placed my hand against the wall and looked inside. The space was crammed full of boxes and filing cabinets, each holding dozens of fat folders. There were photographs, drawings, eyewitness reports, analyses, and follow-ups. Far more information than I'd ever been given access to. It would take a single person days to sort through all of it, if not weeks.

But I only needed one file.

To the woman on the paper, the circle is an impassible barrier. But I looked from a perspective above it. I could see every file, every folder. I didn't need to read them all now. I just needed to find the one file marked "Subject 13". It didn't take long once I understood Miss Vance's filing system. It sat in the third drawer of the first cabinet marked with an "X". There was a reason, I was sure, but I didn't find it interesting.

The door to the record room was locked, of course, and there was an alarm attached. A simple electrical device, easily circumvented, but I feared doing so would make my intrusion too obvious. Fortunately, I had a better option.

I closed my eyes and steeled myself. I saw the file. On the second floor, Agent Fitzgerald dozed in his chair. On the fourth floor, Agents Walsh and Thomas continued their argument, an entirely different conflict from the one they thought they were having. And on the third floor, me, standing in front of a locked room.

"The cup is upside down," I whispered. "The ball is underneath the cup."

A phantom pain shot up my right arm. I ignored it, and the single tear that ran down my cheek. I made my hand open, holding it out. As I had when Miss Vance handed me the files for my class.

"Take the ball out of the cup."

The file cabinet shuddered. There was a barely audible "pop" as air rushed to fill a suddenly created gap. The other files in the drawer fell lightly back.

And a fat file with "Subject 13" typed across the top was in my hand. Full of information Gloria and Luci would find very interesting. With my other hand, I wiped the dampness from my face. I allowed myself a slight smile.

My right arm tingled, but I felt no pain.

21

Despite his dire warnings, I heard nothing more from Agent Thomas for the rest of the week. I saw little more of Agent Walsh. His morning check-ups were perfunctory—he felt so guilty about invading my privacy that he was trying to give me as much as he could. It should have been funny, as privacy was a concept I barely understood, but it wasn't. There were volumes of material he wasn't telling me, but he couldn't hide that the break-in at "Site Two" had the Bureau alarmed. Behind doors supposedly closed to me, the Bureau argued about what it meant, who was responsible, and what would happen next.

They hadn't yet linked Luci and Gloria to the break-in, however, and for that I was silently grateful. They were entirely off the Bureau's radar. To my surprise, so were Lucas and Ralph, at least so far. Professor Blake's name had surfaced, as did a few I didn't recognize, but no action was being taken yet. Just endless circular arguments.

Neither had the Bureau noticed my theft of Subject 13's file. Walsh's reluctance to disturb my room further had its advantages. I spent the remainder of the week poring through the file, taking notes and reproducing documents as closely as I could. I didn't want to risk keeping the entire file—eventually, *someone* was going to want to reference it—but I was bold enough to take a single key photograph. Hopefully it would be all the evidence my friends would need to corroborate the rest.

Friday night, I surreptitiously returned the file. Saturday morning, I met Luci and Gloria as planned. We were there scarcely an hour after the library opened. When Luci and I arrived, Gloria had already laid claim to the same table we'd used before. She was energized from her discoveries, a surprising contrast to the foreboding mood Luci and I felt. She noticed it too.

"What's eating you two?" she asked when we sat down.

Luci's mouth was a tight line. "I ran into Ralph at the Uni cafeteria yesterday. He let something slip."

"Really?" I said, seeing the whole encounter in her mind.

"Well, it wasn't hard," Luci admitted with a casual shrug. "He was aching to tell me, honestly."

"Tell you *what?*" Gloria asked.

"That he and Lucas have the last piece of 'equipment' for their experiment," Luci said. "They're doing it *tonight*."

Gloria let out a low whistle. "That doesn't give us a lot of time."

"And we still don't know how to stop it," Luci said.

A horrible option came to mind, born of foul mood and little time. My fingers twitched, and I suppressed a shudder. I wasn't going to do *that*. Not even to Lucas Dowling.

"I have an idea," I said, "but I'm going to need you to trust me."

"Of course," Luci said without hesitating. Gloria nodded after a moment.

"Good," I said. "But first, let's compare notes. Trying as it's been, I think this week's been fruitful for all of us."

The others nodded. We all laid out our findings on the table. I had my copies of the Subject 13 file, Gloria the primer and her rather copious notes on it, and Luci her photographs from the manor and Professor Blake's stolen correspondence. I went first.

"I actually need you to trust me on two things. One is my plan. The other is that I can't tell you where I got any of this, but I assure you it's real. And very relevant."

Lucia and Gloria exchanged a look.

"I've got a feeling we can guess where it came from," Gloria said.

"It's from the people who are keeping you," Luci said.

"Yes," I said. "They know a lot about this sort of thing."

"And so do you?" Gloria said.

"I really don't," I said. "This past week, I've learned how much I don't know."

"Mm," Gloria said. "These people, can they help?"

"Do you really want to trust the kind of people who could do the sort of things they've done to Amelia?" Luci said.

Gloria looked at me carefully, gauging my reaction. "I will if she does."

I shook my head firmly. "I don't. I don't trust them at all. I don't think they're much better than the Apollonian Society. I don't know their motives, but I do know their methods."

Unbidden, my left hand touched my right arm. The phantom pain hadn't returned, but the memory was there. Luci saw something in my face and covered my hand with her own.

"That's a 'no', then," Gloria said. "I take it they don't know you have this?"

"That's right," I said. "Which means these aren't the original documents. Mostly. I copied them as exactly as I could. Except this one."

I turned the photograph over. It was a close-up of the blurry photo I'd shown the new agents weeks ago. Something not unlike a giant mushroom and not dissimilar from a massive jellyfish grew out of the center of Jonas Richmond's attic. Long tendrils grew from the cap, brushing the ruined floorboard. The whole thing tilted to one side, bent at the middle. That side was clearly rotting.

"Does this look familiar to you?" I asked.

Quietly, Gloria pulled her great-uncle's sketch from her notes and laid it beside the photograph. Uncle Matthew's drawing lacked details, but the shape was the same. Around the base of the thing in the photo, we could see part of a wide circle of strange symbols connected by a complicated arrangement of looping, intersecting lines.

"Amelia, what is this?" Gloria whispered.

"The remains of another experiment gone wrong," I said. "This one from 1935."

I gave them a brief explanation, cribbing from my own lesson of a few weeks ago. I started by explaining the Flatland analogy, then compared it to higher mathematical dimensions. Gloria nodded along, familiar with the concept, while Luci took my word for it.

"I always thought these higher spaces were empty, at least of anything we would consider alive," I said. *That was certainly what I'd been told.* "Most of our knowledge of higher dimensions is theoretical. The math *says* they must be there, we just can't see them."

"But…" Gloria tapped the photograph.

"But at least the Apollonian Society believed otherwise," I said, "and so do its successors."

I pushed one of my files forward. It was a letter, painstakingly copied in my prim handwriting. The original was missing pieces, as if it had been eaten away by something corrosive. It was dated August 9th, fifteen days before the explosion in the Richmond house had been reported.

> J.R.,
> Your estimation of G.L.'s experiment is exceedingly correct. The man seeks to walk before he can crawl!

Certainly, our ultimate ambitions align, but we must exercise caution. We know that the environment of our plane is hostile to the Watchers Above; how much more so must be their native environment to us?

Your own experiment is much more sound. You've learned much from the failed attempts of the past, and I have every confidence this will be the success we have striven for. I wish I could be there to see it, to again encounter such an entity! But caution must come before selfish satisfaction. We will continue to draw W.S.'s eyes away from you so your experiment may proceed without interruption.

I eagerly await your favorable report.

M.T.

Luci said an awful word under her breath. "Maxwell Thorpe!"

"Undoubtedly," I said.

"That makes sense," Gloria said. "It's been nearly thirty years. No way this is only their second try."

"I doubt it's even their fourth," I said. "The Chambers Foundation probably has had pockets of people all over, trying again and again."

"And still failing. Disastrously," Luci said.

"Not just them," Gloria said. "Wasn't G.L. mentioned in one of Blake's letters?"

"Yeah," Luci said, proffering it. "So he's still around too, doing God knows what. Jeez, this is becoming a Russian doll."

"Let's worry about what's in front of us now," Gloria said. She touched the photo. "So, 'Watchers Above'. Can we assume that's what this thing is?"

"If it is, I can't imagine why they'd want to meet it," Luci said. "Thorpe mentions them a lot in some of his letters to Blake. Here, look."

She selected another letter, one of the earliest we'd stolen.

> H.B.,
>
> I fail to see why L.D. would need to know about the Voyagers to conduct his experiment. Frankly, I think you've told him more than he needs to know about the Watchers Above. Remember, he is not meant to be Man's representative to the Outer Planes, a task for which he is manifestly unsuited. He simply needs to innovate a reliable method of establishing contact, preferably without causing another disaster in the process.
>
> Let him focus on the mechanics; that seems to be his joy regardless. Once he reports success, we'll take his method and employ it ourselves. We will address the Watchers Above and finally reap their secrets.
>
> And then, the stars themselves!
>
> M.T.

"Wait, the Voyagers?" Gloria said. "Who are they?"

Something about that tickled the back of my mind, but Luci dismissed them.

"Another doll," she said. "They pop up in a couple of letters, but there's no explanation. There wouldn't be, since they obviously know what they're talking about. They're probably just another kind of person up where they're trying to get to."

"Let's leave it for now, then," Gloria said. "So, we know what they're doing. They're trying to bring something from another dimension of space here. And we know why—they want to learn how to go to that dimension themselves."

"But why?" Luci asked.

"Probably just because it's there," Gloria said. "Remember the photographs in their den and the trophy cases in the library? They're Great White Explorers."

"I guess. They wouldn't be so bad if their experiments didn't keep blowing up in people's faces," Luci said.

Gloria grimaced. "I'm sure there's something else they think they can get out of it. Men like that love going where folks like them have never been before. And then robbing the place blind."

I thought of the presence I'd felt *above*, when I'd let myself become untethered from the Earth. Its hunger.

"I don't think that would end well for them," I said.

"It won't end well for anyone else if this is another bust," Gloria said. "So, we have the what and the why."

She opened the primer. "This is the how. Prospero's Keys are… no, I'm not going to say it. They're at the heart of all of this."

"Prospero…" I said, shuffling through Luci's papers. "I don't recall seeing that name other than in reference to the Keys. A Society member?"

Luci and Gloria stared at me. I could see the reason for their confusion plain as day.

"Oh. He's a made-up person," I said.

"Prospero is the wizard in *The Tempest*," Luci said. "You know, William Shakespeare?"

"Sure, I've heard of him," I said, hesitant. I'd certainly heard people use the name before, at least. "He was a writer."

"Most people wouldn't call him *just* a writer," Gloria said.

"Yes, yes, my education obviously has some gaps," I said crossly. "Sorry, Gloria, you were saying?"

"We came up with a couple of different ways to describe the Keys the other night. I think we were all right, in a way. The Keys are kind of like a sentence, and sort of like an equation, too. These big symbols describe what they're trying to do, and the smaller ones connected to them refine and focus the effect. Together, the whole thing is called a 'seal'."

She tore a blank sheet of paper from her notepad and picked up Luci's photo of the warding script over the manor's back door. She reproduced the script, one looping symbol at a time, flipping back through the primer as she explained what each one meant.

"So, this one in the center is what the book calls the 'Anchor'," she said, drawing the first large symbol in the middle of the page. "It defines the equation. This one's called the Guardian Key. It's supposed to create a barrier."

She drew two more equally large symbols, one on either side. "These are the Refinements. They modify the Anchor. The one on the left determines *how* the barrier works. This one is the Agony Key."

"That one seems self-explanatory," I said dryly.

Gloria flashed me a compassionate look before continuing. "It certainly tells us how the Society thought. There are other options. Forgetfulness is one, or paralysis. I think the Shroud Key would just make whatever the barrier was covering invisible to whomever you don't want coming through."

That got me thinking about the other scripts we'd seen, but I didn't want to interrupt. "And the symbol on the right?"

Gloria paused, unaware I could see how little she wanted to explain what the third key meant or to think about its implications. "It defines who the barrier works against."

I didn't want to say it, but we were going to have to face it eventually. "And who does this one work against?"

Gloria licked her lips. "The book calls it the 'Daimon Key'."

Luci took in a sharp breath. She put a comforting hand on my arm, eyes flashing with offense on my behalf. Honestly, she needn't have bothered, though I appreciated the gesture. "Daimon" was hardly one of the worst things I'd been called.

"I'm sure it's just a bit of poetry," Gloria said quickly. "Especially in the original text this book was copied from. It can be kind of *florid*. The commentary here says it's just a bit of 'uneducated superstition' about the nature of the beings it affects."

Luci looked at me, then back at Gloria. "And that would be…?"

Gloria kept her expression carefully blank, not wanting to upset either of us. "Not native to this world."

I raised my eyebrows. "I was born in Texas," I said. "I think."

The other two exchanged a look. Gloria shrugged. "Well, that explains it."

"Hey!" I said after a moment, mostly because I realized it was expected. Luci and Gloria started giggling, and Luci gave me a quick hug. The tension lifted some, born on a cloud of feminine laughter.

"So we can chalk this up to another thing the Society didn't know as much about as they thought they did," Gloria said, once they'd settled back down.

"Is there a symbol that affects, um, people *not* like Amelia?" Luci said.

Gloria flipped back a few pages. "This one. They call it the Adamite Key."

"Huh. Not sure why anyone would use it," Luci said.

"Actually, it's possible to refine it further," Gloria said. "That's what the rest of these symbols are. They're called 'Structures'. They lay out the mechanics, basically. The Structures in this seal describe the dimensions of the barrier. The funny thing is, I'm pretty sure the original text is old. Centuries old. Before Isaac Newton old. But the barrier this seal creates extends into at least six dimensions."

Luci blinked. "Did they know that?"

"Not exactly. At least, not back then. The Structures that describe the barrier beyond three-dimensional space are called the Temporal and Aetheric Keys. You can see that they're all very similar to the Spatial Keys, though, with just a few slight differences."

"Like a weird mathematical version of word play?" Luci said.

"Yeah, kind of."

"Hm," I said, considering the Temporal Key. "I wonder... if this describes the barrier's extent along the fourth dimension—"

"How long it lasts," Gloria said, off Luci's confused expression.

"Would it be possible to design a seal now and have the barrier put into place, say, thirty years ago?"

Gloria's eyes widened. "That's a *really* good question. I don't see why not, at least in theory, but I feel like it would break important laws of physics."

"Time travel. Have I got that right?" Luci said. "You're talking about *time travel.*"

"Yes," I said. "It was a passing thought."

"Be an interesting solution," Gloria said. "Prevent this whole mess by putting a barrier around the observatory in 1925 but do it now."

"But we can't," I said. "Probably because we didn't."

"You two are speaking in shorthand or something," Luci said, an edge of frustration creeping past her smile.

"Amelia's saying we can't use the keys to prevent the 1925 experiment from happening because it already happened," Gloria said.

"It would violate causality," I said.

Luci thought about that, then nodded. "Okay. So no do-overs. I never believed we could do something like that before, so I guess it's not much of a disappointment."

"There's one other big hurdle," Gloria said. "I still don't know how to make the keys *work.*"

She held up the seal she'd drawn. "This is the exact seal that tried to keep Amelia out of the Society's headquarters, but if we pasted it above that door over there, I bet she could still walk through it."

Luci grabbed my hand and held it tightly, glaring at Gloria. "You are *not* trying that experiment!"

"Trust me, I wouldn't," Gloria said. "This is one time I wouldn't risk being proven wrong. Besides, I've already tried the keys."

"You what?" Luci said.

"I created another warding seal last night, this one using the Guardian, Adamite and Lethe Keys—that one's forgetfulness—and pasted it over my bedroom door," Gloria said. She laughed ruefully. "Didn't work. So much for keeping my little brothers out of my room."

"Do you know what went wrong?" I asked.

"No idea. I'm missing something. There's more to it than just drawing a bunch of lines and circles, but this book doesn't go into that. I guess whoever wrote it figured anyone using it would already know the fundamentals."

"Or it's a precaution," Luci said. "To keep from losing too many secrets at once."

She dug through her photos until she found one of a door. "Still, I guess that explains this. It's the last photo Amelia had me take."

It was the ornate door on the third floor of the Society manor, the one with the complex script—or seal, in Gloria's parlance—that had made my head swim and had erased itself from Luci and Gloria's memory. Gloria took the photo and glared at it.

"Is there a reason you didn't show us this twenty minutes ago?" she asked.

"Because twenty minutes ago, I didn't know why I couldn't remember this door being there," Luci said. "Now I do. Thank you for explaining it."

That mollified Gloria slightly. She started analyzing the seal in the photo, seeing how it worked. "That's the Guardian Key... these are the Adamite and Lethe Keys... and here are a bunch of extra keys I'd need to read up on, but the main business looks like the seal I drew."

"That's impressive," I said. Luci nodded in agreement. "You got really good at this really quickly."

Gloria gave me a wry smile that didn't touch her eyes. "Out here, the schools they send colored kids to aren't worth squat. I had to learn how to pick things up quick on my own."

She handed the photo back to Lucille. "That's an interesting fact. A drawing of a seal by itself doesn't work. Neither does a reproduction, like a photo. It takes something else to get the keys to turn. Must be why they need these big, complicated experiments."

"Should we really be messing with this?" Luci said. "I mean, if this is how the Society burned down the observatory and blew up this farmhouse in Oregon, is this really safe?"

"Safe? I suppose not," Gloria said. "But I don't think it's any more dangerous than electricity. You wire a house without knowing what you're doing, you could burn it down. If you take the proper precautions, though..."

Gloria gestured up to the light above our table. Luci nodded, somewhat mollified.

"That doesn't convince me that Lucas won't blow up downtown Chatham Hills," Luci said. She glanced at the nearby clock. "We've got ten hours at the most. Are we any closer to figuring out how to stop him?"

"We are," I said. "We almost have the puzzle put together. We just need one more piece, and I know where to find it."

Or more accurately, when *to find it,* I thought. I stood up and started gathering my files.

"Ten hours gives us time for one more trip," I said. I knew what our next step should be. "Let's go to the observatory."

"Hon, that place has been a wreck for decades," Gloria said. "How do you expect to find anything there?"

I grinned. "Trust me."

22

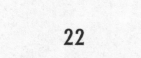

The observatory sat atop Banks Hill to the north of Chatham Hills, about a twenty-minute drive away. Or what should have been. We piled into Luci's friend's car and drove, following Gloria's half-remembered directions. It was a minor miracle we found it at all. Luci missed the turnoff entirely because of the unkempt foliage, taking us on a ten-minute detour that nearly devolved into bickering before I surveyed the area and found the lost road. Luci didn't even blink when I told her to turn around, nor where to find the half-hidden dirt road that went up the hill.

If there had ever been a place to park, it was long overgrown. Weeds and shrubs crowded the remains of the observatory. No one had bothered keeping up the grounds, and no wonder. The observatory was now a shell, a semi-cylinder of burnt and decayed wood, sinking into itself like a rotten tooth. No one could have been here in decades, or so we thought.

Large bills had been pasted all over what remained of the walls, yellow and faded by years of exposure. "No Trespassing." "Condemned – Off Limits." One gave dire warnings as to the consequences intruders would face, topped by an imposing and official-looking seal. I was not surprised. It was the Bureau's.

Luci parked on the dirt road a few yards from the building. We climbed out of the car, Luci and Gloria staring skeptically up at the ruin. I was unconcerned by its appearance. They were right to believe we'd find nothing now, but that wasn't why I'd brought them here.

Luci shook her head. "I hate to say it, but I think this is already a bust."

"What makes you say that?" I said.

She gave me a sharp look. Gloria recognized my attempt at humor but didn't so much as chuckle.

"No one's been here in forever, hon," Gloria said. "Not since Uncle Matthew's day. Kids don't even come up here on a dare."

"I can see why," Luci said, shivering for reasons that had nothing to do with the early autumn air. "This place feels *wrong* somehow."

I didn't disagree. Something about the place made my senses feel *off*, as if I was looking at everything slightly askew. There was a gravity to the place, for lack of a better word, centered on the observatory's interior. It wasn't like the pull I'd felt toward Orr's Used Books that first day in town. This was more like standing at the top of a shallow incline or the lip of a pit that had been imperfectly filled.

"Whatever happened, it can't affect us now," I said, more confidently than I felt. "And I don't think this place is all that abandoned."

"What makes you say that?" Gloria said.

I knelt by the steps leading to the yawning door and pointed. There was a muddy footprint on the top step. There was no way to tell for sure how fresh it was, but it was surely no more than a couple of days old. A sensible shoe. Like the kind worn by the Bureau's agents.

Gloria followed my finger and whistled. "Something to do with the commotion we caused Wednesday night, you think?"

I nodded. "That's my guess, too. Someone checking up after."

"Or going back to the scene of the crime," Luci said. "Okay, I'm convinced. Let's poke around."

I led them inside. It didn't take long to get the layout of the place, even for those with a normal person's sensory range. What interior walls there were had fallen in, the timbers congealing into a mossy mass in the center. There were no unusual marks, no ruined equipment—even the telescope was gone, likely carted away for scrap after the domed roof had caved in. The concrete slab of the foundation was marked with mud and wood rot, but no evidence of fire remained that we could see.

Still, there was that strange, warped gravity, grown slightly stronger as we came closer to the center of the building. I had to stop myself from leaning forward. And there was a smell, a sticky-sweet stench hanging in the air, like perfume long after its wearer had left the room. Only unlike perfume, it made my stomach turn.

"Do you smell that?" I said. "It's foul."

Gloria gave me a quizzical look and sniffed the air. "All I smell is wood rot. It isn't *pleasant*, exactly, but I wouldn't call it foul."

"No, beneath that," I said. "You can't smell it? Like honey gone sour, dripping over rotten fruit."

"That's surprisingly florid," Luci said. "I don't smell anything like that either, sweetheart."

"I suppose I should be used to that," I said. "Although I've never before *smelt* anything others couldn't."

As long as I didn't lose my lunch, the stench gave me something to focus on. It grew stronger the closer I got to the center of the weird gravity. The space around me felt rumpled, almost as if something had pulled it apart and then pushed it back together. The bends and seams still showed.

The bulk of the collapsed roof was in front of where I wanted to be, but that didn't concern me. It wouldn't be there for much longer. I turned to my friends to explain what I intended to do.

"I don't think we need to worry about what the 'authorities' might have found," I said. "They don't know how to look properly. I do, and I think I can show you. But I have to warn you, I've never done this before. I don't know how safe it will be."

I held out my hands. Part of me hoped they wouldn't take them. Part of me didn't want to show them just how weird I was. Part of me wanted them to turn around and leave this all to me. It would be safer for all of us.

The rest of me wanted them to know me. The *real* me, not just the surface bits. And that part sang when Luci took one hand, and a moment later Gloria took the other.

"We've already come this far," Gloria said. "I knew this business wasn't safe when I started poking my nose into it."

"Wherever you go," Luci said.

I blinked back unexpected tears and whispered, "Okay."

Taking my hands wasn't strictly necessary, I didn't think, but it might make it easier for them to visualize. It wasn't my arms that needed to hold them. Stretching myself, I enfolded my presence around my friends. Then I let us fall *backward*.

They both gasped as the world whirled around them, not-green light flickering at the edge of their awareness. Far in the distance, discordant chimes echoed into nothingness. Luci turned to where she thought they were coming from, eyes full of wonder, not realizing that directions as she understood them weren't relevant right now.

"Don't," I said, holding her tightly. My words were not carried by sound waves through the atmosphere. "I don't know what they are, but don't try to follow the chimes. You don't want to get lost here."

Luci gulped and nodded. She tried to press closer to me, though I could see the longing in her eyes. Whatever it was beyond our sphere of awareness, she wanted to know more. I pressed on, hoping to leave the discordant music behind *(before/between/around)* us.

We plunged *down* ever further along an axis at right angles to the space they knew, a dimension they normally traveled in the opposite direction without noticing a moment at a time. Traveling this direction was easier than it had been before, and not because I had grown familiar with it. We slipped almost seamlessly through distortions in space-time, like a trio of marbles following a groove in the floor. I quickly realized I wasn't even propelling us anymore. Once I'd pushed us over the lip, we plummeted through time until we came crashing into the end of the distortion, moments before reality had been torn open.

We sprawled across the concrete slab, now clean and cool. The area around us was dim but lit with electric lights. They glinted off brass and steel armatures that wrapped around the inside of the then-whole observatory walls like a scaffolding, supporting a complex array of glass lenses. Most were focused on the telescope, restored to its place beneath the domed ceiling. Or rather, not yet torn down from it.

We were no longer alone. A half-dozen men and one woman roamed the center of the observatory, making final preparations for a scientific experiment about to go terribly wrong. Seeing them, Luci let out a squeak and scrambled backward. I rose to my knees and touched her shoulder to comfort her.

"Don't worry. They can't see us," I said. "We're... I don't quite know how to explain it. We're out of phase with them or something."

"'Or something'." Gloria scrambled to her feet. "Where are we?"

"It would be more accurate to say 'when'," I said. "We haven't moved in space, relatively speaking. We've moved back about thirty years."

"Thirty... it's *1925?*" Luci said.

"Yes." I gestured to the people in front of us. "We wanted to know how the Society's experiment worked, right? Well, here it is."

My friends stared at the crowd in the center of the room. The men were recognizable from the pictures hanging in the Society's den, but Luci and Gloria could only name one of them. Maxwell Thorpe stood off to the side, gesturing wildly at all and sundry without lifting a finger. The five other men milled about the array of lenses, carefully adjusting this one or that. One woman was also recognizable, but not from any of the evidence in the Society's den. On her knees, tracing a wide circle of symbols in chalk around the center of the room, was a much darker-haired Maxine Orr.

Gloria's eyes widened. "That's—isn't she...?"

"The owner of the bookstore the boys set up shop in," Luci said. "That makes a certain amount of sense, I guess."

"Miss Orr wasn't in any of the photographs," I said, "or Blake's letters."

Luci sniffed. "*That* makes a certain amount of sense, too. Dollars to doughnuts *she's* the brains behind all this."

Maxine certainly had the best grasp of Prospero's Keys. The seal she scribed was composed of dozens of symbols, interlocking with one another and connected by looping lines that crisscrossed the center of the circle in an eye-crossing pattern. The men stepped around it, focusing on the mechanisms and trying not to think about the fact that they barely understood the purpose of half the symbols.

Gloria drew the primer out of Luci's satchel and took a hesitant step forward, then glanced at me for reassurance.

"It's fine," I said. "We're material, but as long as you don't touch them, they shouldn't notice you. Even then, they won't really see you."

I hope, I thought, keeping a careful eye on Thorpe and his cronies. They didn't seem to have noticed us yet, but if anyone could, surely it was one of them.

Gloria knelt beside Maxine, just out of arm's reach. She flipped through the primer and pulled out one of the notepaper sheets she'd tucked inside, taking careful notes of everything Maxine was doing. She pointed out the keys as she recognized them.

"There's the Anchor," she said, but hesitantly. "I think. There are four other keys positioned around the circle that look prominent enough, but I think this is the main one."

"What makes you say that?" Luci said.

"Mostly the way all of this hardware is set up," Gloria said.

Clusters of candles were positioned around those other keys. A smaller lens hung over each candle, as well as the key Gloria identified as the Anchor. The other lenses were angled to focus on the Anchor's lens. That one was tilted up toward the array of lenses around the telescope.

"Also, this one's the Gateway Key," she continued. "It's pretty much the opposite of the key you use to create the wards. If we're right about what they're doing, this has to be the Anchor."

"You're sure?" Luci said.

"Not at all. This seal is much more complex than the others we've seen," Gloria said, "and we haven't had much time to study the keys."

"You're our expert," I said. "What else?"

"I recognize two Refinements." Gloria moved carefully around the circle. She pointed to two large keys, positioned to create an equilateral triangle with the Anchor as the third point. "This one's the Daimon Key. That one over there... is the Midgard Key. I think that means Earth."

"Amelia was right!" Luci said.

"Yes! This seal is supposed to summon something from 'up there' and bring it here. Something very specific, from the number of Structures modifying the Anchor and the Daimon Key. I'm not sure what they *mean*, though. I can't even identify all of them."

"I don't think it matters," I said. "Can you see how to stop it?"

"If you change the right keys, it changes the entire meaning of the seal," Gloria said. "It could make it do something different or make it complete gibberish."

"What would a Gibberish Seal do?" Luci asked. I wasn't sure the capital letters were necessary.

Gloria bit her lip. "Hopefully nothing."

"You don't sound very confident."

"I'll remind you what I just said about time to study."

"I'd say you've devoted more time than most of them," I said. "Let's watch. We'll learn something."

We stepped back to the curved wall, hoping to establish some space between ourselves and whatever was supposed to happen. The members of the Society had similar ideas. As Maxine made her way around the circle, finalizing the connecting lines, the men each stepped back out of the seal. All but one, a sensitive young man named Herbert Townsend. At least, I thought that was his name. He didn't seem very certain of it, or of anything. He radiated nervous energy so broadly that surely everyone else saw it. The others ignored him until Maxine dropped the chalk and stood up.

"Seal's done," she said. "You can start whenever you like, so long as Herbert stops fidgeting."

"Splendid, splendid," Thorpe said, clapping his hands. "Where exactly does Townsend need to stand?"

"Two steps thataway," Maxine said. "Right on that convergence."

Townsend took two shaky steps backward until he stood on the intersection of three lines. Three feet behind him, they fed into the points of another complicated key positioned directly across the circle from the putative Anchor.

"Hmm. Not sure what that's supposed to be," Gloria said. "It's almost like another possible Anchor. Whatever it is, the book calls it the 'Throne Key'."

"Is that a good thing?" Luci asked.

"We're about to find out."

Thorpe folded his hands behind his back and walked halfway around the circle until he stood in front of Townsend. The other men, following a familiar cue, fell into line a few paces to his left. Maxine took up a position on the far wall, folding her arms and watching this business with no small amount of disdain. The others stood quietly, waiting for the Great Man to speak. Which he did, with no prompting.

"Gentlemen," he said, immediately dismissing Maxine. "This is a truly momentous occasion. Within minutes, we shall light a beacon for the Watchers Above. But this, in itself, is no great feat. We have done it several times in the past five years. Twice, we have even been answered. This time, we will do something more. We will open a gate to the Outer Realms and bring one of the Watchers *here*."

He gestured broadly with one hand, indicating the surrounding onlookers. "Many of our fellows have stumbled at the brink of this precipice. Let Dr. Stewart cower in fear of imagined consequences. Let Dr. Lambert chase ghosts and crackpot theories. They will accomplish nothing of note. It is we who will write our names in the annals of scientific discovery tonight!"

"Except for the one who did all the work," Luci said, looking at Maxine.

"*None* of them are going down in history the way they think," I said.

"And that one knows it," Gloria said, gesturing at Townsend.

He was trembling. Second thoughts bounced across the forefront of his mind. Townsend had joined the Society out of a sense of alienation, chasing a need to belong to *something*, to explain why the way he felt so "other". Thorpe had told him he had great potential, but now he questioned what that potential was for.

"M-Max… Doctor Th-Thorpe," he said. "I-is it… is it absolutely n-necessary that *I* be the Throne?"

"What? Of course it is!" Thorpe scowled at the "unmanly" interruption. "We have been *over* this, Townsend! The Watchers Above are not composed of the same matter as the rest of this plane. They need a medium, and you have the greatest psychic potential of the five of you."

Thorpe cared nothing for Townsend's late hesitation. "Buck up, man. You're about to be the first man to make personal contact with an ultraterrestrial entity in the modern era. Don't be a coward now."

I saw what Thorpe wasn't saying and my eyes went wide. "He's the most expendable."

"What?" Luci said.

"Those other men are all from good families. That one's uncle is a congressman. His dad's a judge. His family owns half the mills in Maryland and the last… his father's a gangster, but a very rich one."

Gloria stared at me, believing but not understanding. "How do you know all of this? We don't even know who these men are."

"I do. Now, I mean," I said. "I can *see* it in them. These are men of privilege messing about because they can. Townsend is just a nobody as far as they're concerned. A lonely, lost person they recruited to exploit his gift."

Thorpe cared not a whit for any of this. He turned back to Maxine.

"Is the seal ready for activation?" he said. It was more of a demand than a question.

"Yes," Maxine said. "Just light the candles to power the seal, and—"

"Yes, yes. Focus the energies as required," Thorpe said, brusquely retaking control. "Everyone, to your places."

Thorpe stepped away from the seal, standing not too far from where we stood so he could see the whole enterprise. The other men each took up a position in front of the candles and drew matches from their pockets. Thorpe raised his hands, waiting to give the signal to begin. Townsend stayed alone inside the seal, watching in silent misery.

"What's with the candles?" Luci said. "How are they supposed to power anything?"

Gloria riffed through the primer. "It's not so much the candles. It's the keys around them. They're conduits for something. Power, energy… maybe it's the heat? That must have been what I was missing. Some kind of energy to direct into the system, make the parts *move*."

That made sense. Thorpe made a complex gesture with his hands, like a conductor at the start of a symphony. His minions struck their matches and lit the candles one by one. I could see something shimmering around them. It wasn't simply haze from the flames. The keys around the candles *glowed*.

"Now, focus on our calculations," Thorpe said. "*Visualize* the scene. The pattern of stars marking the region of space where the Watchers wait. Call out to them. The seal and Townsend will do the rest."

The Society members formed their hands into triangles and touched their fingertips to their foreheads. It was a focusing method. I could see them running through complex equations in their minds, over and over again by rote. It might have looked comical until a corona of achingly familiar not-green light began to surround the lenses above their heads. Glimmers of light passed from those lenses to the one above the Anchor. Then a pale column of not-green light shot through the array of lenses above the seal and out into the night sky. Reality warped in its wake.

23

For a moment, nothing happened. Then, distantly, I heard the discordant tinkling of chimes.

The seal lit up, uncanny light blazing from the conduit keys and running along the chalk marks, illuminating every line and key until it met at the point where Townsend stood. He jerked backward but kept his feet planted on the floor. Then he began to convulse, muscles twitching as if a galvanic current ran through him. We three stared in horror as Townsend started screaming.

Then his bones broke.

Another presence entered the room, pouring in from *above* and slipping *on/over/inside* Townsend. His gifted mind recoiled in horror as his body changed to accommodate the alien presence invading him. Bones snapped like dry wood, and Townsend's flesh bulged and warped as the presence forced its way into his tissues.

I could see a single name repeating over and over inside Townsend's mind. Eleanor. A cry for help to a mother? A sister or lover?

No. I didn't think so. I wasn't so certain that he was a "he", after all.

Luci covered her mouth, retching as the presence continued to reshape Townsend's body. Vertebrae popped one by one as Townsend's torso lengthened. Legs and arms corkscrewed around and fused together, forming a single column of tortured flesh. Head flopped forward on useless neck, expanding like a balloon wrapped in skin.

Mercifully, I could no longer sense any presence of Townsend's consciousness in the alien flesh before me. The invader had consumed it as an afterthought to stealing Townsend's body. I bid her a silent goodbye as the mass heaved itself upward.

"What is it?" Luci gasped. "Oh my God, Amelia, what is it?"

"The Watcher Above," I said, my voice a quiet monotone. "Thorpe was right. It can't exist here. So it's building itself a suitable body."

"He knew." Gloria glared coldly at Thorpe. "You were right. Don't you tell me he didn't know."

"I won't," I said.

Thorpe stared at the manifesting Watcher with an expression of unmitigated triumph. I couldn't tell whether he'd expected exactly this, but I could tell that he didn't care. Maxine, on the other hand, stared at everything with the strangest sense of detachment. She hadn't expected what happened to Townsend and was horrified by it. But I didn't think she was particularly regretful, either.

"Our distinguished visitor!" Thorpe shouted. "Welcome to our plane! We who called you here are eager to learn what you have to share about the cosmos!"

The Watcher's presence swept across the room until it focused briefly on Thorpe, like the beam of a lighthouse momentarily pausing. The bulging head flattened, capping the trunk like a fleshy mushroom cap. A half-dozen short tendrils sprouted from beneath the rim, writhing about as if they were tasting the air. The Watcher's growth in three dimensions stopped, but I could see there was more of it hanging above us along other dimensional axes, struggling to fill a vessel that couldn't contain it all.

Its stolen body shuddered. Long rents opened along the trunk. Blood oozed out, quickly thickening into a bright green ichor. The sticky-sweet stench I'd barely detected since arriving suddenly grew overpowering, and now everyone could smell it. Gloria gagged, and Luci clapped a handkerchief over her mouth and nose. Maxine clutched her stomach and turned to vomit, while the men around the seal clutched their heads and convulsed. Even Thorpe was nauseated, though he tried to hide it.

"It's *singing*," I said.

The four men around the seal flung themselves forward. For a second, I thought they were dead; I could see their thoughts blinking out. Then they struggled back to their feet. One by one, they stumbled forward, arms outstretched to embrace the Watcher.

"What are they doing?" Luci said.

"It has to build itself a body. But it's too big," I said. My voice was dull, but I couldn't tear my eyes from what was happening. "It needs more material."

The first of the men, the judge's son, reached the Watcher. He wrapped his arms around its trunk and buried his face in its flesh. In another dimension, the Watcher wrapped a tendril around his body, then plunged it into him. His name had been Lawrence Harris. No more.

The Watcher pulled Harris' body into itself and began to grow again.

"We have to stop this!" Luci said.

"We can't!" Gloria said, sick with horror. "It's already happened."

That was what I'd said. But I couldn't accept it. I couldn't accept that I had to let these men die, even if they were horrible. I couldn't accept that I couldn't have saved Eleanor even if I hadn't been frozen in shock.

"We're here now," I said. "So I think that means that we were there *then*."

I lashed out, grabbing the next invading tendril with my own presence. I wrestled with it, trying to pull it away from its next victim. Albert Dunn, the gangster's son. I could see the Watcher's song in his mind, dripping through it like thick oil. I didn't know how to clean it out without destroying Albert's personality. So I turned my gaze to the Watcher.

And it turned its gaze to me.

I/We aware You.

What? I thought.

You. Gate/Guide/Pathway. Query: open gate yes/no?

"I don't know what you're talking about!" I cried.

"Amelia?" Luci said.

At least, I thought she said my name. I could barely hear her. The Watcher's awareness seeped into mind like fetid water through soil. I had to struggle to keep from drowning in it.

I/We agreement/compact You. You open/lead gate. I/We request passage. In exchange: tribute. Query: open gate yes/no?

"I didn't open the gate!" I said. "I don't know how!"

The Watcher's awareness shifted, lessening its viscous grasp on my consciousness although not releasing it. It probed outside the seal, washing over the others—Luci and Gloria, Maxine Orr, Maxwell Thorpe. I could feel understanding flow through it as it settled on Thorpe.

Comprehension/affront. You open gate no. Animal/native open gate yes.

Inside the Watcher's vast liquid mind, curiosity changed to hunger, like a light dimming. If it had teeth, it would have bared them. And perhaps it was. The green ichor flowed more thickly now, pooling on the concrete at its base.

I/We agreement/compact void You.

In three dimensions, the Watcher's growing body was tethered to the concrete floor. In five, it could reach across a field. It lunged for Thorpe and Maxine, tendrils spreading across space to snare them. I thought they might have stopped at the seal's edges, but no one had thought to include a Guardian Key. Perhaps they'd genuinely believed the Watcher would be happy to see them. And not the way Luci was happy to see a Lane hamburger.

I screamed and threw myself at the Watcher, trying to wrestle it all into three dimensions. Part of me thought it would be somehow easier to contain there, but mostly I was acting out of instinct. In my own body, I grabbed Luci and Gloria to steady myself.

"Luci's right. We have to stop it," I said. "In *our* past, the experiment failed. *We must be the reason why*. Help me figure out how."

Gloria almost started to argue, but I could see her come to the same conclusion.

"Makes as much sense as anything else," she said. She peered at the seal. "The Structures. They're drawing it *down*. If we change them, we might be able to redirect the flow of energy."

"Make the seal push it away instead of pulling it down," Luci said.

"Exactly."

"Perfect. Do that," I said.

I winced as the Watcher struck back at me. Its touch was corrosive, eating away at my presence. Dimly, I wondered if it was going to scar my body. Gloria's eyes filled with concern. She knew I was doing something, she just couldn't tell what. Or how long I could keep doing it.

"This is going to take a minute, hon," she said.

"I'll give you all the time you need," I said. "Luci, get Maxine and Thorpe out of here while Gloria works."

I surged forward. Beneath me, Gloria ran across the room to grab Maxine's chalk, while Luci ran around the other side to grab Maxine. I could see Luci deciding that she was probably the more innocent of the two. I didn't have time to argue. The Watcher was battering me with its strength, bearing down on me with all the force it could muster. I dove into its mind, trying to distract it, trying to find out *why* it was doing all this.

I saw another world, a rocky orb spinning around a distant star. A world dotted with fleshy mushrooms the size of skyscrapers, their tendrils dug deep into its crust. I saw decay surround them, and poisoned seas, and dust-choked skies. I saw the Watcher's titanic form slump and rot as it abandoned that body for the void. One by one, its countless counterparts followed suit. I saw them gliding through empty space, bathing in radiation, probing through other dimensions. I saw the not-green light, and then something my mind interpreted as an eye surrounded by blazing light and warping space.

I saw another world. And another. And another.

I saw the Watchers fall through rents in space like shooting stars. I saw them digging into the crust of a young, wet world. And then they grew. Until there was nothing left to support them, and they moved on. Like cosmic locusts.

The titanic presence I had felt searching for Earth. It hadn't been one entity. It had been a swarm of them.

Selfish satisfaction flowed through the Watcher's presence.

Yes. More.

NO!

This world. It had offered me so little and taken so much in return. But it had given me Luci and Gloria. And I'd be damned if I would sacrifice them to the Watcher's greed.

The observatory shook as the Watcher and I fought. The walls cracked. The ceiling groaned. The armatures shook like tree branches in a storm. A lens snapped off its support and flew through the air, shattering a foot from Thorpe, who stared at it all in rapture. A tributary of the Watcher flowed through his mind as well, though not as deeply as it had the minds of his dead minions.

230

"Come on, stupid," Luci said. She grabbed his arm and pulled him toward the door. He stumbled after her, mostly in shock from the unseen force pulling him away.

"Hope that wasn't important," Gloria said, glancing at the broken lens. "This is the last key! It's almost ready to go!"

"Amelia!" Luci called from the doorway. "Whatever you're doing, it's time to stop!"

Gloria made the final marks. The molecules in the air around us froze for an almost imperceptible slice of a second, then vibrated in a different frequency as the force swirling around the seal suddenly reversed direction. I let go of the Watcher and flung myself backward, following the sound of Luci's voice. I could feel it seeping out of my mind, but it tried to cling to me. My mind felt thick where it gripped me, and I struggled to push it out.

The Watcher screamed as the seal forced it away, blasting it out of our space and back into the ultraterrestrial void where its swarm lurked. A flash of pain ripped through my mind as its grip failed. The swollen, warped remains of Townsend and the others shuddered and collapsed wetly across the concrete as the presence animating them was wrenched out. I didn't see what happened next, as the same force acting on the Watcher flung me away too. I reached out to grab Luci and Gloria, hoping to steady myself. Instead, my awareness filled with not-green light. Somewhere, discordant chimes rang.

And then the three of us were sprawled across the observatory floor again. Only this time, it was covered in dirt and rotten wood.

Luci groaned and pushed herself up. "Where are we?"

Gloria struggled up to her knees. "I think the better question is 'when?'"

I took a deep breath and centered myself, trying to ignore the spikes of pain radiating through my mind and the extent of my form. I focused on both questions, on my position in time and space. I felt the Earth turn beneath me, saw the stars winking to light in the night sky. That wasn't a good sign.

"We're in the observatory," I said. "It's still Saturday. September 25, 1954."

I stood slowly, trying not to overexert myself. Not that I hadn't already done that. I looked at my friends in despair.

"And it's almost seven in the evening," I said.

Lucas Dowling was almost certainly already setting up his experiment. We were a half-hour away from town. And I didn't think I had it in me to fight the Watcher again.

24

Luci tore down the back roads of Chatham Hills in her borrowed car, hands gripping the steering wheel so tightly I thought the skin over her knuckles might split. Gloria sat up front with Luci, trying hard not to comment on her reckless driving. I lay across the back seat, trying to recover my strength. I stared out the windows into the night, my thoughts spinning faster than the wheels.

Had I always known that we weren't alone in the universe? That the Bureau's files didn't describe the detritus of hyper-dimensional storms or meteor strikes, but actual intelligent beings encountering this world? That the Bureau wasn't a disaster relief agency, but a police force for the paranormal?

I think I always knew, on some level. I simply didn't want to face that truth. If I did, I'd have to face a truth about myself, as well. About why the Bureau kept me, about where I came from. About what I am.

I stared at the skin on the back of my hands. Soft. Tender. A light tracery of blue veins showed through the pale skin. If something cut them, blood would flow. Red blood, not some other fluid. Red blood pumped by one heart to carry oxygen through my human body.

"The book's gone," Gloria said, breaking my thoughts.

"What?" I said.

"The book. The primer for Prospero's Keys," Gloria said. "It's gone."

"Where do you think it is?" Luci said.

"Sometime between 1925 and now." Gloria gave a short, mirthless laugh. "I guess it didn't follow us back."

Luci swore and slapped the steering wheel. "Can we still stop Lucas without it?"

"I should be able to," Gloria said. "I remember how the Keys should go. As long as his experiment isn't too different from the one we just saw."

"But it will be," Luci said. "That was the point, right? That Lucas came up with something different. To keep us from doing what we just did to the old experiment."

"But Lucas doesn't know anything about the Keys," I said. "Or at least he's not supposed to. Doctor Thorpe didn't want Professor Blake teaching him anything about the Keys. So the seal should be identical."

"Should be," Luci said.

"If it isn't, we'll come up with something else," Gloria said. "We don't have a whole lot of choices in front of us. Either we do the best we can right now, or we let it all happen tonight."

"There is a third choice," Luci said, her voice bright with false cheer. "We could hope Lucas is about as competent as he seems and the whole thing falls apart!"

"As good as it would feel if that were true," Gloria said, "I don't think we could risk him actually pulling it off."

"You're right, of course," Luci said, though she didn't sound happy about it.

We fell into silence. A mile fell behind us as we brooded.

"What the hell *was* that thing?" Luci said. "Why did the Society want it so badly? Why does Lucas?"

"They're like locusts," I said. "I saw it all in the Watcher's mind. They invade other worlds and… eat everything, I guess. Then they leave and look for other worlds. They can't get to ours on their own, though. I'm not sure why."

"So the Society, what? Sold them ours?" Luci said.

"I don't know. I don't think so. At least, I hope not," I said. "The Society wanted knowledge about other dimensions. I don't want to believe they'd try to trade the whole world for that."

"I don't want to either," Gloria said. Her jaw tightened. "But I do."

"God," Luci whispered.

There was nothing more to say. We sat in silence. As we sped on, I tried to cast my focus to Orr's Used Books, hoping in vain to see where Lucas and Ralph were with the experiment. I could see the building, dark after closing for the night, but no sign of the two boys. It was possible they weren't there after all. Or they were already in their makeshift lab, hidden by whatever design Maxine Orr had worked around her storage room. That had to be the explanation. I didn't recall seeing any seals in the building, but I hadn't known what to look for. Perhaps they were worked in so subtly I couldn't see, or perhaps in thirty years Maxine had come up with some innovations of her own.

I decided not to broach that possibility with the others.

Luci marginally reduced speed once we reached Chatham Hills proper, mostly recognizing that the borrowed car could only handle turns so well. When we reached downtown a few minutes later, she slid the car into an alley two blocks from Orr's Used Books. Hopefully, we were parked far enough away to sneak into the bookstore without being noticed. Luci and Gloria were ready to jump right in, but the sight of a payphone at the corner of a block made me pause.

"What are you doing?" Luci whispered, incredulous.

"Go on ahead," I whispered back. "I just thought of something. Maybe it will help."

Gloria gave me a cautious look. "You're going to call those people, aren't you?"

"Not exactly," I said, "but also kind of yes. I'll explain later. Go! Stay with Luci until I catch up."

The others hesitated to leave me, but the need for haste won out over their concerns. The two hurried into the alley that ran behind Orr's Used Books, while I dug a dime out of my purse and dropped it into the phone. I'd never had a reason to call this number before; I hadn't even been given it, really. I'd plucked it out of his head, just in case.

The phone rang twice. Abandoning my usual calm, I fidgeted with the phone cord, waiting for the other end to pick up. After the third ring, it finally did. The voice on the other phone sounded annoyed and slightly intoxicated.

"Who's this?" Agent Walsh said. "Do you know what time it is?"

"It's seven twenty-four in the evening, Agent Walsh," I said, "and before you ask, no, I am not on the Bureau campus. Before you say anything else, I need you to listen to me."

I paused. There was a moment of silence on the line, broken only by the sound of someone taking a drink. I took that as a qualified assent and continued.

"Agent Walsh. There is something going on in Chatham Hills. It is in relation to the disturbance at 'Site Two', and if there is a Site One and it's what I think it is, in relation to what happened there thirty years ago. Are you following me?"

"Amelia," Agent Walsh said slowly, presumably picking his words with care. "I really need to know what you think is going on."

"We both need a lot of things," I said, "and they don't always seem to coincide. I need something from you now."

Agent Walsh hesitated before speaking. I wished I could see what he was thinking of saying, but I had no idea where to look. I'd never bothered finding out where he lived. It hadn't ever seemed relevant. I supposed it still wasn't.

"I don't have time for you to decide," I said. "Something very bad is about to happen, Agent Walsh. I'm going to try to stop it, along with the 'bad influences' you've failed to protect me from. I need you to make sure they don't get into any trouble."

"This is the Sweeney girl and Miss Lane, I take it?" Agent Walsh said.

"Lucille Sweeney and Gloria Lane, yes," I said. "I don't want to see their names in a Bureau file again, Agent Walsh."

"I can't promise you that, Amelia," Agent Walsh said. "Not unless I know exactly what's going on."

"Something horrible is going to manifest in the used bookstore in downtown Chatham Hills," I said, "and the fact that you've all missed this seriously calls your organization's effectiveness into question. We're going to stop it from happening. Keep my friends out of it."

I didn't wait for him to respond. I hung up the phone and sprinted to the alley, where my friends were waiting. Gloria cast a concerned look at the light pouring out of the single second-floor window overlooking the alley, as if waiting for it to change to an unwholesome color. Luci was already tampering with the back door's lock.

"Take care of what you needed to?" Gloria asked.

"Against my better judgement," I said. "If this all goes badly, we'll need someone to provide backup. Or to clean up the mess, more likely."

"That's not a cheery thought," Luci said.

"I'm not feeling very cheerful right now," I said.

The lock clicked. Luci carefully pushed the door open. The bookstore was dark and entirely empty on the first floor. We crept inside as quietly as possible. Luci and Gloria focused on the stairwell, while I peered into the walls and ceiling, trying to find any hint of seals or other esoteric arts. I saw nothing, or at least nothing that I recognized as being unusual. Perhaps if I looked from a different perspective, but we didn't have time for that. I had to stay with my friends if they were going to have any hope of stopping the experiment.

The second-floor landing was dark. Electric light slashed around the outline of the laboratory door. We could hear sounds behind it, muffled by the walls. Mostly mechanical, intermixed with Lucas' shouting. It was maddening, staring through the wall and seeing nothing but a dark, empty space while knowing something was behind it. Something that caused ripples in space-time; whatever art blocked my vision couldn't hide that. Gradual ones for now, like those made by a dragonfly trapped on the surface of a pond, but they threatened to become waves.

"We still have some time," I whispered, "but not a lot."

"What's the plan?" Luci whispered back.

"You two keep the idiot duo busy," Gloria said. "I'll fix the seal. Need be, Amelia does whatever jinx she did last time to handle the Watcher."

"I like it," Luci said. "Simple."

"Gonna be a lot less simple when we actually do it," Gloria said, her mouth a grim line.

I didn't want to tell her that I didn't think I had the strength, for lack of a better word, to wrestle the Watcher again. I could only hope it didn't come to that. We knew what we were doing this time. There was no way it would get that far.

Luci tried the doorknob carefully. "Locked. Half a moment."

"No time," I said, and *pushed*.

The door cracked in half with a noise like thunder, flying inward and splintering against the floor. I saw the entire apparatus set up and ready to go, and my heart sank. I finally realized what Lucas' innovation was. The summoning seal was in the middle of the floor; I recognized it instantly, but it hadn't been drawn in chalk on the floorboards. It had been inscribed into a steel plate, inset with copper wire. Every curving, twisting line had been perfectly reproduced and perfectly inalterable.

Gloria and Luci caught on as quickly as I had. Luci let out a low whistle.

"Well, boys," she said, "you *have* been busy."

Lucas and Ralph turned, caught in the middle of the final stages of the set-up. The armatures had been set up around the sheet, oriented to focus energies of the seal into a beam aimed at the ceiling and further into ultra-space. An irregularly shaped lump of verdigris crystal the size of my head sat on the Throne Seal. Four cables ran from an extension cord tap to four points around the sheet. Clips at the end of each cable attached them to the seals that served as power conduits. Ralph was attaching the last set of clips, while Lucas was clearly mid-rant. His pale face turned angry red as he realized just who was interrupting him.

"What the hell?" he said. "Lucille and… and the other two? What do you think you're *doing* here?"

"Stopping you from putting everyone in danger!" Luci said. "Ralph, we know what you're really trying to do! It's a stupid idea and it's going to get you killed."

"Don't be absurd," Lucas said. "You uneducated Luddites could never understand my undertaking, and I haven't the time or inclination to explain. Get out of here or I'll—"

"Or you'll what? Call the cops?" Gloria said. "You really want to explain this set-up to the authorities?"

Lucas sneered at her. Then he pulled a piece of paper out of his pocket and unfolded it. I could see the seal inscribed onto the other side. I didn't recognize it at first, but I understood it well enough when Lucas said a word that made the room tilt and my stomach churn. I felt my muscles seize up, like an electrical current was running through my limbs. Luci and Gloria gasped, and I realized they must have been affected as well.

"Lucas!" Luci said, wincing with the effort of making her mouth move. "What do you think you're doing?"

"Handy, isn't it?" Lucas said, pocketing the seal. "Did you know my principals didn't want me to know how to do that? Fortunately, one of the assets they provided was a little more forthcoming."

"You mean Maxine Orr," I said.

Surprise shot across his face before he wrestled control of his expression.

"Miss Orr? The bookstore's owner?" he said, laughing disingenuously. "That old bat has no idea what we're up to. She just needs the rent on the room."

It was such an obvious, ugly lie, but I saw no reason to argue with him. I could see the truth flitting across his mind. Maxine hadn't seen fit to teach him that, at least.

Ralph looked at us miserably. I could see the doubts taking shape in his head. He'd looked up to Lucas but never really trusted him. Neither had he understood what they were doing, not fully.

"Ralph, I know Lucas is too full of himself to listen to anyone," Luci said, "but you're smarter than that! Please, we know what he's trying to do. He's trying to pull an alien from outer space, only it's not the friendly kind. The people he's working for have tried this before, and every time it blows up and gets people killed!"

While Luci pleaded, I grabbed hold of Ralph's mind. It was entirely too easy, pliable as it was. Otherwise, he'd never have fallen under Lucas' spell in the first place.

Listen to her, I thought to him, trying to grab the part of him that still saw Luci as his best friend. *You trust Luci. You're afraid of Lucas. He's going to get you killed.*

Ralph hesitated. He looked at Lucas, blinking rapidly. He licked his dry lips.

"L-Lucas…" he said, his voice quiet and careful, "A-are y-you *really* sure this is s-safe?"

Lucas' usual sneer deepened into a scowl. He stalked across the room and slapped Ralph across the face. Ralph let out a cry of pain, and Luci shouted angrily. Lucas ignored them both.

"*Safe?* Of course it isn't *safe*, you idiot!" he shouted. "We're on the cutting edge of physics here! There's always risk when you're a pioneer. If you're not man enough to accept that, then get out. You've done everything you're good for already."

Ralph's head dropped to his chest. His shoulders slumped, then shook. His mind, too pliable by half, slid back under Lucas' sway. I couldn't push back without risking his mental integrity. I could only watch in despair as Ralph finished attaching the electrical clips.

"It's ready," he said quietly.

"About time," Lucas said. He stalked over to the extension cord tap, then turned to look at the three of us, still frozen under his seal. "I didn't want an audience, but I suppose you're here now. Welcome to the next step in space exploration."

"Lucas," I said quietly. "The thing you're trying to summon can't exist here. It'll have to build itself a body. What do you think it's going to use?"

Lucas looked back at the lump of crystal, which I realized was the compressed remains of the last Watcher. Then he looked at us.

"Well!" he said brightly. "It's a good thing you three came along after all!"

"L-Lucas?" Ralph said.

Lucas ignored him. He stomped on the switch, closing the electrical circuit. Power surged through the seal. The unreal light began to emanate from the keys, converging on the crystal. For a moment, time held its breath. Then the crystal began to glow.

I was the only one who could see the light beams shooting through the lenses, and then up through the ceiling and into the sky. And the only one who could discern the discordant chimes just on the edge of hearing. But I wasn't the only one who felt gravity tip toward the center of the seal as it tore a hole in space-time.

A wrenching, creaking noise ripped through our heads as bubbles began forming along the steel plate's surface, spreading out from the center of the riot of light. It was as if the steel was boiling, without steam or heat. Or liquid.

The crystal burst with a wet sound like an egg splitting, and a blue-green mass poured through the space it occupied. It slapped against the metal plate with a meaty *thunk*, sprouting tendrils that began spreading across the steel. Or perhaps they were roots; they squirmed out for a few feet, spilling over the edge of the plate and sprouting tiny branches that began digging into the floorboards. Space split further as more of the thing pushed its way through the seams.

Lucas stood stock still, staring at the mass as it formed into a column, like a titanic mushroom stalk growing upward until it towered over him. Beside me, I could hear Gloria praying.

More of the fungoid mass pushed its way into our space. The tower of flesh rose above us, a thick cap forming at the top. It split in six directions and sprouted its familiar fleshy tendrils, flopping loosely as it tried to take control of its new body. I didn't think there could possibly be that much mass in the crystal to feed on, but somehow it kept growing.

But it would need to feed soon enough. Or at least, it would want to.

A vent split lengthwise along the Watcher's trunk. It spewed a sickly green cloud of mist at Ralph and Lucas, and finally, someone screamed. I took an unworthy satisfaction in the fact that it was Lucas.

I forced myself to look up. And *up*. In directions the others couldn't see, hundreds of Watchers hung in ultra-space, staring down at our hot, wet world. Hungering after the life that sprawled across it. Waiting for their harbinger to make way for them.

They'd find a way to Earth, and they would take root and devour everything. It couldn't be allowed. I wouldn't allow it.

I could see the energies of Lucas' paralyzing seal playing across my limbs and those of my friends. Somehow, it was working against my body as well as theirs. But my body was much larger than any of them realized. All I had to do was *turn*.

To the others, it must have looked as if my flesh was flowing like wet dough. From my perspective, I simply rotated parts of myself along an axis they couldn't perceive, the greater mass of my form that stretched above-beyond-behind me. Arms lengthened, and then more arms appeared beside them. My height doubled, my mass quadrupled. Someone screamed, and I hoped it wasn't Luci.

The Watcher turned its attention toward me. I could see recognition spread through its liquid mind. The vent on its trunk opened and spewed more of the green mist. It splattered against my body, stinging wherever it touched, and I could feel tiny things within it trying to dig into my flesh. My nerves sang where they found purchase, playing a hymn of consumption.

I didn't care. Better me than my friends. I stared down at Lucille and Gloria, blinking too many eyes. They were still frozen by the paralyzing seal. I could feel their fear and fascination. I saw the questions forming in their minds and was fearful of the answers. I reached out with one of my many limbs. It would be so easy to touch their minds. To make them forget.

No.

The paralyzing energy ran up and down their limbs like a spiderweb spun from liquid electricity. I grabbed the web surrounding Luci and *pulled*. The matrix of power shattered with a sudden burst of energy. For a moment, Luci was suspended in a small, localized windstorm. Then she fell to her knees, retching but mobile. I wanted to hold her, to comfort her as she recovered, but I saw my rugose skin and shuddered. The spines growing from my wedge-shaped head clattered together like bone chimes. I didn't dare touch her. Instead, I tore Gloria free and turned my attention to the Watcher.

The fungoid mass continued to push into our space, though its progress had been sorely hampered. I could *see* the seams in space it burst through; they were now pressing close against it, trapping it in-between volumes it could not normally bridge. I hoped I had not accidentally made this harder on myself. I flung myself at the Watcher, wrapping five arms around its trunk, and braced myself against the solidifying space. Reality rippled as I dug my squirming fingers into it, trying to pull space together like a curtain while I pushed the thing *up* as hard as I could, trying to force it through the hole Lucas had ignorantly torn in space-time. Tendrils ripped up from the floorboards to wrap around my legs, digging into my weird flesh, but I could feel the thing moving… well, backward wasn't *really* the direction, but close enough.

Whatever it had spewed at me was still trying to grow, although it was finding my body a poor planting ground. I could hear a new voice in my head, thick and glutinous, like a rancid syrup flowing along my nerves. This wasn't like before, when I tried to fight the Watcher mind-to-mind. This was in my flesh, such as it was. Not the Watcher's thoughts pouring into mine, but a part of my mind thinking like it.

I/We/You. Embrace/surrender yes.

I won't, I thought back. *This world is not your colony. Neither am I.*

I/We hunger/grow. You fear. You animal/native no. You alone. I/We swarm/nation/family. Embrace/surrender yes.

The Watcher's "voice" didn't have a tone, exactly. But it had a resonance. Something about it was sly. Seductive. It flowed into the cracks in my psyche, the fear and doubt and insecurity. The part of me that, yes, felt isolated from everyone around me. Because I had been isolated. Because I was different. The Watcher's presence teased out those thoughts, amplified them, validated them. Wasn't I more like it than like the humans who infested this world? Didn't I belong somewhere else? Didn't I, deep down, know how to find it?

It was a liar. I knew that. But I was still weak from fighting it before. And while I didn't know whether it'd had thirty years to rest or just thirty minutes like me, it was clearly stronger. At least for now. My grip slackened.

Animal/native open gate yes. I/We agreement/compact void You. But. Query: I/We agreement/compact You new? When world/garden spent. I/We/You open gate yes/no?

I... I...

You I no. You/We yes.

At right angles to everything else, the Watcher reached out its vast arms and dug its fingers into the city. Each digit touched a human mind. More rents opened along the trunk. The Watcher spewed its green mist, the ichor caught on currents that blew through dimensions higher than the third, spiraling away along the creature's limbs. It wasn't waking people up, but they would rise soon enough anyway. Rise and come here.

This body didn't have a mouth, but I still screamed.

25

The high keening tore itself out of my body and shattered the window. In fact, it shattered all the glass for a quarter mile around, though I did not notice at the time. My awareness was entirely taken up by the Watcher. It pushed its presence hungrily against mine. It was becoming difficult to think about anything except the desire to expand. Dimly, I could feel my thoughts sinking into the mental slurry of its infection, burning up and down my nerves like acid.

I reached out for Luci and Gloria, but I could barely perceive them through the murk of the Watcher's assault. I could feel them as vague shadows cast across fetid water, Luci's summer brightness and Gloria's cool brilliance, but I couldn't sense where they were. The boys, on the other hand, pulsed like green flowers on the surface of the swamp.

Beneath the window, Lucas writhed in pain and ecstasy as squirming viridian cilia sprouted from his neck, shoulders, and arms. The strangely fungoid growths grasped blindly at the air, seeking… food? Light? I couldn't begin to speculate. Even noticing the oddness of what was happening to him took such effort.

Ralph was curled in a ball next to the seal, sobbing. Blue-green blemishes spread across his exposed skin. His skin cracked in the middle of the patches, leaking an ichor that looked like no human bodily fluid. The Watcher hadn't touched him, not that I'd seen, but somehow it had infected him as well. His mind was a knot of pain and fear. I longed to soothe it, but even if I could reach him, all I could offer was the lie that everything would be okay.

The Watcher, though, could see my friends very well. A part of its awareness rippled toward them, craving mixed with curiosity. Had it overlooked them earlier, or had Lucas' paralysis seal hidden them as a side effect? I couldn't say. I could only scream and try to dash across the space toward my friends, hoping to shield them from its hunger. It tried to pull me down beneath the surface, drowning me in its bottomless greed. I forced myself through the murk, focusing on the rose-scented golden light that was Luci. I broke through the surface, gasping, and I could *see* them—Luci and Gloria huddled together on the bare floorboards, trying to recover from the paralysis seal. Tears and blood streamed down Gloria's cheeks, while a thin line of vomit ran from the corner of Luci's mouth. They were untouched by the Watcher. Yet. In moments, they would join Ralph and Lucas. If I was weak.

I threw out my hand and grabbed hold of Luci's. I feared she would recoil, but she grasped my rubbery hand as tightly as she could. Gloria followed suit, clasping what might have been my wrist. Not certain what I was doing, I *pulled*.

The Watcher disappeared. Lucas and Ralph disappeared. For a brief moment, everything around me disappeared. And then we were standing in a small, poorly furnished room, decorated only by a rumpled rock and roll poster on one wall. Except where my kitchen should have been, sat the counter from the Lane Diner. A shutter had been drawn over the window to the diner's kitchen. A wet gurgling noise came from behind it and my front door.

I collapsed against the bare floor, my massive body shuddering as I sobbed in utter exhaustion. I was spent and full of despair. My failure was going to cost my friends their lives, as well as a host of other people I'd never know. Any moment, this reprieve would end, and the Watcher would devour us all. Or perhaps it would make me devour my friends. Perhaps there would be no difference between it and me at that point.

Luci knelt next to me, gingerly pressing her soft palm against my side.

"Amelia?" she whispered.

Gloria joined her. "Is that Amelia?"

"Of course it is," Luci said, burying her face against my side. "Who else could it be?"

Yes, I said in my thoughts. They wafted over the others like a cold breeze. *This is part of me. I've never extended it into this space.*

"I don't understand what that means," Luci said.

It's difficult to explain.

I cringed, waiting for her to recoil, to scream. She didn't. She gently ran her hand over my expanded form, amazed by the feel of it. She explored the strangeness of my shape, not in horror but wonder. This was something most unexpected, but she was delighted to discover this new side of me. I shifted to let her come closer and wrapped a limb around her, my many-jointed fingers caressing her hair, face, and neck.

We did not have the time for as thorough an exploration as Luci would have liked (much to my surprise!), nor the privacy. I could still feel the Watcher's infection lapping at the walls like waves. At any moment this shelter could collapse.

Gloria stood a pace away, trying to give us space as best she could in the small room. She slowly turned in a circle, taking in the area, concern written across her face.

"Amelia," she said. "Where are we now?"

This isn't like before, I thought to her. *Physically, we're still in the bookstore's spare room. This is like a shared mindspace.*

"A mind... space?" Luci said, confused. "I'm not sure what you mean."

I... I was afraid. And hurting. So I reached out for help.

Gloria winced. "Amelia, could you please talk? I mean, like a normal person? It's hard to explain, but I don't like how it feels in my head."

"I like it," Luci said. "It's intimate."

"That's all very well for you, Miss Sweeney, but Amelia and I aren't like that."

I'm sorry. I... wait.

We were not, after all, in a physical realm. I appeared in this apocalyptic form only because that was the self I was presenting when I pulled my friends into this mindscape. I could look however I liked. I could change the room as well, but no. There must have been something about this place that I needed, so I left it untouched. The scene rippled, and I was human-shaped again, kneeling on the floor in Luci's arms.

"Is this better?" I said.

"Much," Gloria said. "I'm sorry, but feeling you in my head like that..."

The outside walls grew chilly as the Watcher's infection ran riot. It had taken over a third of my nervous system. My body's defenses were trying to fight back, but they weren't accustomed to whatever was happening to me.

"I know how you feel, Gloria. Believe me," I said.

Luci held me tighter. I rested my head on her shoulder for a moment, breathing in her scent. Strange that it translated to this place, but far from unwelcome.

"So." Gloria sat beside us and gave me a sharp look. "You said you needed help and put us into this 'mind-scape'? Whose mind? Yours?"

I nodded and immediately felt a stab of guilt. I hadn't asked if it would be all right, or even warned them what I was doing. I'd simply grabbed their minds and pulled them into mine. I had endangered my friends even more than they already were.

"I'm sorry. I panicked. The Watcher—"

"It's not the weirdest thing that's happened today," Gloria said. "What is this place supposed to be?"

"It's my—"

The word "home" caught in my throat. My dorm wasn't a home. Not in the slightest. But it was familiar. I didn't feel safe here, but I felt something like comfort.

"This is my dorm room," I said. "This is where I live."

Gloria looked at the lunch counter. She offered me a weak smile. "I beg to differ, honey."

"Yes, it's also your family diner. I think that's coming from you two, actually."

Luci nodded. "It's where we became friends. It's certainly homier than the rest."

"I know," I said. "My comfort is not my keepers' priority. My basic needs are met. Anything more… well. I didn't bring you here to talk about my living arrangements."

"Obviously not, although that's a discussion we're going to revisit in the future," Gloria said firmly. "You brought us here for help. We will, but I think we need a little more information than that."

"Of course," I said, "but it will have to be brief. The Watcher is attacking my mind. It's infected me with a piece of itself, I think. It tried something similar in 1925, but it didn't work. It's learned, or at least tried something different."

"It's attacking your mind," Gloria said slowly. "The same mind we're in now."

"Yes," I said, hanging my head. "I'm sorry, I panicked. I think I can release you—"

"We're not going anywhere," Luci said.

"We're in this together," Gloria said. "Not like we're any safer out there."

Gloria stood and walked over to the diner's counter. She ran a hand along its surface and smiled. The chill of the Watcher's touch lessened. I could hear the clink of utensils on plates, smell her brother's meatloaf. I relaxed ever so slightly.

"I think I understand," she said. "The room is you, but this is coming from us."

"Strength in numbers," Luci said, holding me more tightly.

"Yes," I said. "Working in concert, we can hold off the Watcher. It helps that the two of you aren't infected."

The word "yet" hung between us, unspoken.

Gloria moved to the front door. "What would happen if I opened this?"

I frowned. "The recreation isn't that thorough. If you opened that door, you wouldn't see a hallway. You'd see the Watcher's infection, consuming my mind."

She looked down at the floor. Oily water was seeping underneath the door; slowly for now but threatening to come more quickly any moment.

"And maybe let it in," Gloria said thoughtfully.

"Yes. This space represents my last defenses against the Watcher," I said. "I think I'm abandoning the rest of my nervous system to take a stand here."

"Your last defenses..." Luci said. "But we know better ones! The

Keys! Gloria, couldn't you place a seal around this room? Something that would keep the Watcher out?"

"Would that work?" Gloria said.

I thought of Agent Thomas and Professor Blake and Maxine Orr. About the fact that I'd never been able to see inside their minds like I could everyone else's. It ought to sound ridiculous, but it was the only thing that made sense now.

"Yes. It absolutely will," I said.

"You're very confident," Gloria said.

"I've experienced something like this before," I said. "It'll work. It won't defeat the Watcher, but it will give us some breathing space."

"No, keeping it out won't defeat it at all," Gloria said.

She knelt by the door, pressing the fingers of one hand against the floorboards. She looked thoughtfully at the dingy water still seeping into the room. Luci looked up, alarmed.

"Gloria! Don't touch it!"

"I'm not going to," she said. "We have enough trouble as it is."

Gloria turned, looking at us with a triumphant expression. "Hear me out. What if we let the Watcher in?"

Luci glared at her. "You'd better be able to explain why that's not a terrible idea."

"It's not," I said, catching on to what Gloria was suggesting. "We don't try to keep it out of this space. We lure it in and trap it here, in this corner of my mind."

"Where it's locked up behind the seal," Gloria said.

"This doesn't feel like a long-term solution," Luci said.

"Right now, I don't care about long-term," I said. "What do you need to make this happen, Gloria?"

Gloria concentrated and rubbed her fingers along the floorboard. The air around her fingertips crackled. The fabric of the mindscape rippled ever so slightly as she drew a strong black line across the floor. She lifted her hand and rubbed her fingers together. There was no residue. Gloria grinned at us.

"Don't need anything to write with, looks like. I'm only worried about the Keys themselves. I don't remember the exact Structures that modified the Daimon Key for the Watcher. The book's missing, and I don't have my notes. I mean, this is all memory anyway, right? My memory's good, but it's not that good."

I smiled back. "Fortunately, mine is."

There was suddenly a piece of paper in my hand. The Daimon Key and its associated symbols, reproduced exactly. I handed it to her.

"I don't understand how Prospero's Keys work the way you do, but I've never forgotten anything," I said. "Anything else?"

"How are we going to power the seal?" she asked.

I shrugged. "How do you power your thoughts? This is in my head. I think I can take care of that part myself."

"Don't know how plausible that sounds, but we don't have much else to work with," Gloria said. "Okay, stay close to me. I may need to reference your memory some more."

"I don't see what choice we have *but* to stay close," Luci said.

"You don't seem to be complaining," Gloria said.

Luci stuck her tongue out at Gloria and pulled me further into her lap.

"Just so long as Amelia can still pass me notes," Gloria said.

"I don't actually need to hand them to you," I said. "This is all just an extended metaphor. You're not *drawing* anything, you're working directly on my mind."

"That makes me feel a lot better," Gloria said.

"It will be okay," I said. "I trust you."

Gloria smiled softly and got to work. At first, she traced each key line by line, slowly making her way around the edge of the room. From time to time, she would name a key, or describe it to me, and a sheet of notepaper with the key reproduced would appear in her other hand. After the third time I did that, she had a revelation. She didn't even need to draw. Gloria put out her hand, mainly just to focus herself, and a key appeared underneath it. With that realization, the seal took shape much more quickly.

Which was good, because rents were appearing in the wallpaper on all sides, spilling oily water into the space. I tried to patch the rents as they appeared, squeezing the fabric of the mindscape shut, but it was no use. There was simply too little of me left to control the mindscape. Two opened as quickly as I closed one. And they were becoming stronger. Before our eyes, a huge jet of filthy liquid burst out of the wall and poured into the room.

"Amelia, what's happening?" Luci said.

"The Watcher found me," I said, wincing at the effort of speech. "It's ignoring the rest of my body and focusing its efforts on this redoubt. If it takes this space…"

"It takes all of you," Luci said. "Gloria, it's not going to help at all if I tell you to go faster, will it?"

"Not in the slightest," Gloria said, not looking up.

"Then I won't do that," Luci said. "Amelia, you said you brought us here to make you stronger, right? How do we do that?"

"I don't know for certain," I said. "I barely understand how I do half the things I can do. I think that I've linked your minds to mine. We're still 'in' our flesh, but we can think using one another's brains."

"And that's what you're doing," Luci said. "Using our brains because yours are being taken over."

"It sounds kind of creepy when you say it out loud like that."

"This is definitely third date territory," Luci said with a laugh. "But it's also an emergency. So we need to make the bond stronger, right?"

I started to respond, but Luci didn't give me the chance. She cupped the back of my head and pulled me close, pressing my lips against hers. Everything around me went dark. She drew me into her, bit by bit, until only the barest thread of my consciousness remained in my own flesh. I was her. She was me. We...

We remembered the day we moved to the new neighborhood, after Mom had to leave Dad. We understood why, sort of, but it was scary coming to a new place without him. So we sat in the front room and stared out the window. There was a boy our age on the sidewalk. Two bigger boys were trying to take his model airplane. We decided we wouldn't stand for that.

We remembered the day Agent Pickman called us "him" for the last time. We'd known who we were for years, but no one would listen. Every time it was like getting slapped in the face. And they brought us into the lab and our arm already burned and Agent Pickman scowled and said to take him to get a haircut and we decided no more.

We remembered everything, our joys and fears, our triumphs and failures. This was nothing like what the Watcher was trying to do to us. This was love and sharing and trust. It couldn't last—I could already feel Luci's nerve cells burning out as her body tried to support two full consciousnesses—but it didn't need to. Together, we had the strength we needed.

We reached into the mindscape and dug our fingers into its fabric. With one complicated movement, we mended the seams. The walls and ceiling warped, as if they were melting, but the mindscape held. Then we pushed the fetid water into a single corner, well away from where Gloria was working. It quivered like jelly. We could hear its glutinous voice whispering now, entreating our surrender, but it was no use. Gloria was almost finished.

I retreated from Luci's mind, though I did not break our embrace at first. It was nice, neither of us needing air. Gloria might say it wasn't the time, but I didn't think there was any better time. If all of this failed, I wanted to have as much time loving Luci as I could.

"It's done," Gloria said. "At least, as done as it can be. This is way beyond experimental, you understand? I don't think any of us knows for sure what we're doing."

"It'll be fine," I said. "I think you know more about this than Lucas did, for all his bluster."

I stood up, holding both of Luci's hands, then gently pulled her to her feet. I turned to Gloria to touch her shoulder as well.

"Listen to me," I said. "I'm about to send you both back to your own heads. In case this doesn't work, as soon as you're back, I want you to *run*. Someone should be coming. They'll need to know what happened."

"Someone from the Bureau," Luci said. "I remember enough. You can't expect us to trust those people."

"I don't expect you to trust them, dear," I said. "But someone has to stop the Watcher if we can't."

"Then we will," Luci said. She gave me one last kiss. "I don't like leaving you."

"I know. But we don't have time to argue," I said. "Get ready."

Before either of them could object, I gave them a *push*. They disappeared, and the links between my mind and theirs closed. It was just me and the Watcher now. The gelatinous puddle of its infection wriggled menacingly in the corner. It pulled itself up into a rough approximation of its physical shape.

"You and your threat display can get lost," I said. "Come on, then."

The door burst open. A wave of foul, oil-scummy liquid flooded the space, washing away what little furniture there was. The shutter over the kitchen window flew apart, unleashing another gout of filthy water. The seams in the mindscape Luci and I had sealed tore open, two and three at a time. The Watcher's whispers echoed across the small space, a deafening susurrus that drowned out even the din of the crashing fluid. The room would be flooded within minutes.

Except for a small column of space around me. I had that much strength left. It would fail soon. Fortunately, I didn't need much time.

I closed my eyes and focused on the seal. I saw the entire pattern, a ring encircling the whole space. It just needed a push to become a sphere, and then more. A hyper-dimensional cage made of energy. And I was the source.

Fortunately, I had power to spare.

The Watcher continued to pour into my refuge, screaming for my surrender. It surrounded and enveloped me, surrounding my sphere of blank space. I could feel the pressure of its hunger. It couldn't feel the power building in the seal. Until it was too late.

The seal flared to life.

And I was holding the room in my hands.

Gloria's seal had drawn in not just the Watcher's infection. It had captured the Watcher itself. The lines of the seal traced out the shape of the room in lightning. The trapped Watcher writhed within the glittering cube like an angry goldfish in a bowl, if the goldfish was also the water. It was beautiful, in its way.

The practical side of me wondered how I was supposed to feed it.

Far above me, a riot of lights whirled in the starry sky. I almost wished Luci and Gloria were there to see it; I could never have described the colors that played across the void. Hidden among the dancing aurorae, the host of Watchers Above lurked, waiting for the open gates that would let them ravage the Earth. Gates that would never again open, if I had any say in it.

I held the Watcher's cage up to the gamboling lights. I stretched my presence *up* and *out*, and the lights surrounded me like a shimmering mist, encircling the nowhere space I occupied. The Watchers Above grew closer. The swarm thrashed and roiled in the sky, but from a safe distance. I smiled and cast one limb out. They scattered, a school of gleaming, predatory fish fleeing a hurled stone. I pulled my limb back and drew myself up, assuming what I hoped was an imperious expression.

"I'm waiting," I said.

There was movement in the aether. Exotic radiation passed between them, tinging the aether with radio static. Watchers slid through the space in streams, twisting and turning through an endless variety of shapes. Their debate was clearly inconclusive.

Finally, a single Watcher descended. Its tendrils twitched warily. Immaterial effluvia dripped from the tips, coalescing into an iridescent cloud that formed a halo around my head. An invitation to parlay.

"Well?" I said.

I/We greetings You. I/We peaceful intent approach/emerge.

"Is it undiplomatic to call you a liar?" I said. "Sorry, but I'm exhausted, so you're going to have to accept me speaking plainly. You're an invasion force, a colonizing party, and I'm not letting you have this world."

The Watcher radiated a negative.

I/We agreement/compact You.

"That's what they said," I replied, gesturing to the sealed Watcher. "I didn't buy it then, either. We don't have any agreement."

The Watcher shivered. I could feel its confusion, its disbelief.

I/We agreement compact You.

"*No*, we *don't*," I said.

The Watcher's tendrils thrashed. It was clearly becoming agitated.

I/We agreement/compact You. You open/lead gate. In exchange: tribute.

Agreement/compact span myriad spawnings.

Agitation ran through my limbs. The sealed Watcher sloshed in its cube, causing it to emit staticky bursts of alarm. I realized I was letting the other get to me. I willed myself to stillness, trying to tease out the essence of what it was saying.

"I don't know who your people made an agreement with, but it wasn't me. I don't entirely understand why you think it was, or who I represent, so let me make it clear. I am Amelia Temple, and I represent myself. And in that capacity, let me say that I will not open any gate for you, nor allow your people to invade this world."

I/We discord/despair. Agreement/compact no, I/We extinction/decoherence.

I paused, looking up at the huge host of Watchers, a swarm seeming without end. Was it true? Was the choice between every life on Earth, or every life here in the aether?

"No, I don't think so," I said. "I don't think that's true at all. You may believe it's true, but I think it's just because no one's ever told you that you can't have it all. No one's ever been able to place a limit on your greed."

I held up the sealed Watcher and gave it a slight shake.

"You are all going to have to learn to play nice with the others, understand? And I'm keeping your friend until they do. If they can learn how to coexist instead of consume, maybe they can teach you. In which case, you'll be welcome on Earth. I think humans can use that kind of shaking up.

"Now go tell the others. Earth is off-limits."

The Watcher hesitated until I traced a finger along one line of the seal. Then it fled, seeking the safety of its defeated army. I let myself fall away, the kaleidoscope sky stretching back up to fill the heavens. I heard the ethereal chimes again. This time, they didn't seem so discordant. Instead, they seemed strangely pleased. The impossible colors swirled around me, forming a funnel as I fell back to Earth.

When I opened my eyes, I was back in the lab. The aftermath of the experiment was eerily quiet. The Watcher's body, now mindless, was slumped over and already beginning to decompose. Ralph still lay insensate next to the equipment, which someone had shut off. Most likely Luci and Gloria, who to my utter lack of surprise were still there, waiting for me to return.

There was no sign of Lucas Dowling.

"Where is he?" I said.

Luci, who had been waiting for me to show a single sign of still being me, flung herself at me and threw her arms around my neck. "Oh thank God, it's you."

"Of course it's me," I said, petting her hair as she covered my face in kisses. "But seriously, where's Lucas?"

"We don't know," Gloria said. "Mister High and Mighty was already gone when we woke up. How did the seal work?"

"Even better than I expected," I said.

Even as I said that, I gave the window a wary look. Now I wondered whether Gloria's seal had really trapped *all* of the Watcher.

"So, what happened to that thing?" Luci said.

"It's up here," I said, tapping my head. "In a manner of speaking."

She made a face. "That sounds like a temporary solution if I ever heard one."

"We'll start working on a more permanent one tomorrow," Gloria said. "In the meantime, we have more pressing concerns. Amelia, we called for a doctor while you were… doing whatever it was you were doing. They should be here soon."

"We need to decide what to tell them," Luci said. "Normally I'd be all for cutting and running, but someone needs to do something for Ralph."

"I know," I said. "But I have a feeling the doctor won't be the first person to arrive. We should have some help figuring out what to say."

"Or someone to completely pass that problem off to?" Luci said.

"Precisely. In the meantime, let's make Ralph comfortable."

We weren't sure whether it was a good idea to move him, but none of us felt sanguine about leaving Ralph so close to the Watcher's corpse. We settled on moving him to the center of the room, covered with a blanket that had once covered a piece of forgotten furniture. Luci found a small bowl and filled it with water from the washroom, then began dabbing the angry, sick blemishes growing across his skin. Meanwhile, Gloria and I began searching the room for anything we didn't want falling into the wrong hands.

And so we waited for the authorities to arrive.

26

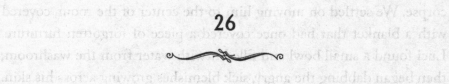

I stood in front of the burned-out shell of Orr's Used Books, peering through the broken glass of the storefront window. Shelf after shelf of ruined books lay toppled across the store. The ceiling in the back had partially caved in; though it wasn't visible from the street, the wreck of Lucas Dowling's makeshift laboratory had crushed the first-floor storeroom. The twisted remains of the focusing apparatuses lay melted and cracked over ash-filled boxes that once held unshelved books. While it had been mostly scoured by the fire, I could feel the blistered residue of the Watcher's ichor still clinging to the charred floorboards.

Luci had left a message for me at the Bureau. She was going to see Ralph at the hospital today, where he was recovering from "smoke inhalation". I had declined to join her. I didn't know what to say to him if he ever woke up. It felt wrong, not being there to support her, but she said she understood. It was, after all, partly his fault we'd gone through all of this.

There was a polite cough behind me. I knew Agent Walsh had been standing there, of course. I'm sure he knew it as well. Still, easiest to play along with the social game.

"Hello, Agent Walsh," I said.

"Returning to the scene of the crime?" he said.

"Just curious about what else goes on in the world," I said. "Did you ever find out who was behind all this?"

He gave me a sharp look. I responded with a winsome smile.

"The Bureau has its suspicions," he said. "There are a couple of likely suspects. No one you would know, of course."

I nodded, quietly grateful that he'd kept his word. Luci and Gloria were out of it.

"I would like to know how the fire started, though," he added.

I shrugged. "These things happen when people mess around with matters they don't properly understand."

Time is just another direction. By turning my attention just *so*, I could see the afterimages of that night. See the experiment begin. See the Watcher attack Lucas and Ralph. See myself fighting vainly back, and then reaching out to my friends to save me. And then what came after.

Agent Walsh arrived first. I breathed a sigh of relief when it was his automobile that pulled up outside the bookstore. I'd been half afraid he would pass my warning on to the Bureau instead of coming himself.

That someone from the Bureau had arrived first was probably a good thing. I had hesitated to think how to explain the remnants of the boys' experiment when the doctor arrived, let alone the Watcher's decaying corpse, but it meant I was going to have to introduce my friends. Luci wasn't going to leave Ralph until the doctor had come, and Gloria wasn't the type to leave without the rest of us. At least we had someone reasonable to deal with.

"He's here," I said to them. "The man from the Bureau."

Luci wrinkled her nose in distaste. "Are you sure about this?"

"Yes," I said. "The man who's come is one of the good ones. He's… sort of my guardian. And he's promised to keep the two of you out of the investigation."

That was a bit of a stretchy truth. Agent Walsh hadn't actually agreed to anything yet, but it sounded good enough to mollify Luci. Gloria was keeping her feelings and expression carefully guarded. I couldn't blame her, but neither could I see any way out of involving the Bureau.

I left them on the second floor and went downstairs to meet Agent Walsh. I found him just outside, shining his flashlight through the shattered glass door. He jumped a bit when the beam hit my face. I barely noticed the light.

"Agent Walsh," I said quietly. "I'm glad it was you."

"I wasn't going to expose you to Thomas or the others," Walsh said, trying to sound gruff. "We'll talk about your curfew later. What happened?"

"It'll be easier to show you," I said.

I led him upstairs. He sucked in a sharp breath the moment he saw the Watcher's corpse. His hand flew to his service pistol, until he realized it wasn't moving, or doing anything except slowly decompose. I rolled my eyes at him. Just what had he thought a firearm was going to accomplish?

"Is that Subject 13?" he said.

"Or one of its relatives," I said. "It's entirely possible it's been the same entity each time, going back to 1925."

Walsh paused. I could feel him formulating the question. I wasn't supposed to know about "Site One" or the experiment that occurred there. Then his eyes fell on Luci and Gloria, and he decided now wasn't the time to pursue that line of questioning.

"These must be the famous Lucille Sweeney and Gloria Lane," he said, moving his hand well away from his pistol holster. "I've heard so much about you."

"Good evening," Luci said. "We've heard absolutely nothing about you."

Agent Walsh nodded. It was what he'd expected. "My name is Patrick Walsh. Special Agent Patrick Walsh." He quickly flashed his badge, then knelt beside Ralph and felt for his pulse. "Is this the Connor boy? What happened to him?"

Luci looked at Gloria, then at me. "We're not sure."

"He's been infected by something," I said. "Spores, probably. The W—the subject released some sort of effluvia. We think he got a whiff."

"What about... there was another one. Dowling?" Agent Walsh glanced around the room. "Where's he?"

"We don't know," I said.

"He ran off when it all started going wrong," Luci said. "Like a rat on a sinking ship."

"Was he infected as well?" Agent Walsh asked.

I considered the question very carefully before I answered. Obviously he had been, more severely than Ralph or even me. It was an open question whether there even still was a Lucas Dowling. Did I want the Bureau pursuing this, though? What would they do to find him? What would they do if they did?

It wasn't worth finding out.

"I can't say for certain," I said, "but Ralph is passed out while Lucas was mobile enough to do a runner. I think that leans toward 'no'."

"Hmm. You're probably right," Agent Walsh said. "We'll still want to find him, but that can't be our priority. I take it you've called for a doctor?"

"One's on the way now," Luci said.

Agent Walsh nodded. "Do you know who?"

"We just called the operator and asked to send a doctor to this address."

He made a face. "He really should be seen by one of our doctors.

Amelia, I'd expect you to know better than that."

I kept my expression and voice carefully neutral. "I was otherwise engaged at the time. There was a lot going on."

"Well, it shouldn't matter. If you just asked for a doctor, it'll probably take a lot longer to get one out here. I'll call the office for support and run interference when the civilian doctor shows up."

Agent Walsh stood and pointed at the Watcher's corpse. "Now, what about that?"

"It didn't survive long," I said. "It encountered a hostile environment."

"Like those fish they keep dragging up from the bottom of the ocean," Agent Walsh said. "Well, it didn't kill everyone for a hundred yards around this time. That's something."

"Nothing comforting," Luci said, placing a protective hand on Ralph's shoulder.

"I think Amelia could tell you that I'm not good at comfort," Agent Walsh said. "But I am good at handling situations. We'll get this cleaned up and your friend taken care of as best we can, Miss Sweeney."

"And in the meantime, I suppose you have some questions for us?" Luci said.

Agent Walsh turned to me. I lifted my chin and held his gaze. I could have made him decide what I wanted. It wouldn't have been difficult. He was sympathetic enough. He wouldn't even know I'd done it.

But I didn't. I let him come to his own conclusion.

"No," he said. "I promised Amelia that I'd keep the two of you out of this. Unless you have a particular desire to make a report, you're free to go."

Luci looked to Gloria. She didn't want to leave before a doctor came for Ralph, but she understood Gloria's discomfort with the federal agent's presence. Gloria had slowly moved closer to the door. Her expression was carefully blank, which was out of character enough for

Luci to pick up on it. But what would happen to Ralph when she left? Torn, she looked to me.

I knelt beside her and placed a hand on her shoulder. "Leave the rest to me, dear. I'll make sure he's taken care of."

Luci's eyes brimmed with gratitude, as well as tears. "You're sure?"

"Of course. And it's best if you two leave. The sooner you do, the easier it will be to keep you out of the reports."

"Amelia's right, Miss Sweeney," Agent Walsh said. "If you and Miss Lane are still here when our man from Medical arrives, we're going to have to explain you."

Luci hesitated, but after seeing Gloria's face, she conceded the point. She squeezed Ralph's shoulder once, hoping somehow to reassure him, then rose to leave. For a moment, she looked as if she wanted to kiss me, until her eyes flicked to Agent Walsh. I shook my head slightly. She closed her eyes, disappointed but also understanding.

Ever so gently, I reached into her mind and brought up the memory of our first kiss.

I love you, I thought to her.

She smiled and clutched my hand. Then she followed Gloria's lead out the door and down the stairs. Agent Walsh watched them go with an odd expression.

"I'm curious as to just how those two got involved with this," he said.

"Luci was worried about her friend," I said, gently touching Ralph's arm. "And for good reason. Gloria got involved because Luci was, same as me."

"I see," Agent Walsh said. He walked carefully around the makeshift lab, taking it all in. "All right, Amelia. Tell me everything."

I took a deep breath and considered what to lie about.

"Are you going to be out for much longer?" Agent Walsh asked.

"It's barely past noon," I said. "Nearly six hours to my curfew. Unless that's changed?"

"It hasn't," Agent Walsh said, somewhat cross. "I explained to my superiors that I was the one who took you off-campus that night."

"I wasn't aware of that," I said. "Did I have a portentous dream?"

He gave me a sharp look. *Don't push it.*

I shrugged. "Probably not too much longer, honestly. Although I will need to find a new bookstore. Perhaps it's time to consider extending my allowable travel range? I'll need to go to another town."

"I'll think about it," he said. "Well, I'm off. I'll see you on Monday."

"Have a nice weekend, Agent Walsh," I said.

He gave me an awkward wave before walking to his car. I watched him leave, though I kept my face turned to the ruin of the bookstore. He wasn't that bad of a man, all told. Patronizing and presumptuous, but at least he treated me like a person. Maybe a little bit more than that, honestly. He could very easily have turned me in to the Bureau or dragged Luci and Gloria into the investigation. He was taking a big chance by keeping our secrets.

I couldn't help but wonder what the hidden cost would be.

Once he was gone, I approached the bookstore's broken door, put a hand on either side of the frame, and leaned in. "He's gone," I said, just slightly louder than a speaking voice. "You can come out now, Maxine."

For a moment there was silence. Then there was a shimmer in the gloom, and Maxine Orr stepped out from behind a ruined bookshelf. She gave me a funny look, as if I was a particularly clever pet.

"Didn't think anyone could see me," she said. "I have to say, I'm impressed."

"I couldn't see you," I said. "Sight isn't my only sense."

"So I guessed," she said. "And here I thought you were just another teeny-bopper."

"I don't actually know what that is," I said. I looked up at the collapsed ceiling. "You set the fire after we left."

"Yep. Figure the reasons why were obvious enough," Maxine said. "You wanna come in for a cup of coffee or something? I've got a little time before I have to go."

I followed her into the ruin, more out of curiosity than anything else. I suppose I wasn't surprised when she opened a closet in the back to reveal a much larger space than could have fit inside the back of the store. A space conveniently untouched by fire. I couldn't see any seals, but the way it warped the space around it was entirely too familiar.

It wasn't that much bigger, mind. Just room for a pair of bookshelves, a small table and a kitchen counter. More of a private reading room than anything else. I was surprised to see two chairs. Maxine offered me one of the seats, then pulled a hotplate and kettle out of the counter's cabinet space.

"I s'pose I'm partly to blame for this," she said, as she began fixing up the coffee. "An old friend asked me to give the Dowling boy a few pointers in esoteric physics. Well, not so much a friend. Frankly, I never liked any of the old sick crew. They were just useful."

"Esoteric physics?" I asked. "Is that what you call it?"

Maxine shrugged. "Less-educated folks used to call it 'magic'. You think it's a coincidence the Keys are named after a wizard?"

"What? I..."

She gave me a look that could cut glass. "Don't try to snow me, sister. I know what happened to Henry's grimoire. I know Dowling didn't get his hands on it, so I reckon you girls are the most likely culprits."

"I don't know what you're talking about, Miss Orr."

"Suit yourself. It's all the same to me," she said. "I certainly don't need that book anymore. Like I said, I was just doing Henry a favor."

"Uh huh," I said.

Maxine poured two cups of coffee and set one down in front of me. "I got sugar but no cream. Deal with it."

"I'll take a little sugar, if you don't mind."

She handed me the sugar pot and sat down. "So what's 'uh huh'?"

I measured out two spoonfuls and gave the coffee a stir. I sipped it slowly, not meeting Maxine's eyes. Drawing it out before I answered.

She snorted. "You think you're clever, that it?"

I let out a sigh of approval, more theatrical than anything else. The coffee wasn't very good. "I think you were bored. I think you wanted back in the game. And I think that makes you dangerous."

Maxine glared at me over her coffee cup. She let out a slow breath. "Is that so? You think you're one to talk to me about dangerous?"

I folded my arms on the table and leaned forward. "So you know who I am."

"I've got a couple of educated guesses."

"Then that puts you ahead of me," I said.

Maxine set her coffee cup down. She crossed her arms and leaned back in her chair. Her head cocked to one side as she looked at me, measuring me. "So ask me what you want to ask, girl."

"I don't know what I want to ask," I said. "I can't see it in your head like most people. My senses just slide right off you. I hate that I'm getting used to that."

"Interesting," Maxine said. "Not surprising, though."

"The thing is, I could probably threaten you into telling me what I want to know," I said. "The Bureau would probably *love* to interview you."

"The Bureau," Maxine said with a dismissive snort. "Hmph. A bunch of revenuers scrabbling in the dust to sort out things they don't understand and jumping at shadows the whole while. I'm not scared of them. Keep your threats."

"Even after what they did to the Apollonian Society?" I said, rolling the dice.

She gave me a humorless grin. "The boys they have now don't have the same killer instinct, my girl."

"Are you sure about that?"

"I was there and you weren't, so yeah," she said, taking a long swig of coffee. "Got no interest in them poking through what's left of my work, mind."

"So…?"

"So what? You can tell your Bureau whatever you like. I'm leaving town today. I just came to pack up what was important. Didn't expect to find you, although I suppose I shouldn't be surprised."

She put down the coffee cup and gave me a piercing look, as if weighing something inside of me.

"You could come with me," she said. "I can offer you far more than the Bureau can, and I figure you'd make a better apprentice than anybody else Henry Blake could scrape up."

I almost dropped my cup. Leave? Just like that? And with Maxine Orr? It was a more tempting offer than any I'd ever received. Except for one. I thought of Luci. I could feel her, a distant light in rose-gold. It would barely take a moment to throw my perception her way, see her sitting alone in a hospital waiting room. Was this knowledge enough to leave her?

"I'm sorry," I said. "I can't."

"You can," she replied with a sniff. "You just chose not to."

"Just like you chose not to tell me what you know about me," I said.

"Just so," Maxine said.

She smiled again, this time with some humor. Then she stood, downing the rest of her coffee in a single gulp. She wiped her mouth with the back of her hand and tossed the empty cup on the counter.

"I'm going to grab what's important from out of here and then hit the road," she said. "You mind helping so it's only the one trip, or do you have somewhere better to be?"

I stood, leaving my half-finished cup where it sat. "Where are these books going?"

"In the immediate term? Back seat of my car," she said.

I glanced at the alley behind the store. "The black one parked out back?"

"Can't imagine who else would be parked back there."

I glanced at the two bookshelves. I didn't know which of the books were important. I supposed it didn't matter. There was a sudden popping sound as air rushed in, and the books were gone.

Maxine glared at me. "They'd better be in my car."

I shrugged. "Maybe they are. Maybe they're in-between here and the aether. Guess you'll find out in a minute."

I turned and walked away from her. I could feel her eyes on me as I left, burning holes in between my shoulder blades. Maybe she didn't know as much about me as she claimed. Maybe she was too dangerous to be left running around loose. I didn't know. Still don't.

But I wasn't prepared to do the things it would take to stop her for good. So I settled for some minor inconvenience. Her books would pop up in that car. Eventually. She looked healthy for her age, she'd make it to 1964 easily.

I stepped out of the ruin of Orr's Used Books and onto the sidewalk. The crisp autumn air felt nice on my skin. Cool. Cold. Cold like the very edge of a ripe planet's atmosphere, caught between life and the void…

I looked inward at my new companion, sloshing around irritably in the back of my mind.

Cut it out, you, I thought.

I turned and made my way down Main Street. Luci would be returning from the hospital soon, while Gloria was in the middle of her shift. I'd meet them both at the diner for a late lunch. And then we'd talk about what we were going to do next.

It was a weird world, after all. Too weird to be left to the people in charge.

ACKNOWLEDGEMENTS

Believe it or not, this book began as an attempt to break my writer's block.

I was stuck on a sci-fi novel without much of a beginning or end, just an interminable tangle of a middle. With no way forward, I decided to try a different project entirely and remembered an idle thought I'd had a couple of years before. I quickly had an image of a quiet, drab young lady sitting alone in a barely furnished dorm room. Then I imagined her in a mad scientist's lab, trying desperately to stop him from unleashing something dangerous. It was just a matter of getting her from point A to point B.

You've just finished the result. I hope you enjoyed it.

This book wouldn't exist without the support of my amazing wife and incredible cover artist, Frankie Valentine. She's been my number one fan for over twenty years now, always encouraging me to keep writing, always believing that my work would find an audience. I love you more than anything else in the world, Frankie.

I'm also tremendously grateful for the support of my found family, Kelsey and Ryan, who are second only to Frankie in supporting my writing. I promise the next Amelia Temple book is coming soon, you two. Leave me alone. Love you!

Thanks to my amazing alpha and beta readers, this book has improved by leaps and bounds as it evolved from a short story to a novella to the short novel you've just finished. Lindsey, Lis, Crystal, Hannah – thank you so much for your feedback and encouragement. Anything that's still wonky is my fault, not yours.

Any work of fiction owes a tremendous debt to the works that inspired it. There's a lot of Neil Gaiman in the Amelia Temple Series, and some Stephen King and Madeline L'Engle. Ruthanna Emrys' Innsmouth Legacy stories made me ask, "What if 'The Dunwich Horror', but a trans woman?" and Mike Mignola's *Hellboy* made me ask, "And then what if she worked for the BPRD?" And of course, the short stories of H.P. Lovecraft inspired most of us in turn. Hope you don't mind me dabbling my nasty transsexual fingers in your pool, Howard Phillips, ya dead racist bag of dicks.

Thank you to the Newport News Library System for including me in the Local Authors Showcase 2022 and putting me in touch with Narielle Living of Blue Fortune. Thank you, Narielle, for believing in this little book about a lesbian monster girl and my gender dysphoria. I'm beyond grateful for you taking a chance on me.

And thank you, you beautiful disaster, for reading this book. You rock!

ABOUT THE AUTHOR

Vivian Valentine is a rad trans lady who loves monsters. When she was a child, she found the Crestwood House Monster Series at her local library and it's all been downhill from there. Now everything she likes is horrible. When not writing, Vivi enjoys card and board games and plotting out more tabletop RPG campaigns than she will ever have time to run. Vivi lives in Virginia Beach with her amazing wife Frankie and their son, as well as an ever-growing collection of action figures. *Beneath Strange Lights* is her first book.

CPSIA information can be obtained
at www.ICGtesting.com
Printed in the USA
BVHW081702220223
659023BV00009B/226